FALLING FOR THE BOSS'S SON

HEAD OVER HEELS

BOOK 1

SHERRI HAYES

Falling for the Boss's Son (Head Over Heels #1)

By Sherri Hayes

ISBN (ebook): 978-1-948471-10-7

ISBN (paperback): 978-1-948471-11-4

Cover Design by Get Covers.

Editing by Lawrence Editing.

This is a work of fiction. Names, places, characters and incidents are the product of the author's imagination and are fictitious. Any resemblance to actual persons, living or dead, events or establishments is solely coincidental.

ABOUT THIS BOOK

Jesse Masters is used to getting what he wants, and he wants Cassie. There's something about her that captivates him. The chemistry between them is undeniable. He knows she wants him, too. He can see it in her eyes—feel it every time her body is near his. But their budding romance faces a major obstacle: Cassie works for his father.

Cassie Ross has sworn off relationships. She caught her last boyfriend in a compromising position with another woman, and she has no interest in going down that path again. Then she meets Jesse. He's charming and his kisses leave her breathless. He seems perfect, except that his father is her boss and Jesse has just accepted a position at the same company.

Is she willing to put her heart on the line and submit to Jesse's desires? Or will she let fear and her past stop her from finding love?

Falling for the Boss's Son is the first book in Sherri Hayes's sizzling Head Over Heels series. If you like workplace romances, he falls first, and dominance and submission, then you'll love this smoking hot love story.

CHAPTER 1

CASSANDRA ROSS HUGGED the blanket a little tighter to her body and reached for her popcorn as her favorite episode of *Buffy the Vampire Slayer* began to play on the television. She was in desperate need of girl power after the week she'd had. Her favorite heroine kicking some ass would hopefully make a dent in her mood.

As the musical score played and introduced the cast, Brie strolled into the living room. Her best friend was five-foot-seven and had the body of a model, which was on full display in the red dress she wore. Her boyfriend, Kaden, would be drooling the moment he saw her.

Cassie popped a piece of popcorn in her mouth. "Hot date tonight?"

"Sort of."

Brie took a seat on the couch beside her, and Cassie got an uneasy feeling in the pit of her stomach. Her friend was blunt to a fault. The fact she was chewing on her lower lip, destroying her freshly applied lipstick, didn't bode well.

"What is it?"

"I need a favor."

"What kind of favor?"

Brie took hold of Cassie's hand. "I need you to come with us tonight."

"You want me to come with you on your date? Why? Are you planning to break up with Kaden or something?" Cassie paused and her voice rose half an octave. "What did he do?"

Her friend shook her head. "He didn't do anything. Things with Kaden are great."

Cassie liked Kaden. He was good to Brie. But he was a man after all, and men did stupid things sometimes. Even to women they claimed to love.

"A friend of Kaden's is throwing a party tonight. I have no idea how many people will be there, but I got the impression most of them are going to be guys." She stood and put her hands on her hips. "You have to come with me."

"Why don't you just tell him you don't want to go?" Cassie asked.

"He said he can't wait for his friends to meet me, and I don't want to be that girlfriend who can't support her man." She pressed her palms together in a praying gesture. "Please, come with us."

Her eyes were pleading, and Cassie could feel her resolve slipping. "I was going to watch Buffy." It was lame even to her ears.

"We can watch Buffy tomorrow night." This time, Brie reached for Cassie's hand. "Besides, what better way to show Greg you're over him than to go out and have a good time."

"You had to bring him up, didn't you?"

Brie shrugged.

Sighing, Cassie turned off the television, threw her blanket on the couch, and stood. "How long do I have to get ready?"

Brie grinned. "Kaden said he'd pick me up at seven."

Cassie looked at the clock and her eyes widened. "That's twenty minutes from now."

"I know. I still have a few things to do and I'm running out of time." Before Cassie could say boo, Brie was halfway down the hall. "You'd better hurry."

Blowing out a breath, Cassie carried her popcorn into the kitchen, then headed toward her bedroom. It was a good thing she wasn't a high-maintenance kind of woman because if she were, there'd be no way she could get herself ready in such a short amount of time.

She was in the bathroom twisting her hair up when the doorbell rang. Cassie ignored it and continued to get ready even as she was mentally kicking herself for agreeing to go. Brie would owe her big time.

Someone knocked on the bathroom door as she put the finishing touches on her makeup. With one last quick look in the mirror, Cassie pulled it open to find Brie, polished and perfect. Not a hair was out of place.

She smiled as she took in Cassie's appearance. "You're going to have Kaden's friends groveling at your feet tonight."

"Very funny."

"I'm serious," Brie said.

Not in the mood to discuss all the reasons why that wasn't true, at least not when she was standing next to Brie. Cassie swiped her bag from the counter. "Are we ready to go—"

Brie had pulled her in for a hug, cutting off her question. "Thank you for doing this."

"That's what friends are for, right?" Cassie hugged her back.

It was a short drive to their destination. This friend of Kaden's lived in a high-rise condo building not far from downtown. Cassie had never been here before, but from the looks of the elevator alone, it was way above her pay grade.

The back of the elevator had a beautiful fan pattern that screamed expensive, as did the marble on the floors. She felt out of place.

Even though her dad had money, he didn't flaunt it. His house, while large, wasn't decked out in opulent finishes. It felt nice and comfortable.

The doors to the elevator opened to a long hallway. It was modern and dripped with high-end finishes.

Brie's heels clicked on the floor as they walked to the opposite end of the hall. Cassie had chosen flats. If she was going to spend the evening keeping her friend company, then she was going to be comfortable doing it. She wasn't there to impress anyone.

Kaden knocked and a few seconds later, a woman opened the door. When she saw Kaden, she smiled. "Hey. You made it." She took a step back, motioning for them to come inside.

"I didn't know you were going to be here," Kaden said to the woman.

"Yeah, well, my big brother sucks at party planning."

Both the woman and Kaden laughed.

Cassie raised an eyebrow in question to Brie, but her friend wasn't looking at her.

"Where's the birthday boy?" Kaden asked.

Birthday boy?

Again, Cassie looked at Brie, but she was still focused on the woman.

Brie held out her hand, inserting herself between Kaden and the woman. "Hi. I'm Brie. Kaden's girlfriend."

The woman didn't miss a beat. She took Brie's hand in hers. "It's nice to meet you, Brie. I'm Beks."

Beks's gaze shifted to Cassie.

Kaden cleared his throat and made the introductions. "Beks, this is Brie's best friend and roommate, Cassie."

Someone shouted Beks's name from across the room and she rolled her eyes. "Excuse me, I'm being summoned. There are drinks and hors d'oeuvres in the kitchen. Help yourselves." Then she was gone, blending into the crowd of people mingling in the living room.

Kaden placed a hand on the small of Brie's back and guided her toward the kitchen. Cassie had no choice but to follow.

The condo was what she'd expected. Open floor plan. Lots of windows looking out over the city. The sun was dipping down below the horizon, casting a reddish-orange glow into the room.

Brie handed Cassie a drink. "I didn't think there'd be this many people here."

Most of the partygoers were in the living area. While Cassie had no idea the exact number, there were at least thirty people. Most of them were men and appeared to be in their late twenties to early thirties. She only counted three other women, one of whom was Beks.

"I should probably try to find Jesse," Kaden said. Then he glanced at me. "Do you mind if I steal Brie for a few minutes?"

What was she supposed to say? No? "Sure."

"We'll be back before you know it." Taking Brie's hand in his, Kaden headed into the crowd.

They weaved around two people, then bumped into a man with long brown hair. Both men grinned and then embraced. She wondered if that was Jesse.

Cassie took a sip of her drink. She knew no one at this party besides Brie and Kaden, and she didn't know Kaden all that well. Her friend had only been dating him for a few months.

After chatting with the man with the dark hair for several minutes, Kaden and Brie disappeared into the crowd. Sighing, Cassie walked to the nearest window to look out. The building sat on a small hill, giving it a great view of the city.

She had no idea how long she stood there, sipping her drink and watching the sun as it lowered in the sky before she felt someone come up beside her.

"Beautiful view, isn't it?"

Her gaze met crystal blue eyes and she almost choked on her drink as her heart rate doubled. His blond hair had a slight wave to it, making her want to run her fingers through it to see if it was as soft as it looked.

He smiled, making her stomach do a somersault. "I don't think we've met." He held out a hand to her and she took it out of habit. The heat from his palm radiated up her arm and went straight to that spot between her legs that had her pressing her thighs together. "I'm Jesse."

* * *

Jesse took in the woman standing beside him. She was gorgeous. The dress she wore hinted at a body he wanted to explore and the way his pulse raced at her touch had him wanting to spend the rest of the night getting to know her in every way possible.

"Um. I'm Cassie." Then her eyes opened wide. "You're Jesse?"

"The one and only." He smiled. "Well, not the only, but the only one here tonight that I know of."

She removed her hand from his and glanced around the room. "Kaden was looking for you."

Kaden was one of his best friends in high school. They'd kept in touch over the years and now that he was back in Kansas City, he was hoping they could hang out. But the look of concern on Cassie's face had an uneasy feeling brewing in his gut. "Are you here with Kaden?" His old friend had said he'd planned to bring his girlfriend with him tonight.

Cassie's gaze returned to Jesse's. "Yes." She paused. "I mean. I am. Sort of. His girlfriend, Brie, is my best friend and she didn't want to be the only woman here, so she asked if I'd come with them. I hope that's okay."

The more she talked, the more he smiled. She was cute when she was rattled. "So you're *not* his girlfriend?"

She shook her head. "No."

Jesse took a sip of his drink, holding her gaze. "Are you anyone's girlfriend?"

Their gazes held for what felt like an eternity as he waited for her to answer. "No." The sound came out as no more than a whisper, but he heard her.

"There you are." Kaden's voice broke the spell between them and Cassie turned to face the window again.

Jesse faced his friend. "Hey."

They patted each other on the back before Kaden wrapped an arm around the woman at his side. She was wearing a sexy red dress that hugged her curves, leaving little to the imagination. The woman was pretty, but she didn't call to him like Cassie did.

Being the gentleman his father taught him to be, Jesse extended his hand to the woman. "And you must be the girlfriend I've heard so much about."

The woman blushed and glanced at Kaden before returning her attention to Jesse. "That would be me. I'm Brie."

"I'm glad you could come tonight. Kaden needs someone to keep him in line."

Brie laughed. "Isn't that the truth."

"Hey."

Jesse and Brie chuckled.

Cassie turned around to join the group and Jesse's focus was on her. Not that it had ever left her. Not really. She clutched her drink in both hands as she faced her friends.

Kaden hugged Brie to his side. "I see you've met Cassie."

"Yes," Jesse said. "We were just getting to know each other."

Brie raised her eyebrows, curiosity written all over her face. "Is that so?"

Cassie spoke up, "I think I could use a refill on my drink. If you'll excuse me."

Before any of them could respond, Cassie was several feet away, her back to him.

"I should probably get a refill, too. It was nice to meet you, Jesse." Brie followed her friend.

Kaden watched his girlfriend until she'd caught up with Cassie, then he turned back to Jesse. "What was that all about?"

Jesse lifted his drink to his lips and grinned. "You know her better than I do."

He glanced at the two women where they were huddled together at Jesse's kitchen island. "I think you may have spooked her, man. What did you say to her?"

"I didn't say anything."

"Are you sure? She looks…nervous."

She looked on edge, which told him their brief interaction affected her as much as it did him.

"How long have you known her?" He figured as long as Kaden was there, he might as well take the opportunity to do some research.

"Only a couple of months. She and Brie are pretty tight, though. They've been roommates for the last five years. Brie told me when we first met that if her friend didn't like me, then we weren't going to work."

Jesse chuckled. "Had to get her friend's approval, huh?"

"Yeah."

Brie linked her arm with Cassie's and led her back to where Jesse and Kaden stood by the window. She released her friend and moved to stand beside Kaden. Placing her hand on his arm, Brie leaned up and whispered something in Kaden's ear.

His friend's expression changed and his eyes heated. He cleared his throat. "We need to...I'll catch up with you later." Lacing his fingers with Brie's, they headed down the hall toward Jesse's bathroom. It didn't take a genius to guess what they'd be doing in there.

Cassie stood beside him, once more clutching her glass.

"Would you like something else to drink? Wine, perhaps?" His suggestion had nothing to do with the wine. Yes, he did prefer wine over the liquor-laden punch his sister had concocted for the party, but in truth, his motivation had more to do with getting her alone.

"What?" Her hazel eyes sparkled in the lights reflecting off the glass, drawing him in.

"My sister insisted punch would be better for the party, but personally, I prefer wine." He offered his hand, silently asking her to take it.

She hesitated for a moment, then placed her hand in his. The instant their skin connected, a rush of excitement rippled through his body again.

Ignoring the rest of his guests, Jesse led her across the room to his study. The room needed a lot of work. Most of the bookcases were still empty. The boxes full of books were still sitting in the corner, waiting to be unpacked.

He released his hold on her to close the doors behind them. The last thing he wanted was for one of the partygoers to interrupt them.

She took in the floor-to-ceiling woodwork. As much as he loved his new condo, this was his favorite room. The rest of the place was very modern, but this still had a traditional elegance with a modern flare. It was the perfect balance of old and new, and he loved it.

But his focus wasn't on the fine woodwork or the piles of boxes begging him to unpack them. All his attention was on the beauty standing in the middle of the room with her back to him.

Her black dress hugged her ass in a way that had his hand itching to touch her again and his groin tightening. She didn't have the exaggerated curves her friend had, but there was more than enough there to hold on to. The thought of drilling his cock into her from behind had him hard in a matter of seconds.

Knowing he had to control himself, Jesse walked to the far wall where he kept his wine collection. He selected a favorite of his and removed two glasses from the cabinet.

She came to stand beside him, watching him pour the wine. "Good thing I like red."

He handed her a glass, then held his up for a mock toast, clinking their glasses together. "A good thing indeed."

They ended up on the couch along the far wall. A tall window brought in the light from outside and they were able to see the city skyline, although they didn't pay much attention to it.

Cassie twirled the stem of her wine glass between her fingers. "You grew up around here?"

"About ten miles outside of the city." He took a sip of his wine. "What about you?"

"I moved to Kansas City with my mom when I was fourteen."

He wondered if something had happened to her father or if her parents were divorced, but for some reason, that felt too heavy and tonight he didn't want that. "Where did you live before you were fourteen?"

"St. Louis." She looked at him from beneath her lashes and he felt the muscles in his stomach tightening again. "My mom met David and his job transferred him here, so we moved."

"Was it hard to leave all your friends?"

"Of course, but I went back to visit them when I was with my dad."

That answered his question on whether her parents were divorced.

"How—"

The doors to his study swung open, causing them both to look up.

His sister, now looking slightly pissed off, stood in the doorframe, hands on her hips. "Why are you hiding in here? This is your party. You're supposed to be mingling with guests."

Knowing his time alone with Cassie was over, he stood and offered her a hand up. She'd relaxed as they'd sat and talked, but now the awkwardness was back.

"Um. I should go find Brie and Kaden." She set her glass of wine on the desk and brushed past his sister.

Beks raised an eyebrow in question, but he ignored her as he put the wine bottle away and made his way back to the party.

CHAPTER 2

CASSIE SPENT the rest of the evening avoiding Jesse and pretending she didn't notice all the questioning looks she was getting from Brie. Her friend had noticed her absence, but apart from asking where she'd been, Brie hadn't said much. Then again, they hadn't been alone.

All that changed after Kaden dropped them both off at their apartment. Cassie thought he'd come in—spend the night—but Brie told him she had to be up early in the morning. The universal woman code for I'm not in the mood tonight.

As soon as the lock clicked shut, Brie zeroed in on her. "I've been patient all night. Where did you disappear to?"

"I didn't disappear." Cassie padded to the kitchen for some water.

"You were gone for at least thirty minutes."

Had it been that long? It didn't seem like it. But she tended to get lost in Jesse's eyes every time she'd meet his gaze. It was as if he'd cast a spell on her or something.

When she didn't say anything, Brie softened her tone. "Did you two..."

Cassie met her friend's gaze. "No." She paused. "He offered me some wine and we talked."

"You talked?"

Finishing her water, she placed the glass in the dishwasher and headed toward her room. Yes, all they did was share a glass of wine and talk, but it had felt intimate somehow.

She was halfway out of her dress when Brie appeared in her doorway, her hip leaning against the frame. "Are you going to see him again?"

"It wasn't like that." It was never like that. Not for her. Guys either weren't interested in her the way she was in them, or they wanted more from her than she was willing to give. Her dad had taught her not to settle. She deserved someone who treated her like she was special to them.

As her dad's words filtered through her brain, her thoughts returned to Jesse. While she was with him, she felt a connection she'd never experienced before with a man. It was both equal parts amazing and a little frightening.

Brie walked across the room and took Cassie's hands in hers. She led her to the bed and sat down, taking Cassie with her. "Look, I know things didn't work out with Greg."

"Or Trent. Or Brian. Or—"

"I know you've had bad luck in the men department."

Bad luck was putting a pleasant spin on things. Her last boyfriend, Greg, was supposed to be out of town on business when she spotted him having dinner with another woman. She'd followed them back to his place, waited for twenty minutes, then went up. He'd given her a key, so she'd let herself in.

Looking back, she wished she'd stayed in the car. The whole experience had been humiliating.

"I don't know if I'm ready to go through that again."

Brie gave her a hug. "You'll find the right guy and he'll treat you like a queen."

Cassie really hoped so, but she wasn't betting on it.

Two days later, Cassie was at work, sitting behind her desk, when her boss called her into his office. She'd worked for Blake Masters for three years and for the most part, she liked her job. Her boss was a little anal when it came to his schedule, but other than that, he was easy to work for.

"You wanted to see me, Mr. Masters?"

Blake Masters sat behind a huge wooden desk, papers spread out before him. He looked up as she entered and ran a hand through his blond hair. "Yes." He motioned for her to take a seat.

Cassie had brought her tablet with her so she could make notes. She took a seat across from him and waited.

"You may have heard rumors that my son is taking over the accounting department." He waited for me to nod before he continued. "He's not officially starting until next week, but I want him to feel comfortable here."

"Yes, sir." From her understanding, Mr. Masters's son had moved away for college and an internship abroad. He was now coming home to learn the business, one department at a time, and eventually take over.

"He's still getting settled in his new place, but he's planning to stop by this afternoon. I have a meeting across town I can't get out of, so I need you to do the honors of showing him around."

Not that she had an issue giving his son a tour, but hadn't his son been there before? Mr. Masters had built his company from the ground up. Granted, it may have grown since his son was there last, but it couldn't have changed that much, could it? "Of course."

"Great." Mr. Masters stood, and she followed. He removed his jacket from the coat rack in the corner and slipped it on. It was eleven and his meeting didn't start until twelve thirty. "I'm going to grab an early lunch before I head to my meeting. If you have any issues, text me."

"Yes, sir."

Given her boss wasn't in the office and Cassie had no idea when his son would show up, she logged out of her computer and headed to lunch. Her favorite restaurant was within walking distance. After grabbing a sandwich and some chips, she made her way back to the office.

She ran into one of the other administrative assistants in the elevator. "How's your day going?" Stephanie asked once the doors had closed.

"Good. Yours?"

Stephanie chuckled. "It's Monday and I'm trying to get everything ready for the new boss. I heard he's supposed to visit today and I want everything to be in order. You never get a second chance to make a first impression. Especially when it's the boss's son."

Cassie nodded. She was worried about her own first impression. Granted, she wouldn't be reporting directly to him, but it wouldn't do if her boss's son hated her either.

The elevator doors opened on the third floor and Stephanie hurried out, leaving Cassie alone. Moments later, she was at her destination.

As soon as she stepped off the elevator, she felt a change in the air. The office was buzzing with an unusual energy.

She made her way down the hall to her desk. As she rounded the corner, she noticed someone was in her boss's office.

Setting her food on her desk, she squared her shoulders and prepared to be as intimidating as possible. "May I help you?"

The man turned around and those sea blue eyes she'd dreamed about for the past two nights greeted her. His blond hair was slicked back and he was wearing a suit and tie, but there was no mistaking it was Jesse.

From the look on his face, he was as shocked to see her as she was him. "Cassie."

The way he said her name made her feel as if her stomach were full of butterflies.

He walked toward her, his gaze never leaving hers.

Cassie tried to get her bearings. She had a job to do. "What are you doing here?"

"You work here?" he asked, ignoring her question.

"Yes." Cassie forced herself to look away. She couldn't think when he was staring at her like that. "If you're looking for Mr. Masters, I'm sorry, but he isn't in at the moment. If you'd like, I can schedule a time for you to meet with him."

Jesse stepped forward, closing the distance between them. He didn't touch her, but he was close enough she could feel his breath on her cheek. "Cassie, look at me."

She didn't want to be rude, so she turned to face him. He was right there, and she could feel the same pull toward him as she had at the party.

He lifted his hand as if to touch her but closed his fist instead before lowering it back to his side. "I didn't realize you worked for my dad."

It took a moment for what he said to sink in. "Your dad?" She swallowed. "You're Mr. Masters's son?"

The right side of Jesse's mouth pulled up into a half smile. "I am."

"You're going to be taking over as head of accounting."

It was a statement rather than a question, but he answered it anyway. "Yes."

He was going to be working in management, which meant she'd be seeing him, interacting with him on a regular basis.

Heat flooded her cheeks as she remembered some of her dreams about him over the last two nights. Her very inappropriate dreams.

"You're very cute when you blush."

That, of course, only made her cheeks heat more. How was she supposed to be around him when she'd imagined him naked? Naked and doing all sorts of nasty, wonderful things to her body.

Then she remembered she'd agreed to give him a tour of the building and she started to hyperventilate.

* * *

Jesse had been enjoying her discomfort at seeing him again until she began gasping for breath. He took hold of her shoulders and guided her to her chair. "Put your head down."

She did as instructed, resting her chest on her thighs as she continued to hyperventilate.

Kneeling beside her, he ran a hand along her back. "Slow, deep breaths. Breathe in. Breathe out."

Slowly, her breathing returned to normal, and she sat up. Her face was flushed and some of her hair had come loose from the clip that had been holding it back.

She licked her lips, drawing his gaze to her mouth. He wanted to kiss her. "Are you okay?"

"Yeah." She averted her eyes, glancing around.

He followed her gaze, but they were alone. Most of the executive floor had gone to lunch.

That thought brought all the wicked ideas he'd had to the surface, but he pushed them to the side. "Want to tell me what that was all about?"

She shook her head. "Not really."

The last time he'd had the urge to touch her, he'd held back. This time, he didn't. Cupping the side of her face, he turned her to look at him. "I tried to find you again Friday night, but every time I'd spot you across the room, you'd disappear."

"I'm sorry."

His thumb caressed her cheek as he held her gaze. "What are you sorry about?"

"This isn't a good idea."

He didn't have to ask her what she was talking about. "I think it's an excellent idea." Granted, the fact they'd be working for his father did make things a bit more complicated. "And that still doesn't explain why you ran away from me the other night. I thought we were enjoying ourselves."

"We were." She tried to look away again, but he wouldn't let her. "I was."

"Then why?" He brushed his thumb over her tempting lips. It was taking everything in him not to kiss her. "I want to understand."

Her eyes fluttered closed. "I don't have the best track record with men and you're my boss's son."

"You didn't know that Friday night."

She looked at him again but didn't say anything more. The look on her face spoke volumes, though. Even without the added barrier of him being her boss's son, she was scared. What she felt, her attraction to him, scared her.

It made him wonder about the other men she'd dated. Then again, he wasn't sure he wanted to know. He didn't want to think about her with anyone else. "Let me take you to lunch."

Her gaze went to the sandwich on her desk. "I don't think we should."

The sound of heels clicking on the tile floor drew both their attention. Cassie sat up in her chair and he let his hand fall from her face.

"Hi, Jennifer. Mr. Masters is out of the office this afternoon. Is there something I can help you with?"

"I was hoping I'd catch him before he left. I wanted to run some numbers by him," the woman said.

Cassie's fingers flew over the keyboard. "I can make some time for you tomorrow morning at eight thirty. Will that work?"

"Thanks, Cassie. I appreciate it."

"No problem."

He could hear the woman's heels clicking on the floor again as she walked away.

Cassie looked down at him where he still kneeled next to her desk. "She's gone. You can get up now."

It wasn't exactly what he wanted to do, but he figured pulling her out of her chair, tossing her onto the ground, and ravishing her wasn't the best idea.

Once he was on his feet again, he rested his hip on the edge of Cassie's desk. She wasn't looking at him. As much as he wanted to push her about lunch, he had bigger goals in mind.

He placed his index finger under her chin, making her meet his gaze. "I'll be back in an hour so you can take me on that tour." He could feel her gaze on him as he strode toward the elevator, but he didn't look back. Not until he was inside the elevator. He met her gaze and held it until the doors closed, cutting their connection.

Cassie was at her desk when he returned. She'd fixed her hair, the loose strands back into the clip, and she'd put on fresh lipstick. As good as she looked, he preferred it when she was a little disheveled.

"Good afternoon, Cassie."

She jumped at his greeting, placing her hand on her chest.

"Were you daydreaming about me?"

To his surprise and great delight, color filled her cheeks.

He smiled, knowing he'd flustered her again.

Pushing away from her desk, she grabbed a notebook and pen from her desk, clutched them to her chest, and came to stand beside him. "We should probably get started with our tour if you're ready."

Her attempt to keep things professional amused him, but he let her have it. There would be time to push her later. For now, he did need to get a lay of the land, so to speak. He hadn't been to his father's office in over five years. A lot had changed since then.

"Lead the way, Ms. Ross."

He fell into step beside her as she headed toward the elevator. "You don't have to call me that, you know. Everyone here, including your dad, calls me Cassie."

"I know."

When he didn't say more, she glanced over at him.

He met her gaze, then pushed the down button on the elevator. They waited in silence until the doors opened and they stepped inside. "What floor?"

"Let's start from the bottom and work our way up," she said.

"Sounds good."

Three hours later, they returned to the executive floor. He must have said hi to at least a hundred people. Some had worked there since he was a kid and remembered him from his high school days. Others were new to management and had wanted to introduce themselves. He had gotten a warm welcome, but it was exhausting. He was good with names, but not even he was going to remember them all.

Cassie had also introduced him to his administrative assistant. Her name was Stephanie and she'd been working in the position for a little over a month. While she was new to being an administrative assistant,

Cassie said she'd started in the mailroom and worked her way up. He admired her desire to improve.

"Did you have any questions for me?" Cassie asked as she rounded her desk.

"Will you go out to dinner with me?"

She frowned. "I meant, do you have any questions for me in regards to the people you met today, the office, that sort of thing."

"I knew what you meant."

"Then why…"

"You know why."

The hustle and bustle of the office around them faded into the background as they stared at one another from across her desk.

She was the one to break it. "Jesse, I think we need to keep things on a professional level. Whatever this is between us? It'll pass. You'll lose interest, and we'll still have to work together. I can't jeopardize my job."

He noticed she said he'd lose interest. It was yet another insight into her relationship history. "Why do you think I'll lose interest?"

Taking a seat at her desk, she began typing. "Men always do. They're fickle like that."

"I don't think you've been dating the right kind of men."

Cassie looked him straight in the eye. It was the first bit of backbone he'd seen from her and he had to admit it was hot as hell. "And you think you're the right kind of man?"

"Yes."

She snorted.

"Come to dinner with me," he said. "One meal. And if I can't change your mind, then I'll never bring it up again."

Her mouth twisted as she considered his offer. "Just dinner. That's it?"

"Just dinner. I promise I won't even kiss you good night unless you want me to."

A long silence met his proposal as he awaited what felt like an eternity for her answer. "All right."

"All right?"

She nodded. "All right, I'll go to dinner with you. One time."

Jesse smiled. His mind was already racing with ideas on where he could take her. He wanted it to be somewhere special and where they wouldn't be interrupted. "I'll pick you up at seven. I'll need your address."

"I can meet you there."

"This is a date, remember? I'll pick you up."

He could tell she wanted to argue with him, but she let it go. Grabbing a Post-it note, she scribbled down her address. Granted, he could have gotten it from Kaden, but he wanted her to be committed to the date.

Giving the paper no more than a glance, he tucked it into his pants pocket before giving her a wink and turning on his heel toward the elevator. "Until tonight."

CHAPTER 3

Cassie was an emotional wreck by the time she arrived home. The apartment was quiet, which meant Brie wasn't there yet. Part of her wanted to tell her friend everything and get reassurance that she wasn't making the biggest mistake of her life, but the other part of her didn't want anyone to know.

Going straight to the bathroom, Cassie turned on the shower and stripped out of her work clothes. She couldn't believe she'd agreed to go to dinner with Jesse. It was beyond stupid, especially given he was her boss's son. But she couldn't seem to say no to him. Not Friday night when he'd led her into his study or when he'd asked her to dinner.

She let her head fall forward against the fiberglass wall as water sprayed down her back. What was wrong with her?

A door opened and closed next to the bathroom and she knew Brie was home. There was no way to hide her date from her friend given Jesse was coming to pick her up, but she had no idea what to say. Tonight's dinner was a formality. They were going to be working together. Not directly, but that was a moot point. His father was her boss. There was no way anything between them could work.

"Cassie, you in there?" Brie's voice filtered through the closed door.

"Yes." Cassie stood and reached for the shampoo. "I'll be out in a minute."

"Everything okay?"

"Fine."

There was a long pause. "Okay. I'm going to start dinner."

"Thanks." Cassie figured agreeing was easier than trying to explain through a closed door why she wouldn't be eating dinner there tonight.

She rinsed the soap from her hair and grabbed the conditioner. Once her hair was coated, she snagged her razor. She might as well make sure everything was clean and tidy, just in case, right?

That thought brought her up short. Why was she primping for a first date? She wasn't even sure she wanted to make a good first impression with Jesse.

Okay, that was a lie. She did want to look good for him, even though she knew she shouldn't.

Before she could talk herself out of it, she shaved her legs and armpits, even tidying up the little patch of hair covering her sex. Why, she had no idea. Even if the date went well, it wasn't as if she was planning to sleep with him.

She finished rinsing off, toweled herself dry, and then made her way to her room to try to find something to wear. Cassie had no idea where he was taking her, but she had a feeling it would be somewhere fancy.

Normally, she'd wear her black dress, but she'd worn that to the party. She was standing in front of her closet, still trying to decide, when Brie knocked on her door. "Come in."

Brie opened the door and stepped into Cassie's room, noticing her friend contemplating her clothing choices. "Are you going out?"

Cassie bit the side of her lip as she flipped through her options. "Yeah."

"On a date?"

"Yeah." At the back of her closet, she pulled out a blue dress she hadn't worn in a while. It wasn't that she didn't like the dress, but it made her feel self-conscious. The skirt was a couple of inches too short for her liking and the neckline dipped a hair too low.

"It's Monday."

She glanced over at Brie before bringing her attention back to the dress. "I know."

Brie released a loud breath. "Do I need to drag it out of you?"

"Sorry." Cassie turned toward her friend and held the dress up against her. "Do you think this is too much?"

"No. And you didn't answer the question."

Cassie removed the dress from the hanger, unzipped the back, and stepped into it. "What question?"

"Who are you going on a date with tonight?"

"Oh." Cassie pulled the dress over her hips and torso, removing the towel as she went. "Jesse."

She was hoping Brie wouldn't make a big deal about it, but she should have known better.

Her friend squealed. "I knew it. I knew there was something going on between you two."

"There's not."

"Uh-huh. That's why you're wearing your sexiest dress."

"He's already seen my black dress and it'll seem weird if I wear one of my work outfits."

Brie rolled her eyes. "Okay. Sure."

"Really. It's no big deal. It's just dinner."

"You like him, though, right?" Brie asked.

"Whether I like him or not is irrelevant."

"Why?"

Cassie took a seat at her desk and pulled out her blow-dryer. "Because he's Mr. Masters's son."

That brought Brie up short for a few moments and she was silent as Cassie blew her hair dry. It wasn't until she unplugged the dryer and placed it back in the drawer that her friend spoke again. "Does that really matter?"

"I can't date my boss's son, Brie."

"But you're going on a date with him tonight," she said, stating the obvious.

"It's one dinner."

Brie stared at her for a long time. She opened her mouth, then closed it before backing out of the room.

Cassie tried not to think about what was going through her friend's mind or the fact that she was most likely on the phone with Kaden right now sharing the news. Time was ticking away and Cassie wasn't ready for her date with Jesse.

At seven o'clock on the dot, the doorbell rang. "I'll get it," Brie yelled.

Cassie had locked herself away in her room on the pretense of getting ready, to avoid any further inquiries from her friend. She could hear Brie talking to someone in the living room and knew it was time to come out of hiding. Like it or not, Cassie had agreed to this.

Grabbing her purse, Cassie headed to the living room where Jesse waited. He was talking with Brie, but his gaze fixated on Cassie the moment she walked into the room. She gipped her purse, trying to slow her heartrate as his gaze raked over her. "You look amazing."

"Thank you."

"Well, you two should probably be going. Wouldn't want to be late for your reservations," Brie said, pushing them both toward the door.

"After you," Jesse said, holding the door open for her.

As she brushed by him, she tried to ignore the way her body reacted to being close to him again, but it was impossible. She'd made out with guys before and hadn't felt this alive and Jesse wasn't even touching her.

The door closed behind them, and she felt him come up behind her. He placed a soft hand on her lower back, guiding her toward the elevator. She wanted to lean into him, but she stopped herself. Dinner. That's all it was. One dinner, then they could concentrate on being work colleagues.

"How was the rest of your afternoon?"

"Fine."

He chuckled. "You can relax. I'm not going to ravish you in the elevator. Although I wouldn't be opposed to that."

Cassie swallowed. Why did that turn her on?

They stepped off the elevator and he guided her to an electric blue Ford Mustang. It wasn't exactly the type of car she'd pictured him driving. He'd struck her as more of an Audi type of guy.

Jesse opened the passenger door and waited for her to slide into the seat before going to the driver's side and getting behind the wheel. The engine roared and she could feel the rumble deep in her core. Or maybe that was because she was sitting so close to Jesse.

He glanced over at her as he pulled up to a stoplight. His gaze lingered on her exposed thighs, and she pulled at her skirt.

The smirk on his face said it all as he accelerated with the change of the light. "You have a killer body. You shouldn't try to hide it."

She didn't know what to say to that, so she stayed quiet.

This only seemed to amuse him more.

Knowing she needed to change the subject, she straightened in her seat and did her best to keep her voice even and unemotional. "So where are we going to dinner?"

The smirk returned. "Just a little place I know. I want us to have some privacy."

Being alone with him was the last thing she wanted. Okay, that wasn't true. She wanted to be alone with him. She wanted to know what it felt like to have his lips, his hands on her.

But that was the problem. She shouldn't want that. He was her boss's son. Not to mention the fact that she didn't know him well enough to want those things.

Her body, however, didn't agree. It wanted Jesse's touch. And it didn't matter they'd only known each other for a few days.

* * *

Cassie was quiet for the rest of the ride to the restaurant. Jesse could almost hear her brain working, trying to talk herself out of her attraction to him. He couldn't explain it either.

The restaurant he chose was a farm-to-table place in the heart of the city. It was one of those places one would miss if they didn't know it was there.

Jesse found a place to park and helped Cassie from the car. Her skirt rode up again, revealing more of her creamy thighs. His gaze lingered until she pulled the fabric down as low as it would go.

"I shouldn't have worn this dress," Cassie muttered.

"I'm very glad you did." He laced their fingers together, brought her hand up to his mouth, and placed a kiss on her skin.

Her gaze met his and he watched as she swallowed. She felt it too. She didn't want to, but she did.

They made their way along the sidewalk until they reached the restaurant. The sign out front read Maxine's Farm to Table.

Jesse opened the door with his free hand. "Have you ever been here before?"

She shook her head. "No."

"Then you're in for a treat."

Betty, Maxine's sister, greeted them and took them to their seats. The restaurant only had ten tables and given it was a Monday, only half of them had people at them.

"What can I get you to drink?" Betty asked. "We have a lovely selection of wine."

"I think I'll stick to water," Cassie said.

Jesse nodded. "The same for me."

Betty smiled and went to get their waters.

"Do you come here a lot?" Cassie asked.

"I've been here three times since I've been back in the city."

She nodded and picked up her menu. "What would you recommend?"

He liked that she'd asked him. "Everything is delicious, but I'd highly recommend the basil tomato soup to start and their filet mignon for your main course."

Betty returned with their drinks. "Did you need a few minutes?"

Jesse met Cassie's gaze over the table.

"I'll start with the basil tomato soup and then the filet mignon," Cassie said.

Jesse handed his menu to Betty. "I'll have the same."

"Are the green beans and mashed potatoes good for both of you?" Betty asked.

They both nodded and Betty vanished into the kitchen to put in their orders.

Cassie scanned the room, taking in the intimate space. "I never would have known this place existed. How did you find out about it?"

"A friend brought me here for lunch a few weeks ago." He took a sip of his water before diving into what he really wanted to know about. Her. "Do you have a favorite restaurant?"

She shrugged. "I have a favorite pizza place. I'm not sure I'd put it on the same caliber as this, though."

"Pizza's important. One of the major food groups."

Cassie smiled and it lit up her face.

Betty brought their soup and he waited for Cassie to take a spoonful before diving into his. She hummed as soon as her lips closed around the liquid.

"Good?"

She nodded and went in for another bite. "Very."

He chuckled and filled his spoon.

They spent the rest of the meal talking about his time in Europe and her life after college. It was the best first date he'd ever had and he didn't want it to end.

As they made their way to his car, he slipped an arm around her waist. She leaned into him for a moment, then straightened herself.

Jesse waited until they were at his vehicle before turning her to face him. He kept one hand at her waist and brought the other to cup her cheek. "What's wrong? Didn't you have a nice time?"

"I did have a nice time."

His gaze searched hers. "Is this still about my dad?"

She nodded.

"What happens between us has nothing to do with my father."

Cassie leaned into his touch as if she were trying to memorize the way it felt to have his hands on her. "It does."

Stepping closer, he pressed his body against hers, letting her feel what she did to him. "This has nothing to do with anyone else. This is only you."

There was no mistaking what he meant. His hard length rested against her belly, leaving no doubt he wanted her.

Instead of trying to pull away, she closed her eyes and whispered his name.

That was all he needed. He lowered his mouth to hers, savoring the soft feel of her lips as they moved against his.

Her fingers dug into his sides, holding him to her, silently begging him for more. He didn't want to deny her, but he also didn't want them to be arrested for public indecency.

She whispered his name again and he cursed the fact they were standing on a sidewalk in the middle of the city. Her hands hadn't left his sides, and he was tempted to ask her to come back to his place. But he didn't want only one night with her.

Breaking the kiss, he rested his forehead against hers as they both caught their breaths. "I should get you home."

Before she could respond, Jesse pressed a kiss to her forehead and backed away. He reached for the door handle and helped her inside. When he slid behind the wheel beside her, he started the car and reached for her hand, giving it a squeeze, then pulled into traffic.

Neither said anything on the drive back to her apartment. Jesse wondered if she was struggling with the same emotions as he was. She hadn't let go of his hand, which he took as a good sign, but he knew, despite their kiss, she still had reservations.

He parked and walked her up to her apartment. With their fingers tangled together, they rode the elevator to her floor. It felt as if their time was coming to an end, and it was the last thing he wanted.

They arrived at her door, and she turned to face him. "This is me."

His gaze lowered to her lips and her tongue darted out to wet them as if she knew exactly what he was thinking. He looked into her eyes, hoping to see the same heat and desire he felt. "I'd like to take you out again."

"Jesse."

He crowded her against her door, bringing their noses together. "Say yes."

She held his gaze for a long moment. "It's not a good idea. I—"

He cupped her face with both hands. "You have to feel this between us."

Her fingers gripped his shirt, holding on to him as if she didn't want to let go. He didn't want to let go either.

"I do feel it."

"Then come out with me again." Jesse wasn't above using everything in his power to persuade her to give them a chance. He tilted her head to the side, brushing his lips along her cheek, down to her neck, and up to her ear. "Are you free this weekend?"

"Yes."

Her back arched, pressing her breasts against his chest as he tugged her earlobe into his mouth and sucked. "I'll pick you up Saturday morning at nine. Wear something comfortable."

"Okay."

Jesse was so hard he was about to burst. He was going to need a long shower to take the edge off, but he knew it still wouldn't be enough.

Taking a step back, he put some distance between them and took her keys from her. He unlocked her door before placing them back in her palm.

Cassie reached for the handle, but he stopped her. She turned, meeting his gaze once more.

He grazed his lips over hers, needing to feel her mouth one more time before he said good night. "Think of me tonight when you touch yourself. I'll be thinking of you."

Then, before he could talk himself out of leaving, he left her standing outside her door and walked to the elevator.

When he turned to look down the hall, she met his gaze for a moment before ducking into her apartment. He pressed the button for the ground floor, not able to wipe the shit-eating grin off his face.

CHAPTER 4

BRIE WAS SITTING on the couch when Cassie walked through the door. Pointing the remote toward the television, she clicked it off and waited.

Instead of answering her friend's unspoken question, Cassie headed to the kitchen to get some water. She needed to cool off and gather her thoughts.

"Well?"

Cassie removed a glass from the cabinet and filled it with water. "Well, what?"

"How'd the date go?"

"It went fine." Cassie took her glass and left the kitchen. She didn't want to answer questions about her date with Jesse.

Of course Brie followed her to her room. "Are you going to go out again?"

That was the million-dollar question. She was already fretting over agreeing to go with him on Saturday. Should she cancel? Maybe she should drive down to St. Louis and see her dad for the weekend.

"Hello?"

Cassie shook her head. "I haven't decided yet."

"Did something happen? Was he a bad kisser or something?"

The memory of his lips on hers had Cassie's skin tingling all over again. "No."

"No something didn't happen, or no he's not a bad kisser?"

Setting her water on the nightstand, Cassie went to her dresser and removed a set of pajamas. Brie meant well, but Cassie didn't want to talk about her date. She still wasn't sure how *she* felt about it. "Can we talk about this tomorrow? I'm exhausted and I have work in the morning."

Brie held up her hands in surrender. "Fine. I'll let you off the hook for tonight, but tomorrow you're telling me everything. I want details." She backed out of the room with a knowing smile on her face. "Sweet dreams."

Details. Normally, she'd be excited to share the possibility of a new relationship with her best friend, but for some reason, this time, she didn't want to. She wasn't sure if it was because mixing business with pleasure was a bad idea or if it had to do with the way her body responded every time he was around.

Either way, it was going to have to be a quandary for tomorrow. She really was tired.

Changing into her pajamas, Cassie went to the bathroom to remove her makeup and brush her teeth. When she came out, Brie's light was still on, and she could hear her talking to someone—most likely Kaden.

Cassie turned off the light, crossed the hall to her bedroom, and crawled under the covers. She could still hear Brie talking in the next room as she closed her eyes.

Soon, her friend ended the call and all was quiet. There was no sound other than the hum of electricity in the apartment. Perfect for a good night's sleep.

Only an hour later, Cassie was still awake. Every time she closed her eyes and tried to relax, her thoughts would drift to being pressed up against Jesse's car, wedged between the cool metal at her back and his warm body at her front. She relived every detail of their kiss over and over again.

Her body responded to the memories, and her pussy began to

clench with the desire to feel his hard length inside her. It was crazy. She'd never wanted to sleep with a guy this soon. With Trent, it had taken months for her to feel comfortable enough to even consider opening herself up like that.

But with Jesse, it was different. Everything was different. The way he touched the small of her back as they walked together. How he'd held her. How he'd kissed her. She'd never felt so…cherished and turned on at the same time.

Her cheeks heated as she recalled his parting words. She could almost feel his breath on her face as he whispered them to her. *Think of me tonight when you're touching yourself.*

A shiver rippled through her body and her sex pulsed. She shouldn't have liked him saying that to her. But her body said otherwise.

Cassie looked toward her nightstand. In the back of the drawer was a vibrator. A birthday gift from Brie.

Before she could change her mind, Cassie dug through her drawer until she located the vibrator. It fit in the palm of her hand and was in a U shape.

She turned it on and spread her legs wide. As the toy worked its magic, she remembered how Jesse's erection felt as it pressed against her. The thought had her body temperature rising even more.

Slipping a hand under her shirt, she palmed her breast, massaging it, then took her nipple and twisted it as she tugged. The sensation went straight to her clit.

She did it again, this time imaging it was Jesse's hand.

A soft moan left her lips as she pressed her thighs together, seeking friction. But something stopped her from pushing herself over the edge just yet. She imagined Jesse would want to touch her more before he sent her flying. Cassie wasn't sure why she thought that, but given how he'd kissed, she had the feeling he wouldn't rush things.

As she continued to play with her breasts, the pressure continued to build. She was practically humping the air by the time she pressed the vibrator against her clit.

She was breathing hard as she raced toward her climax, tweaking her nipple between her fingers to the point of pain. Keeping her eyes firmly closed, she fantasized Jesse's cock was inside her. That his mouth was on her breast, teasing and tugging.

It felt so good, but she needed more.

Turning the vibrator on high, she rubbed her clit harder, faster. She arched her back as sensation took over.

"Are you gonna come for me, baby?" His voice rang clear as day in her head. It was like he was right there beside her in the bed, watching her.

That thought turned her on even more. She was so close.

The vibrations had her hovering on the edge, and she knew it wouldn't take much more. Removing her hand from her breast, she pushed two fingers inside her pussy and began riding her fingers with an abandon she'd never felt before.

Her sex clamped down on her fingers as she imagined Jesse hovering over her. She could feel his lips trailing down her neck to her breast, whispering how good she felt wrapped around him. How he wanted to feel her come.

A whimper left her lips as she increased the pressure on her clit a little more, and that was all it took. Her orgasm hit her hard, the pure force of it causing her to gasp.

As she came down from her climax, she lay there, contemplating what had happened. Her fantasies in the past typically involved nameless, faceless partners. But since she'd met Jesse, they'd changed.

Tonight's fantasy had been all about details. His eyes. His hands. His mouth.

It would be easy to write it off as physical attraction, but it was so much more than that. She liked him. A lot.

Cassie had no idea what she was going to do, but she didn't have the energy to think about it now. Rolling onto her side, she placed the vibrator on the table beside her bed and closed her eyes. Her breathing slowed as she let sleep take her to more dreams of crystal blue eyes.

* * *

Jesse woke up the next morning with a smile on his face. He had a list a mile long of things he needed to get done before he officially started his new position on Monday, but all his thoughts drifted back to Cassie. His hands itched to touch her again, but he knew he had to play his cards wisely. She was hesitant, and he understood that, but he wasn't willing to ignore his attraction to her.

Grabbing his keys, he left his condo and drove to the florist. First things first, he wanted to send her some flowers to thank her for their date and to let her know he was looking forward to Saturday. He was tempted to send them to her at work but didn't want to spook her even more.

"I need these to be delivered to this address tonight at six thirty," Jesse told the woman behind the counter after selecting the bouquet he wanted.

"We normally make all our deliveries during business hours."

"I understand, but this is a special circumstance. I have no issue paying more for the inconvenience." He smiled, not afraid to use his charm to get what he wanted.

The woman stared at him for a long beat before blinking and nodding. "I can deliver them on my way home."

Jesse's smile widened. "Perfect."

With that task marked off his list, he moved to the next— the DMV.

Three hours later, his stomach was growling. He needed food.

As he walked to his car, he pulled out his phone. He typed out a quick text to his dad, asking if he wanted to grab lunch.

His phone dinged as he clicked his seat belt in place.

Dad: Are you close by? My next meeting isn't until 2.

Jesse: I can be there in twenty minutes.

Placing his phone in the cup holder, Jesse backed out of the parking lot and made his way through traffic to his father's building. He found a place to park in the garage and rode the elevator up to the executive floor.

The doors of the elevator opened, and his gaze went to the end of the hall. Cassie sat at her desk with her head lowered, her dark hair cascading around her shoulders. She'd worn it down today, as she had at the party, and he wanted to run his fingers through it.

He never took his gaze off her as he closed the distance between them. As he approached, she looked up. Her eyes widened when she saw who it was, and he heard her breath hitch. "Good morning, Cassie."

"Um." She blinked a few times before she turned her attention back to whoever was on the phone. "Yes, I'll pass that along to Mr. Masters and have him get back to you as soon as possible." She hung up and turned her attention to him again. "What are you doing here?" Jesse didn't miss the way her gaze drifted toward his father's closed door.

"I'm meeting my dad for lunch."

"Oh." A look of what he thought might be disappointment crossed her face.

He leaned forward so what he was about to say wouldn't be overheard. "Were you hoping I was here to see you?"

"That's absurd." She took a stack of papers from one side of her desk and moved them to the other. "Of course not."

Her discomfort told him more than she probably wanted him to know.

Unfortunately, his fun at seeing her squirm was cut short when his father's door opened. Blake Masters strolled out of his office, smiling when he saw his son. He turned to Cassie. "If Forester calls again, tell him I should have the report by the end of the day."

Cassie nodded.

Blake clapped his son on the shoulder, and they turned toward the elevator.

They ended up at a steak house across town. He hadn't been there in years, but the hostess had recognized his dad. "Come here a lot?" Jesse asked.

His dad chuckled. "Every now and then."

Jesse snorted.

Blake smiled and changed the subject. "Are you settling into your new condo? Beks said your party was a success. I'm sorry your mother and I couldn't come."

His father had to fly to New York the day before and had asked his mother to accompany him. It was rare for his mother to stay home these days when his dad had to travel. With no young children needing her attention, his parents spent as much time together as they could. He didn't understand the significance of that when he was younger, but he did now, and he wanted that for himself.

"Oh, that reminds me, your mom wanted to know if you could stop by on Saturday. She found some boxes tucked away in a closet that belong to you."

The server came to take their drink orders, breaking the flow of conversation. Once they were alone again, Jesse responded. "I can't on Saturday, but I'll try to swing by on Sunday."

"I'll see if your sister can stop by as well and you can both stay for dinner."

While his parents had been excited Jesse had the opportunity to work in Europe, they were thrilled to have him home. They'd missed him. "Sounds good."

Their drinks came and they placed their orders. As they waited for their food, Jesse shared some of his ideas for the accounting department. Like it or not, he knew he had something to prove. He was the boss's son and he wanted to show everyone he was there because he could do the job, not because Daddy was signing his paychecks.

"What did you think of your team?" Blake asked.

Conversation pulsed again when their food arrived. After assurance they had everything they needed for the moment, their server disappeared, and they both picked up their utensils to dive in. "No red flags as of yet."

"Your assistant, Stephanie, has a lot of ambition."

Jesse nodded. "Cassie told me she'd only been in the position for a little over a month."

His dad stopped his chewing and stared at his son for a long moment. He had no idea what his father was looking for, but Jesse continued to eat his food. Eventually, his dad did the same.

There were so many questions he wanted to ask about Cassie, but he didn't. She was already nervous about them dating.

They finished their meal discussing a much safer topic…Beks. His sister was a bit of a wild child. While he'd been in Europe, she'd been hopping from job to job. Dad had tried getting her to come to work for the company, but she had no interest in finance or business in general. To be honest, he didn't know what she was interested in.

Jesse walked his dad back to his office, hoping to see Cassie again, but she wasn't at her desk. It was after one, but he figured maybe she was still at lunch.

Blake stopped outside the door to his office. "I'll let your mom know about Sunday and text you the time. Don't be late."

"Not me you have to worry about."

His father nodded. "True."

They said goodbye and Jesse made his way back to the elevator. He shoved his hands into his khaki pants and rocked back on his heels.

The elevator doors opened, and he came face to face with Cassie. She stood frozen, like a deer in the headlights, and he took advantage. He stepped inside the elevator and closed the doors before she could move.

"Hey." She reached for the button to open the door again, but he closed his hand over her wrist and brought it back to her side. "What are you—"

Jesse used his body to back her up against the wall. "I was hoping I'd see you again before I left."

She looked up at him, her breathing labored as if she'd walked up ten flights of stairs instead of taking the elevator. "You were?"

"Yes."

The elevator began to move, and he wished they'd have more time alone.

As the doors opened, he took a step back. A woman entered, one he recognized from the accounts receivable department. She seemed surprised to see him but smiled. "Hello, Mr. Masters." Then she looked at Cassie and her smile fell a little. "Are you all right?"

Cassie straightened. "Yes. I'm fine." She glanced over at Jesse, then back at the woman. "How're things in accounting?"

The woman relaxed again. "Well," she said, leaning in as if imparting some big secret. "Word is we're getting a new boss."

Cassie played along. "Really?"

The woman nodded, sending me a sly smile as the elevator doors opened again and she exited.

Jesse laughed. "What was her name?"

"Beth."

"I like her."

"She's married with two kids." Cassie's voice was devoid of emotion. Too much so.

He met her gaze. "Jealous?"

"Of course not."

Jesse brushed his fingers along the back of her hand. He wanted to do more, but he knew better. "You have no reason to be jealous. I'm not interested in Beth like that."

Their eyes met and held. He didn't break the connection as he hit the button for the garage level.

Cassie didn't move as he continued to caress her hand and he wondered if she could feel the same tingles going up her arm as he felt going up his.

The elevator doors opened, and a rush of wind blew inside from the garage. Then, unable to resist, he took a step forward and pressed his lips ever so slightly to hers. "Saturday."

Before he could be tempted to do more, he turned on his heel and marched out of the elevator.

CHAPTER 5

CASSIE DIDN'T UNDERSTAND how a simple touch from him made her brain go haywire. The logical part of her said she needed to snap out of it. It wasn't smart to allow a man to have so much control over her. Giving him so much power was dangerous to her heart.

But the logical part of her took a back seat whenever she was around him. She could still feel the way his fingers had brushed against the back of her hand.

It didn't make sense. She'd been attracted to guys before, but it had never been like this. Never this intense. It was almost as if he'd put her under some sort of spell.

To make matters worse, flowers showed up for her not long after she got home from work. It was an arrangement of pink and white tulips. She'd taken one look at them and known they were from Jesse.

Nestled in between the delicate petals was a note. Cassie removed the folded paper from the tiny envelope.

Until Saturday.

Cassie hadn't had a lot of time to process her feelings over the note and the flowers before Brie came home. She looked at the flowers, then at Cassie, and grinned. "He sent you flowers."

Instead of responding, Cassie picked up the flowers and carried them into the kitchen. She removed them from the crystal vase they'd arrived in, changed the water out, and added the little packet of nutrients.

"Now you have to tell me everything," Brie said.

"There's not much to tell. We went to dinner, and he brought me home."

"Dinner."

After placing the flowers back in the vase, Cassie carried them into her bedroom.

Brie followed.

Cassie placed the arrangement on her dresser. She grazed her fingers along the top of the petals and was once against transported to the feel of him touching her.

"You really like him, don't you?"

The sound of her friend's voice pulled her out of the memory. "He wants to see me again on Saturday."

"That's great."

Cassie shook her head and leaned back against the dresser to face her friend. "No. It's not."

Brie's brow furrowed. "Why? Because his dad's your boss?"

"Exactly. This is a disaster. Or, at the very least, a potential disaster." Cassie threw herself on her bed and covered her face with her hands.

"You don't know that. Maybe it'll work out."

Cassie peeked through her fingers and gave her friend a skeptical look.

Brie kicked her shoes off and climbed onto the bed next to Cassie. "I know you've had some...bad luck in the relationship department, but there are good guys out there. Maybe Jesse's the one."

"And what if he's not, Brie? What if I continue seeing him and things go bad like they always do? At best, I have to face his dad every day. At worst, I'm out of a job."

"You can't be so negative."

Cassie looked at her friend in disbelief.

"I know it's a risk, but there are always risks in life. Sometimes you have to take a chance. The question is, is Jesse worth the risk?"

That was the million-dollar question.

Four days later, Cassie still didn't have the answer. She'd tossed and turned in her bed Friday night, too anxious to sleep. When the sun began streaming through her bedroom window, she gave up the pretense of sleeping and headed into the bathroom to shower.

Three hours later, she was in the kitchen sipping coffee and eating a Poptart when Brie padded out of her room. Her friend had been out with Kaden the night before and hadn't gotten home until almost one in the morning.

Brie took one look at Cassie dressed in her jeans and favorite forest green top and smiled. "What time's Jesse supposed to pick you up again?"

"Nine."

Walking over to the coffee machine, Brie popped a pod into the contraption and pressed start. "Have you heard from him since he sent the flowers?"

"No." And for some reason, that disappointed her. She'd wanted to thank him for the flowers, but she'd quickly realized she didn't have his number. Sure, she could get it. Human resources would have it on file, or she could ask Mr. Masters, but neither of those options felt right.

The machine finished brewing Brie's coffee and she topped the mug off with a healthy amount of milk. "I'd ask why you didn't call him, but I already know the answer."

At eight fifty-six, there was a knock on their door. Butterflies began churning in Cassie's stomach as she got up to answer it.

Jesse stood in the hallway dressed in dark blue jeans and a bluish-gray button-down shirt. The top few buttons were undone, and she could see a hint of his chest hair beneath. He looked better than she remembered.

His blue eyes drank her in, and she swayed toward him, her body wanting him to touch her again.

They were still staring at each other when Cassie felt Brie come up behind her. "Morning, Jesse."

He tore his gaze from Cassie to glance at Brie. "Morning."

"Did you want to come in?" Brie asked.

"Thanks for the offer, but we should be on our way."

"Oh. Well, maybe next time." Then Brie handed Cassie the purse she'd left on the kitchen table and hurried her out the door. "Have fun, you two."

The door closed behind them, and Jesse chuckled.

Cassie grimaced. "Sorry about that."

"It's fine." He placed a hand on her lower back as he'd done on their date Monday night and heat radiated along her spine and down to her lady parts.

She met his gaze. His eyes darkened, looking more like a stormy sea than a bright blue sky. The butterflies in her stomach began working overtime.

"If you keep looking at me like that, we won't be going anywhere other than to my condo."

Cassie leaned into him, thinking maybe that wouldn't be so bad.

His forehead came down to meet hers and she closed her eyes, savoring the feel of him this close again. She was ready to say screw it and drag him back into her apartment when a door at the other end of the hall slammed shut. It was the dousing of cold water she needed to cool her libido.

She took a deep breath and straightened. "We should go."

There was a long pause before Jesse reached for her hand and they began walking toward the elevator. She needed to get her head on straight and stop allowing him to muddle her brain. He was her boss's son. She needed to remember that.

But that was difficult to do when all she wanted was to melt into him.

Tucked into the leather passenger seat of his mustang, Cassie watched out the window as they left the parking garage. "Are you going to tell me where you're taking me?"

He glanced over at her before pulling out into traffic. "Worried?"

She shrugged. "Maybe a little."

Jesse laughed. "I figured we'd start with something fun."

"Such as?"

"You'll see."

Cassie snorted. "See. Secretive."

He reached for her hand and gave it a squeeze. "I promise if you don't like it, we can leave."

Ten minutes later, they pulled into a parking garage at Crown Center. "We're going shopping?"

Finding a spot, he turned off the engine and climbed out of the vehicle. Coming to her side of the car, he opened the door and helped her out. "Not exactly. But if you want to go shopping later, I'll happily watch you model sexy dresses for me."

She met his gaze, knowing he was serious.

Before she could respond, Jesse pressed his lips to hers for a soft kiss. "Don't distract me." Then he took her hand, and they were off.

As they made their way out of the garage, Cassie took a few moments to clear her head. He was mistaken about who was distracting who.

They ended up at the aquarium and she wondered if Brie had shared with Kaden how much Cassie loved the ocean. "How did you know this is one of my favorite places in the city?"

He smiled and kissed her temple. Brie had definitely spilled.

After getting their tickets, they began walking through the aquarium. He didn't rush her, allowing her to take her time at each of the exhibits. And when they reached the ocean tunnel, she got lost in the experience. Sea creatures swam around them, making her feel as if she were really inside their world. One day, she wanted to learn to scuba dive so she could swim alongside them instead of watching behind glass.

Jesse moved behind her. He wrapped his arms around her waist and let her lean against his chest as she watched the creatures glide through the water.

Kids brushed past them as they made their way through the tunnel with their parents, but she was barely aware of them. Between the water surrounding them and Jesse's heat against her back, she felt more relaxed than she had in a long time.

"Which one is your favorite?" Jesse asked.

"I love sharks."

She felt him smile. "Not what I expected."

"They're so misunderstood. People have been made to fear them, but all they want is to live their lives like every other sea creature."

They stood there for a long time, watching, before making their way out of the tunnel. She'd been through the exhibit more times than she could count, but this time it had been different. Jesse was with her. She wasn't sure the aquarium would ever be the same again.

The sunlight blinded them when they exited the building over an hour later. Cassie shielded her eyes to give them time to adjust. It had grown considerably warmer since he'd picked her up that morning.

He led her away from the aquarium toward the stores and restaurants. "Do you like Mediterranean food?"

"Like hummus and gyros?"

The side of Jesse's mouth quirked up in a half smile. "Yeah."

A few minutes later, they were at a Mediterranean restaurant she'd never noticed before. It was small but not quite as tiny as the place he'd taken her to on Monday night.

Without asking her what she wanted, he placed their order.

* * *

One of Jesse's favorite things to do was to try new restaurants. When he lived in Europe, it wasn't the monuments that drew him in, it was the food. So much can be learned about a place through eating the food.

Jesse held out a chair for Cassie and waited for her to sit down before taking his own seat. "Have you been here before?"

"No. Have you?"

He smiled. "No."

Cassie glanced up at the menu, then back at him. He was expecting her to question his ordering for both of them, but she didn't. "How did you know I love the aquarium?"

"A little birdy might have told me."

The woman behind the counter approached their table. She placed a bowl of hummus and some pita bread on the table, then left.

Jesse motioned for Cassie to help herself.

She tore off a piece of the bread and scooped up some hummus. Her gaze lifted to his as she took a bite, then lowered to the table. She was still looking down when the woman brought their salads.

When Cassie reached for her fork, Jesse covered her hand with his. "Are you upset I asked Kaden about you, or is something else bothering you?"

"Jesse, we shouldn't be doing this. I shouldn't be doing this." Then her voice lowered to a whisper as if she didn't want anyone to hear her confession. "But I can't seem to say no."

"I don't want you to say no."

Her fingers flexed in his hand. He held her gaze and knew her thoughts were going back to the last kiss they'd shared. He could have pushed things. Could have asked her if he could come in when he dropped her off at her apartment Monday night.

They were still locked in their own world when the woman brought the rest of their food. "Can I get you anything else?"

Jesse dropped Cassie's hand. "No, I think we're good for now."

The woman nodded and went back behind the counter.

He picked up his fork and dug into his salad. "Eat your lunch. You may need your energy later."

Cassie blushed as she picked up her fork and began eating her salad.

Several minutes passed and the pink was beginning to fade from her cheeks. He finished his salad and moved on to the lamb. The food was good, but it didn't compare to what he'd had in Greece. Cassie had never traveled outside of the US, and he had a sudden desire to whisk her away on a private jet to see all his favorite places.

She caught him staring at her. "Do I have something on my chin?"

His lips curled up into a smile. "No. I was thinking I'd like to get you on a plane and take you to all my favorite places."

"Oh." She glanced out the window and her body went rigid.

Jesse followed her gaze, hoping to find what had caused her reaction, but he didn't see anything out of the ordinary. People were walking down the sidewalk, going in and out of shops, but there was nothing that stood out. "What's wrong?"

She shook her head and turned her attention back to her food. "Nothing."

"Cassie."

Her gaze met his. "My ex, Greg, is across the street with…"

"With?" he prompted when she didn't continue.

"The woman I caught him in bed with."

Kaden told him Cassie had some bad history with men and that, according to Brie, the last guy she'd dated was a douchebag. "How long were you together?"

"Three months." She looked out the window again, and her eyes narrowed. Was she still hung up on the guy?

Jesse zeroed in on the couple in question. The guy was tall and lean, with dark hair and a beard that looked in need of a trim. A woman, almost a foot shorter than him, stood tucked into his side.

The sound of a fork scraping against a plate brought his attention back to Cassie. Her mouth was set in a thin line.

"Are you all right?"

"Fine." Cassie stabbed a piece of chicken as though she wanted to kill it all over again. She was not fine.

"Cass?"

Cassie raised her gaze to his and blew out a breath. "Sorry."

"Why are you apologizing?"

"I shouldn't let them get to me. It was better I found out before I slept with him."

Jesse took a few moments to process that information. "You two never had sex?" Luckily, there wasn't anyone else sitting near them.

"No." Cassie blew out a breath. "Best decision I ever made."

They finished their meal and walked out into the shopping center.

Jesse reached for her hand, lacing their fingers together as they passed by the various store fronts. When he saw a bakery up ahead, he steered them in that direction.

The place was packed. People were lined against the far wall, waiting for their turn.

Jesse walked to the rear of the line and positioned Cassie in front of him. He circled his arms around her waist and brushed his lips against her ear. "What looks good?"

Cassie gripped his arms as if she were afraid he'd pull away. She didn't have to worry, though. He had no intention of running away from her.

"The salted caramel cupcake sounds good."

"Hm. Do you like sweet and salty things?"

The question was meant to be suggestive, and he heard her breathing kick up a notch. "Yes."

He kissed her ear and kept her close as they moved toward the front. When it was their turn, he ordered a salted caramel cupcake for her, along with a few others for them to try.

She didn't say anything as they got their cupcakes and headed outside the building. There was a nice seating area with tables scattered around. They sat side by side at one of the tables and he pulled out the first cupcake, her salted caramel. He tore the paper away from one side and presented it to her.

Cassie reached to take it, but he pulled it back.

She met his gaze, a question in her eyes.

He brought it closer to her mouth, holding it there.

Understanding what he wanted, she opened her mouth and took a bite.

Icing coated her lips and she had a little on her nose. She reached for a napkin, but he was quicker. Jesse took a napkin and cleaned the icing from her face.

"Thanks."

"You're welcome." If they'd been alone, he would've licked it off her. The napkin, however, would have to do for now. "Ready for another bite?"

CHAPTER 6

THE ONLY OTHER time Cassie had felt this conflicted was the day her parents told her and her brothers they were getting a divorce. Back then, she'd worried about not seeing her dad every day. Feared their relationship would change.

It was a child's fear and one her parents worked hard to dispel. Her dad had gone out of his way to continue being part of her life—even after her mom and stepdad moved them to Kansas City.

"How was the big date on Saturday?" Brie asked as she poured her coffee into a large tumbler Monday morning. Her friend had been gone on Saturday by the time Jesse dropped her off and she'd texted Cassie that night to let her know she was staying at Kaden's. Brie hadn't returned home until late last night and by then Cassie was already in bed.

When Cassie didn't answer, Brie frowned. "Do I need to have Kaden kick his ass?"

"What? No." Cassie realized she was going to have to give her friend something, but she wasn't sure how much she wanted to share. "The date went..."

Remembering how Jesse had wiped the frosting off her face, how his gaze had lingered on her lips, making her forget where they were.

That happened a lot when she was with him, and she wasn't sure it was a good thing. At the time, it felt wonderful, but it wasn't good. She couldn't lose herself in him. That wasn't…smart.

"The date was…" Brie moved her hand in a go on gesture.

"It was nice."

"Nice."

"Yeah." Cassie took a bite of her Poptart. The date had been nice. And sweet. And the best date she'd ever been on with a guy.

Luckily, they both had to get to work, so she was spared having to go into the details. She knew Brie would want more information, but she was going to enjoy her reprieve.

The executive floor was quiet when Cassie arrived at the office. It was early and only a few people were at their desks.

Cassie made her way down the hall to her desk and booted up her computer. She went through her normal routine, getting her coffee and going through emails while making her to-do list for the day.

Mr. Masters had an off-site meeting, which meant it was the perfect time to get some paperwork done. A few people stopped by over the course of the morning, looking for her boss, but only one of them left a message.

She was halfway through the end of month report when her phone rang. "Blake Masters's office."

"Is my father at his desk?" The sound of Jesse's voice on the other end of the line, low and soft as if he were sharing a secret with her, had her body heating up.

"Jesse." There was a long pause on the other end of the line and she forced herself to answer his question. "No. Your dad had a meeting this morning."

"Cass, is everything all right?"

She sat up straighter and attempted to make herself sound like the professional she was supposed to be. "Of course."

He was quiet again for a long moment. "I think we need to talk. Have lunch with me."

She swallowed and glanced around the office as if someone could hear their conversation. "I can't. I have a working lunch with…Mr.

Masters." She'd almost said she'd be having lunch with his dad, but she'd caught herself.

Jesse wasn't deterred. "Tonight, then. Dinner."

Cassie chewed on her bottom lip, no doubt destroying her lipstick. She wanted to say yes, but there was that stupid voice in her head telling her it wasn't a good idea.

"Come to my condo and I'll make you dinner." He paused and lowered his voice to a whisper as if he were imparting a great secret. "I promise not to poison you."

That made her laugh a little.

The sound of feet approaching caused her to look up. It was Jesse's dad. Her boss. He wasn't looking at her. His head was down, and he was reading something on his phone.

"I have to go," she said.

"You haven't answered my question. Dinner?"

She knew she shouldn't, but her mouth and her brain didn't seem to be communicating. "Okay."

Then, before he could say anything else, she hung up.

Blake Masters stopped in front of her desk and met her gaze. "Any messages?"

"Miss Layne from HR asked that you give her a call when you have time. She seemed a little distressed when she stopped by."

He nodded. "Anything else?"

I'm kinda, sorta dating your son? It was at that moment it dawned on her that Jesse had called to talk to his father and she'd hung up on him. "Your son called looking for you, but he didn't leave a message."

Blake Masters nodded and made his way toward his office. "Give me a half hour, and then we can get started on the second quarter reports."

"I'll order lunch. Did you want your usual?"

Her boss grinned. "Don't fix it if it isn't broken."

Cassie dialed her boss's favorite deli and placed their lunch order. As she waited for the food to be delivered, she finished what she'd been working on before Jesse called.

Two hours later, she had a pad full of notes that would keep her busy the rest of the afternoon. The one thing she'd learned about Blake Masters over her time working as his assistant was that he liked to be prepared. She'd spend hours researching things for him so he could be ready for a meeting.

As they were finishing up, Mr. Masters leaned back in his executive chair and met her gaze across the desk. "Have you thought about your future at the company?"

Of course her thoughts went to Jesse. Did her boss know? "What do you mean?"

"You've got a good head on your shoulders, Cassie. And while I'd be happy to have you as my assistant for the next twenty years, I also think you have talents beyond being my gatekeeper."

"Thank you, sir, but I'm happy where I am for now."

He nodded. "You'll let me know if that changes."

Cassie exited Mr. Masters's office and was surprised to find Jesse standing beside her desk. He was wearing a dark blue suit, and his hair looked a little rumpled. She imagined him running his hands through it. Her insides warmed remembering how she'd run her fingers through his hair on Saturday when he'd kissed her good night.

Their gazes met and she could have sworn his eyes darkened as he took her in. She licked her lips and swallowed. "What are you doing here?"

A slow smile pulled at his lips. "I came to see my father."

Of course he'd come to see his dad. "He's in his office."

Jesse nodded and walked toward her. She should move, but for some reason, she was frozen in place.

Her breath hitched as he came to a stop a few inches away. His eyes were intense, penetrating. "You hung up on me."

She swallowed. "I'm sorry. I—"

He placed his index finger over her lips, sending heat straight to her core. "We'll discuss it tonight. Six-thirty."

Dinner.

She nodded.

Jesse reached around her and swiped a sticky note and a pen from her desk. He scribbled something on it, dropped the pen on her desk, and handed her the note. Without another word, he went to his father's door and knocked.

Cassie looked down. His address. She'd been so flustered, she hadn't even thought to ask him for it.

Mr. Masters's voice sounded from inside the office. "Come in."

Jesse didn't look back at her before disappearing into his dad's office and closing the door.

Cassie blew out a breath and tried to clear her head. She had a pile of work to do and yet all she wanted was for Jesse to take her in his arms and kiss her again. The brief touch of his finger against her lips wasn't enough.

Forcing her feet to move, she took a seat behind her desk and pulled up a blank document. She'd managed to clear her head enough to enter in the notes from her meeting and start working on the list of action items her boss had wanted when Mr. Masters's office door opened.

She looked up from her screen, trying to prepare herself to see Jesse again. Her gaze zeroed in on him but was quickly pulled away when she realized he wasn't alone. Blake Masters strode out of the office behind his son. The two standing next to each other in their suits was striking.

"I'll get the official proposal to you by the end of the week," Jesse said to his father.

Blake Masters nodded, then turned his attention to Cassie. "I'm heading out. Call my cell if anything comes up."

"Of course."

The two men headed toward the elevator. She couldn't take her eyes off them. They waited for the elevator, then stepped inside. Her gaze locked with Jesse's and the side of his mouth quirked up. She'd been caught staring again. But even still, she couldn't look away. She held his gaze until the doors closed, removing him from view.

* * *

Jesse strolled into his condo a little after five. He removed his jacket and tie, then rolled up his sleeves and started working on dinner.

His mother had made sure he knew how to cook. She'd insisted it would come in handy throughout his life and she hadn't been wrong. In college, he'd been one of the few students who could cook a meal from scratch.

He wasn't a chef, but he could hold his own in the kitchen. Tonight, he'd settled on ribeye steak, sauteed green beans, and mashed potatoes. There was a knock at the door just as he was checking to make sure the steaks were ready. He set them on the cutting board to rest and went to let Cassie in.

She stood on his doorstep in a simple black dress. The fabric hugged her body and drew his gaze to the way her chest moved up and down. She clutched her purse in front of her, clearly nervous.

"Perfect timing. Dinner's almost ready," he said, taking a step back, inviting her in.

He expected her to hesitate, but she didn't. "It smells wonderful."

Jesse closed the door and went back to the kitchen. "I hope you like steak."

Cassie smiled and took a seat at his island. "I love steak."

He drained the potatoes and threw them in his mixer along with salt, pepper, butter, and some milk. Once that was mixing, he gave the green beans a final toss before removing them from the heat.

"You know your way around a kitchen."

He glanced at her before checking on the potatoes. "Does that help my chances?"

Cassie smiled. "Maybe a little."

Jesse chuckled. "I like an honest woman."

Satisfied the potatoes were ready, he plated their dinner, then carried it to the dining room table. Cassie followed. He laid the plates on the table, one across from the other, before pulling out a chair for her.

He made sure she was settled, then went to get the iced tea he'd picked up from the store. As much as he'd loved to dip into his wine collection, he wanted them both levelheaded and completely sober tonight.

Cassie waited for him to take his seat. "Thank you for dinner."

Jesse picked up his fork and nodded for her to do the same. "You're welcome."

They each cut into their steaks and he watched as she took her first bite. She closed her eyes as the steak hit her tongue and his mind went to a certain body part of his he'd like to have those lips wrapped around. Then she hummed and the sound went straight to his cock.

He hadn't planned for tonight to be about sex, but his libido was having other ideas. It had been a while. He hadn't been with anyone since he'd been home.

Her gaze met his and darkened. He knew she felt the same pull he did, but he also didn't want her to do something she didn't want to do. "I like you, Cassie. I think you know that."

She looked away. "I like you, too."

"Do you like me enough to risk things going wrong somewhere down the line?"

"I'm here, aren't I?"

Jesse cut another piece of his steak. "That doesn't answer my question."

She pushed her green beans around her plate. "I can't seem to say no to you."

"While I like the idea of you not being able to say no to me, I also don't like the idea of you being uncertain about being with me. I want you to be certain."

Cassie didn't comment for several minutes. She took three more bites of her food before responding. "We could get in trouble."

"Fraternization is discouraged. Not forbidden. Besides, we don't technically work together." He knew it was a fine line. Given his management position and that she worked for his father, they would no doubt interact in a professional capacity on a regular basis.

Again, she was quiet for several very long moments. "Would we keep it a secret?"

His first instinct was no. He didn't want to keep her locked away like some dirty secret. But he also understood the implications of going public. "Is that something you'd want?"

"I don't know."

He nodded. "If it were up to me, then no, I wouldn't want to keep you a secret."

"So you'd tell your dad about me? Us?"

Jesse laid his hand over hers. "I would."

She stabbed another piece of her steak and popped it into her mouth. He could tell she was thinking about what he'd said. If anything, he admired her for taking the time to weigh her options. He wanted her to agree, but he also wanted her to be sure. He was tired of the hot and cold vibe he kept getting from her.

"Can I ask you something?" she asked.

Jesse finished his dinner and pushed his plate to the side. "You can ask me anything, Cass." In fact, he had no doubt if they did decide to move forward with their relationship, she'd have quite a few questions.

"Would there be anyone else? I mean, would you be seeing anyone else besides me if we…"

Remembering what she'd told him about her ex, he couldn't blame her for asking, but it still stung a little. He would admit he'd played around with women in his early twenties, but they'd been aware of what had been on offer. He hadn't been interested in anything long term and neither had they. It had been about mutual pleasure.

Cassie was more than that. She was the type of woman he could see himself with for the long term. "If you're asking me if we'd be exclusive, then the answer is yes. I wouldn't be seeing anyone else in a relationship or sexual capacity besides you." He paused and waited for her to look at him. "And I'd expect the same in return."

Her eyes widened, but she didn't answer.

"Is that a problem?"

"No." She shook her head. "I mean, I wouldn't do that."

Jesse smiled and stood. "Are you finished?"

She looked at her plate and began to get up.

He stopped her. "I've got it."

"Thank you."

After rinsing their plates and loading them into the dishwasher, he filled two bowls with ice cream and carried them back to the table. Placing one in front of her, he took his seat again. "I hope you like chocolate."

Her lips curled up into a smile as she picked up her spoon. "Who doesn't like chocolate?"

"My mom."

Cassie sent him a skeptical look.

"I'm serious. She prefers vanilla."

"She doesn't know what she's missing."

Jesse chuckled. "No, she doesn't."

Cassie made it through half her ice cream before she spoke again. "Does this mean we're dating?"

"You haven't changed your mind on me again, have you?"

She shook her head. "No. I haven't changed my mind. I'm still worried, but the thought of seeing you at work but not being able to touch you again... to have you touch me..." Her gaze met his, her hazel eyes darker than usual.

Jesse put a spoonful of the rich ice cream in his mouth. "Is that something you think about a lot, Cassie? Me touching you?"

"Yes."

He could see the pulse in her neck beating out a rhythm. She was aroused and he knew it wouldn't take much to get her into his bed. And he did want her in his bed, but he also wanted to do things the right way.

Licking the last of his ice cream from his spoon, he stood and held out his hand for her. She took it and rose to stand beside him. Jesse slid an arm around her waist and pulled her against him. It had been two days since he'd kissed her, but it felt like weeks. He needed a taste.

She released a sigh the moment their lips touched. He could taste the chocolate ice cream lingering on her tongue. Her arms circled his neck and her fingers brushed through his hair as he pulled her closer to him. His erection pressed against her stomach, begging to be let free. The desire to feel her warmth surrounding him was almost too much and he knew he needed to get a grip on things before he lost control.

Breaking the kiss, he gazed into her eyes for a long moment, then kissed the tip of her nose. "How about a movie?"

She blinked. "A movie?"

He cleared his throat and took a step back. "You like movies, right?"

"Yes, but—"

Jesse took her hand and led her to his large couch. He made sure she was comfortable, then reached for the remote.

CHAPTER 7

"Is this going to be a dirty movie?" Cassie asked. Things had been heating up a moment ago, and now she felt he was pulling away. Why had he stopped?

Jesse paused and lowered the remote. "Did you want to watch a dirty movie?"

"No. I just don't understand why you suddenly want to watch a movie, that's all."

He'd planned to wait to have this conversation, but he supposed now was as good a time as any. She might decide to change her mind about a relationship after all.

Placing the remote back on the coffee table, he shifted in his seat to face her. "I want you to be completely comfortable with me, Cassie. From the little you've told me, your last relationship wasn't full of a lot of trust or communication. That's not what I want for us. In fact, to have the kind of relationship I desire, we both need to be completely open and honest with each other."

Cassie nodded. "I know I'm a little hesitant sometimes. I don't mean to be." She paused. "I just don't want to get hurt again."

He took her hand in his. "I'm aware of that, which is why I'm trying to go slow with you. I need you to trust me."

Her brow creased in confusion. "I don't understand."

"I'm a Dominant, Cassie. Do you know what that means?"

She didn't answer right away. He could almost see her brain working. "Like the guy in that movie?"

Jesse grinned. "Yes and no. A Dominant's first and foremost responsibility is to take care of the needs of his submissive."

He waited for her to process what he'd said, giving her time. When she met his gaze again, he could see her anxiety. "And you want me to be your submissive?"

"Yes, I do."

She didn't pull her hands away from his, which gave him hope she wouldn't get up and run screaming from his condo. Instead, she seemed to be taking in the new information, weighing it in her mind. "What would I have to do?"

"That would be negotiated. We would sit down and talk about our sexual history, then discuss what it is we like, what we're okay with, and the things we never want to do."

"Would you order me around, tell me what I'm allowed to do?"

He could tell by the tone of her voice she wasn't thrilled with that idea.

"Only when it comes to sex." He gave her hands a squeeze. "Other parts of your life wouldn't change unless you decide you want them to. Outside of the bedroom, we'd be like any other couple that's dating."

Cassie's long pauses were understandable. He was giving her a lot of new information to consider. "When would we...I mean, how would we start?"

He released one of her hands so he could cup her face. "I'll give you some papers before you leave tonight. I want you to read over them and fill them out to the best of your ability. It's called a limits list. It will let me know what you're interested in exploring. If there's something you don't understand, leave it blank and we can discuss it. All right?"

She took a deep breath and nodded. "I think I can do that."

Jesse trailed his fingers down her cheek and rubbed his thumb along her jaw. "Are you ready to watch that movie now or would you like me to drag you over my lap and spank you?"

Her eyes went wide as she froze.

He chuckled. "I'm kidding. We'll save the spanking for another time." He winked, dropped his hand, and retrieved the remote. "What are you in the mood for? Action? Drama? Sci-fi?"

To her credit, she blew out a breath and turned her attention to the screen. "Action sounds good."

Jesse flipped through the selections until he found something that sounded appealing. As the movie started playing, he reached for Cassie. She leaned against him, resting her head on his shoulder as she watched the movie play out on the screen.

An hour and a half later, Cassie sat up, smiling at him. "That was amazing."

"It was. I'd heard good things about it, and now I understand why."

Cassie stretched and his gaze went to the hem of her dress. She'd spent most of the movie curled up against his side, but in the last fifteen minutes or so, she'd squirmed in her seat as the climax of the movie had unfolded. The movement had caused her dress to creep higher and higher. Now it was bunched to the top of her thighs.

"Do you mind if I use your bathroom?" she asked.

Her question drew his attention away from the temptation. He knew he needed to be patient—that the wait would be worth it, but damn it was taking all his willpower to keep his hands to himself. "Of course. It's down the hall. Second door to your right."

She smiled at him, stood, and sashayed down the hall.

Jesse turned off the television and went to get the empty bowls of ice cream they'd left on the table. He rinsed them before putting them in the dishwasher and grabbing a towel to wipe down the counters.

That's where Cassie found him. To his surprise, she came up behind him and circled her arms around his waist.

He dropped the towel on the counter, turned to face her, and pulled her closer.

She gazed up at him, biting the side of her bottom lip. "Thank you for dinner. And the movie."

"No need to thank me. I like cooking for you."

Cassie smiled, but he could sense something was on her mind.

He pressed his forehead against hers. "What is it?"

"What if I can't do the submissive thing?"

Jesse pressed a soft kiss to her lips. "Do you remember when I walked you to your door after our first date and I told you to think of me when you touched yourself?"

"Yes." The admission came out in barely a whisper.

"Did you follow my instructions? Did you think of me while you brought yourself to orgasm?"

Her eyes closed as she swayed in his arms.

"Did you obey me, Cassie?"

She sucked in a breath, and he felt a shiver run through her body.

"Answer me."

"Yes."

Jesse covered her mouth with his. She opened for him, and he slid his tongue inside, stroking and tasting. His hands wanted to explore every inch of her, but he kept them on her back and hips. As much as he wanted to take things further, he knew it would be better... smarter...to wait.

He broke the kiss. "It's getting late. You need to get your rest."

She met his gaze, her pupils dilated with arousal. If he led her to his bedroom, she'd follow.

Placing another brief kiss on her now swollen lips, Jesse took two steps back, forcing himself to put some distance between them. "Wait here."

Jesse strolled into his study, still feeling the tingle of her lips against his. He was rock hard and would need to spend some quality time with his hand after she left, but it would be worth it. He had to keep reminding himself.

Going to his desk, he unlocked the bottom drawer and removed the blank limits list he'd printed out for her. He hadn't planned to give it to her quite this soon, but maybe it was better this way.

When he exited his study, she was exactly where he'd left her. Cassie met his gaze and held it as he crossed the room until he was standing in front of her. It was only then she seemed to notice the papers in his hand.

He handed them to her. "This is the limits list I was telling you about. Fill it out as best as you can and be honest. That's the most important thing. Don't mark something as okay because you think that's what I'd want."

She took the papers. "Okay. I'll be honest."

Jesse smiled. "I want you to text me when you get home so I know you arrived safe."

"I will." Cassie picked up her purse, folded the papers, and stuffed them inside.

He walked her to the door, admiring the way her ass swayed beneath the fabric. It was a good visual he'd use later tonight.

She began to leave, then stopped, meeting his gaze. "What about work?"

He'd been expecting her to ask and he'd been thinking it over. "We'll need to tell my dad and inform HR. I'll see if I can get some time with my dad tomorrow. Once that's done, we'll tackle HR."

A little worried wrinkle appeared on her forehead. "Do you think he'll be upset?"

"My dad?"

"Yeah."

Jesse thought about it. Blake Masters was a strange bird sometimes. He honestly had no idea how his dad would react, but he wasn't overly concerned about it either. His father was more likely to be upset with him than he was with Cassie, if he was bothered at all. He was hoping, however, that since his dad liked Cassie, he'd be okay with Jesse dating her. "No."

Cassie seemed to relax a little. "Okay. Well, I guess I'll see you tomorrow."

She started to walk out the door, but he hooked his arm around her waist and crushed her against him. He needed one more kiss.

Her arms went around his neck as she melted into him and kissed him back. They were both breathing hard when he finally let her go. He brushed his thumb over her bottom lip. "Drive safe."

Jesse stood in the doorway, watching her make her way down the hall. She glanced back at him before stepping onto the elevator. He had a moment where he wanted to chase after her, throw her over his shoulder, and carry her back into his condo, but he wanted to do this right and that meant taking it slow.

* * *

Cassie woke the next morning with a smile on her face. She'd texted Jesse the night before to let him know she'd gotten home safely. He'd replied immediately, telling her he'd stop by her desk at noon to take her to lunch.

Her nerves about them dating had everything to do with how other people would react. When they were together, only the two of them, Cassie wasn't thinking about who Jesse's father was. She was too busy enjoying being with him.

Brie was pouring cereal into a bowl when Cassie emerged from her room, dressed and ready for the day. She'd taken a little extra time with her makeup, wanting to look good for her lunch date. Her friend took one look at her and whistled.

Heat rushed to Cassie's cheeks.

Her friend laughed. "Want some cereal?"

"Sure."

Brie took another bowl out of the cabinet and topped it off with cereal as well. Then she went to the refrigerator and poured milk into both bowls before carrying them over to the small table.

Cassie managed to eat two bites before the questioning began. "You got home late last night. I'm guessing the date went well."

"Yes."

"Did you…" Brie lifted her eyebrows in a suggestive manner and gave a little wiggle in her chair.

She took another bite of her cereal. "No."

Brie gasped. "You turned him down?"

"No." Cassie's thoughts went to the papers he'd given her. They were folded and tucked in her purse. She needed to look at them, but

63

part of her was weary of what she'd find. What if there was crazy stuff on there? And what if he wanted to do that stuff with her? To her?

"I don't understand. The guy's clearly into you. And he invited you to dinner at his place. You're telling me he didn't make a move on you?"

Did he make a move on her? Did telling her he was a Dominant and he wanted her to be his submissive and do who knows what to her count?

Cassie didn't know the answer.

She could probably ask Brie. Her friend was better at relationships than Cassie and she knew Brie and Kaden had a healthy sex life. For all Cassie knew, Kaden was a Dominant, too. But for some reason, Cassie didn't want to talk about it with Brie. "We ate dinner and watched a movie."

"That's it?" A crease formed on her friend's forehead. "No dry humping or fingering you while you sucked him off?"

A picture formed in Cassie's mind and heat rushes between her legs. She hadn't missed the bulge in Jesse's pants the night before.

Clearing her throat, she picked up her spoon and took another bite of cereal. "No."

It was strange. When she'd started dating Greg, she'd been anxious to get Brie's take on everything that had happened between them. Where he'd taken her for their first date. How he'd asked her to come back to his place. She'd wanted her friend's opinion on all of it.

But with Jesse, it felt wrong somehow. She didn't want to share.

"Ugh! You're killing me. I want details."

Cassie scooped the last of her cereal into her mouth, chewed, and swallowed before answering. "He says he wants to take it slow." Of course Cassie wasn't sure how slow given what was burning a hole in her purse right now.

Brie was quiet while Cassie took her bowl to the sink. After a long moment, her friend pushed back her chair and carried her dishes over as well. "Maybe he's gay."

It was a good thing Cassie was done eating or she might have choked. "He's not gay."

Her friend raised a skeptical eyebrow.

"Trust me. He's not."

Brie still didn't look convinced.

"Look, I've gotta go or I'm going to be late." Cassie grabbed her purse from the back of the chair. "I should be home after work."

"Spaghetti for dinner?" Brie asked, letting the pervious topic go.

Cassie removed her lipstick and rubbed it over her lips before dropping the cylinder back into her bag. "Sounds perfect. Later."

She slipped into her parking spot in the company parking garage, then headed up to the executive floor. One of the perks of being an administrative assistant to the president of the company was she got her own parking spot close to the elevators. She didn't have to fight for a space and walk the length of a football field in heels.

Normally, she loved that perk, but today she thought the walk may have helped to calm her nerves. Or maybe not.

Jesse wasn't worried about his father's reaction to them dating, so she was trying to be positive. He knew Blake Masters better than she did. Maybe he'd even be happy for them.

The elevator doors opened and she made her way to her desk. Cassie waved to Anu, one of the other administrative assistants, as she passed by.

As Cassie rounded her desk, she noticed the single daisy. She picked it up and held it to her nose, then took a deep breath. The beautiful fragrance made her smile, as did the simple gesture.

She looked around to see if Jesse was still on the executive floor, but she didn't see him. How early had he come in to make sure the flower would be on her desk waiting for her?

Cassie was still grinning an hour later when her boss strolled up to her desk. "Good morning, Cassie."

"Good morning, Mr. Masters."

"My son called me this morning asking if I had some time on my schedule today. I told him I could do lunch. He said it was important, so it might run long. Could you call Paisley Grant and see if we can push our meeting back to two?"

Cassie smiled, but her stomach began doing flip-flops and not in a good way. "Of course."

"Thank you." He took a sip of coffee from the mug in his hand. "I'll be in my office if anyone needs me until my conference call at ten."

She nodded, but he was already walking away.

As soon as her boss's door was closed, Cassie picked up her phone and sent a text to Jesse.

Lunch? - Cassie

She tapped her foot as she waited for him to respond.

I told you I was taking you to lunch. - Jesse

Yes, but you didn't tell me it would be with your dad. - Cassie

Does that make a difference? I thought we agreed to tell him about us. - Jesse

Her fingers hovered over the screen as she contemplated her answer.

I thought we'd be meeting with him in his office or something. - Cassie

Trust me. - Jesse

Trust him. It's what he'd asked of her last night. He wanted her to be able to trust him. The question was, could she do that? This was a big leap considering her job could be on the line.

As she thought of last night...of how right it had felt to sit there on the couch with him watching a movie. And how when he held her and kissed her everything else faded away. There was only one way she could reply.

Okay. - Cassie

Then, she remembered the flower.

Thank you for the daisy. I love it. - Cassie

You're welcome. - Jesse

I'll see you in a few hours. - Jesse

CHAPTER 8

THE MORNING FLEW by and before Cassie knew it, her boss was exiting his office. He straightened his suit jacket, making sure his collar was lying flat. "Were you able to get in touch with Mrs. Grant?"

"Yes. She said she'll see you at two."

Blake Masters nodded and headed for the elevator.

Cassie blew out a breath and looked at the clock again. She had no idea what Jesse had planned. Having lunch with her boss to tell him she was dating his son wasn't exactly on her list of fun things to do, but Jesse had told her to trust him, so that's what she was going to do.

Or at least, that's what she was going to try to do.

At eleven fifty, the door to the stairwell opened, drawing her attention. Jesse stepped out and his gaze locked on hers. Despite her nerves, Cassie's heart rate kicked up a notch.

Jesse stopped two feet in front of her desk. "Ready for lunch?"

"Not even a little bit." Cassie grabbed her purse and stood anyway, rounding the desk to join him.

They walked side by side to the elevator, not speaking, but getting a few looks as they passed the other offices. Most of the executive assistants were still at their desks. She tried to ignore them and act like what she was doing was perfectly normal. Like she went to lunch with the boss's son every day.

After waiting for what felt like forever for the elevator to arrive, the doors opened, and they slipped inside. "Relax."

Cassie glanced over at him. "I'm trying."

"Would you like me to provide a distraction?" The sparkle in his eyes left no doubts as to what type of distraction he had in mind.

"No. Thank you."

Jesse chuckled. "Suit yourself."

The elevator doors opened, and they made their way to his car. He opened the door for her and waited until she lowered herself into the passenger seat before rounding the vehicle to get behind the wheel.

As soon as they were out of the parking garage, Jesse reached for her hand. He brought it to his lips and placed a kiss on the back of her palm. "Sure you don't want to take me up on my offer to relax you?"

"I'm not sure anything would relax me at the moment."

"You have little faith in my abilities. We're going to have to change that." He gave her hand a squeeze and lowered it to rest on his thigh.

"It's not that I doubt your…talents. It's more I'm not sure I can get my mind to shut off. I keep wondering what your dad will think when we walk in together."

To her surprise, Jesse pulled up in front of one of the fanciest restaurants in the city. "We're about to find out."

As soon as he came to a stop, a valet was at her door, opening it. She stared at him wide-eyed for a moment before standing. "Thank you."

"You're welcome, Ma'am."

Jesse came to stand beside her and laced their fingers together. He gave her hand a squeeze. "Just follow my lead."

She took a deep breath and nodded.

After giving his name to the hostess, they were led to the back of the restaurant, away from all the other guests. They stepped through a doorway and Cassie spotted Blake Masters. He was sitting alone, sipping a glass of red wine. One of the perks of being the boss, she supposed.

When he noticed Jesse, he smiled, but then he realized his son wasn't alone. A look of confusion took over his expression and she forced herself not to look away as they closed the distance.

Blake Masters wasn't a stupid man, and it didn't take him long to notice Jesse was holding her hand. He set his glass on the table and held his son's gaze.

They seemed to be having some sort of stare down she wasn't a part of. It was only their server coming to the table to get Cassie and Jesse's drink order that broke the tension.

Jesse ordered them both water, then helped her into her seat. Blake Masters still hadn't uttered a word.

As if nothing was wrong, Jesse picked up his menu. Not knowing what else to do, she did the same.

"The lamb here is very good," Jesse said.

She nodded and continued to scan over the menu. Or, at least, pretended to. She could feel the vibrations coming off Blake.

No one said a word until the server returned to take their lunch orders. With the menus no longer in front of them, there was nothing else to do but address the elephant in the room.

"Cassie and I are seeing each other."

Blake said nothing for several moments. "How long has this been going on?"

"We met at my birthday party. Her best friend is dating Kaden." Jesse appeared to be unaffected by his father's stiff demeanor.

Cassie wasn't. Her palms were sweating, and she was waiting for her boss to tell her she no longer had a job. But she was trying to do as Jesse asked. This was his father after all.

"You know fraternization is discouraged. It doesn't matter that you technically met before Jesse took over the management position."

"Yes, we know," Cassie said.

Jesse picked up his water and took a sip. "That's why we're meeting with HR this afternoon. We want everything to be out in the open. But we wanted to let you know first."

"You know how this will be perceived, the speculation, especially for Cassie," Blake said.

Cassie frowned. She hadn't thought of anything beyond potentially losing her job.

Jesse placed a hand on her thigh as if he could sense the thoughts running through her head. "If something happens, we'll address it. Until then, nothing should change. She works for you, not me."

"It won't matter. You're my son and it will be implied that as your girlfriend you'll be able to use your influence with me on her behalf."

"I don't expect any special treatment," Cassie said.

Before he could respond, their salads arrived. Everyone remained quiet until they were alone once more.

Blake draped his napkin across his lap and picked up his fork. "Again, it won't matter." Then, he turned his focus on Jesse. "I do hope you know what you're doing."

"I do."

They held each other's gazes for a long moment before both men seemed to relax and dig into their salads. Cassie had no idea what had just happened, but she was sure something had. Blake stabbed a piece of lettuce with his fork. "You know you're going to have to bring her over for dinner."

Jesse smiled. "We'll check our schedules."

An hour later, Cassie was sitting next to Jesse in his car and they were heading back to the office. She was glad at least that hurdle was over, but she couldn't help but replay Blake's warning. Was there someone specific she needed to watch out for, or was it more of a general note of caution?

She was so lost in her thoughts she didn't realize they'd pulled off to the side of the road. "What—"

Cassie wasn't able to get anything else out before Jesse's lips covered hers. All her swirling thoughts went out the window at the feel of his mouth moving against hers.

"Feeling better?" he asked several minutes later.

It took her a moment to realize he'd asked her a question. "Why'd you do that for?"

"You looked like you needed it."

Had she needed it? Maybe she had. "We were going back to the office."

Jesse smiled, his eyes lighting up with his amusement. "I decided to take a short detour. I'm trying to be good and not kiss you at work."

"Oh."

He gave her another lingering kiss, then turned to face the road and maneuvered back into traffic. Two minutes later, they were driving into the parking garage.

Walking into the building felt different now that they weren't keeping things a secret. She could tell he wanted to hold her hand because he kept brushing the back of his hand against hers.

They rode up the elevator to the executive floor and he followed her to her desk. "Our appointment with HR is at two. I'll meet you there."

She nodded. "Thanks for lunch."

"Don't spend the next hour worrying about what will happen, okay? Things will be fine. You'll see. Soon, it'll be normal for people to see us together around here."

Cassie really wanted that.

There was still that lingering voice in the back of her head, wondering about the list he gave her and if she'd be able to meet his expectations. She'd never been a submissive before and her limited knowledge came from movies and television shows.

Before she could let her mind go too far down the rabbit hole, her boss emerged from his office. He took one look at his son, then at her, and back at his son. "Don't you have some work to do?"

Jesse smiled and straightened, then his gaze met hers. "I'll see you at two."

He headed toward the elevator, and she turned to see what her boss needed.

* * *

All things considered, lunch with his dad went as well as could be expected. His dad had always encouraged him to weigh the pros and cons of a situation, what he wanted, and how it would affect others before deciding on a course of action.

Pursuing Cassie was no different. He wanted Cassie. There was no hesitation there. She was beautiful, sweet, and had a humble air about her he found appealing. She wasn't afraid to speak her mind, something he needed in a partner given his sexual preferences, but she wasn't obnoxious about it.

As for how their relationship would affect others?

Besides the obvious speculation it would cause, Jesse didn't see it having any effect on anyone other than maybe his father. Cassie was good at her job. She'd been his dad's administrative assistant for long enough and each knew what the other's expectations were.

When it came to everyone else in the office…

As far as he was concerned, him managing the accounting department was more of a potential minefield than him dating his father's assistant.

He made his way to his office. Stephanie, his administrative assistant, looked up from whatever she'd been working on as he approached. "Welcome back. How was your lunch?"

"Very good." He paused beside her desk. "Could you see if Shannon has yesterday's figures ready for me yet? I wanted to try and look them over before my two o'clock."

"Sure." She stood and went off in search of Shannon.

Normally, he would have gone to Shannon's desk himself and asked for the report, but he already had three missed calls from his mother. It didn't take a genius to know his dad had talked to her after leaving the restaurant.

They'd been married for thirty-five years and there were no secrets between them. Growing up, he'd hated it. There was no going to one parent to ask permission to do something, then if he didn't get the answer he wanted, go to the other parent. Blake and Florence Masters didn't play that game. The one time he'd tried it, he'd ended up not only losing his gaming system for the week, but he'd also had to weed his mom's flowerbeds.

Lowering himself into his highbacked chair, Jesse dialed his mother. She answered on the first ring.

"I was beginning to wonder if you were avoiding me."

He chuckled. "Never. I just got back to my desk."

"I'm sure you know why I called. You need to bring Cassie to dinner so I can meet her."

"Mom, you know Cassie. She's dad's assistant."

"I'm perfectly aware of who she is," his mom said. "But it's not as if I've sat down and gotten to know her. I've only seen her in passing and exchanged pleasantries when I came to the office to see your father."

"Fair enough." He'd come with his mom to see his dad at the office many times over the years and he'd never spent much time wondering about who his dad's assistant was. "When would you like us to come?"

"Friday night. Six o'clock. Don't be late."

The smile wouldn't leave his face. His mom was giving him a hard time, but he knew she was secretly thrilled. She wanted grandbabies. "I'll talk to Cassie and make sure she doesn't already have plans. I'll call you back after work to confirm."

Jesse hung up with his mom and logged into his computer. He was going through his emails when Stephanie walked in with the reports he'd been waiting for. "Thanks."

He expected her to leave, but she remained in his office.

"Did you need something?"

Stephanie shifted her weight, a sign she was nervous about whatever it was she was about to say.

He stopped what he was doing and gave her his full attention. "You aren't quitting, are you?"

Her eyes went wide. "What? No. I just…"

Jesse raised an eyebrow in question.

"I stopped by the break room, and I overheard something." She glanced at the picture of him graduating college he had hanging on the wall, his dad's arm around him and a big smile on both of their faces. "They said you were seen leaving the building with Cassie Ross, your dad's assistant." She paused. "And they were speculating on how you spent your lunch break."

"Close the door."

It took a moment for his words to register, but when they did, Stephanie did as he asked and shut the door.

"Have a seat." Jesse motioned to the seat across from his desk.

Stephanie lowered herself into the chair and folded her hands in front of her as if she were waiting for him to reprimand her.

"Cassie Ross and I are dating. We've been dating for a couple of weeks now and my two o'clock meeting today is with HR to let them know about our relationship." His timeline was a little exaggerated, but it sounded better than saying they'd met a little over a week ago. "As for lunch today, we met with my father to tell him about our relationship."

"If you're telling HR today, then why the secrecy?" Stephanie asked.

"I don't want to fuel the rumor mill. Nor do I want people hovering outside my office trying to listen in to find out any tidbit of information they can. However, as you'll be the buffer between me and those who are so eager for information, I figured you should know the situation."

She nodded.

"I appreciate your discretion on this." It was a request, but it was also a reminder he didn't want her blabbing about his personal life in the break room.

"Of course, Mr. Masters. I won't say anything."

"Thank you."

Forty-five minutes later, Jesse stood outside HR, waiting. They had an appointment with the HR manager in two minutes and Cassie wasn't there yet. He checked his phone again, but there were no messages.

With less than thirty seconds to spare, she came rushing down the hall.

"Are you all right?"

She nodded. "Yes. Sorry I'm late. Corrine needed my help with her computer."

Her hair had come loose from its clip and he wanted desperately to brush it behind her ear. "Are you ready for this, or do you need a few minutes?"

"I'm ready," Cassie said. "Let's get this over with."

The meeting with the HR manager had him feeling as if he'd been sent to the principal's office. Courtney Layne would have made a good headmistress at a private girls' school. She wore a tailored suit, her makeup was on the heavy side, and her hair was pulled up tight into a bun.

They'd each been given a copy of the employee manual and read the section regarding fraternization. Then she'd gone farther, saying she expected us to remain professional while on company property. She clearly didn't have an issue with him being Blake Masters's son.

Cassie let out a loud breath when they left the HR department.

"Feels like we just left the principal's office."

He'd been hoping to lighten the mood, and it worked.

Cassie laughed. "Yes, it does. I was kind of expecting it, though."

"Why's that?" he asked, moving them toward the elevator.

"There was a couple in shipping and receiving last year. It didn't end well and one of them quit. Your dad considered changing the policy to forbid fraternization, but changed his mind when he realized there are five married couples that work for him."

"That many?" They got into the elevator, and he punched the number for the executive floor.

She nodded. "There's also a mother and daughter."

His hand brushed against the back of hers as they stood side by side in the enclosed space. It was testing his discipline not to touch her the way he wanted. He could see why working together would be an issue. He'd want his hands on her all the time.

Deciding to switch the subject, he moved to a more pressing matter. "My mom would like us to come to dinner on Friday night. She wants to meet you. Are you available?"

"Your mom comes in at least once a month. She's already met me."

"She's met you as my father's assistant. Now, she wants to meet you as my girlfriend."

Cassie gazed up at him. "Is that what I am?"

Jesse clenched his fists to keep from reaching out. "I thought I'd made that clear last night."

She didn't look away until the elevator doors opened. There was no one waiting on the other side, but she left his side before turning to face him. "I guess that makes you my boyfriend, then, huh?"

Jesse smirked. "Yeah, I guess it does."

Smiling, she turned to go.

"You haven't answered my question. Friday night? Dinner?"

She looked back, meeting his gaze, and nodded as the elevator doors closed between them.

He shook his head, laughing as he headed back to his office.

CHAPTER 9

IF CASSIE HAD THOUGHT Tuesday was bad, Wednesday was a nightmare. Every time she left her desk, she got side glances and whispers.

She was happy to find the elevator empty when she headed down to IT. It would only take a minute to get to her destination, but she was grateful for that small moment. For some reason, she hadn't thought it would be this bad.

Even Jesse was encountering some of it, and he'd texted to see how she was doing. That alone made her day better. She couldn't imagine any of her previous boyfriends checking in with her like that.

Jesse had wanted to take her out to lunch, just the two of them, but then he'd been called into a meeting. Considering the previous manager of his department had been fired, Cassie had no doubt Jesse had his hands full.

She exited the elevator and made her way down the hall. IT was tucked away in a corner on the second floor, away from all the other departments. It was also freezing and she'd forgotten to bring her sweater.

Grayson Hyde, the head of IT, was bent over a computer, his

glasses halfway down his nose. He didn't look up when she approached. "Hi, Grayson."

His only response was a grunt. This wasn't unusual. He got hyper focused when he was working on a problem.

"I have some papers I need you to look over and sign."

"Put them on my desk."

"Mr. Masters needs them this afternoon."

Grayson sighed and stood to his full height, which wasn't much more than hers. He took the papers, scanned the contents, and scribbled his name.

She took them from him and slid them into a folder. "Thank you."

Cassie turned to go and was met with four very curious faces peeking out of nearby cubicles. They all ducked back into their respective offices when they realized they'd been caught.

She bit the inside of her cheek as she marched toward the elevator, her irritation growing. It wasn't as if she was screwing her boss. She was dating his son. It wasn't a big deal.

But clearly, it was. At least for her coworkers.

Most of them, anyway. Alinda still greeted her with her usual smile when they'd run into each other in the break room, and Nester hadn't batted an eye when she'd almost bumped into him as she'd rushed into the elevator earlier. It gave her hope that maybe once people got used to the idea of her and Jesse being an item things would calm down. Go back to normal. She hoped.

When she returned to her desk, her boss's door was open, so she took him the paperwork he'd needed from Grayson. He was working on his computer. "I have the paperwork you asked for from IT."

He took the papers. "Thank you."

She nodded and turned to go. That was another thing she was grateful for. Her working relationship with her boss hadn't changed in all this. He still treated her the same. Still greeted her the same way he always had when he came in and still had the same expectations of her. It was the stability she needed as she spent most of her day at her desk doing work for him.

With only a few minutes left of her workday, Cassie began shutting down her computer and straightening her desk.

She removed her purse from the drawer where she kept it and stood. When she looked up, she came face-to-face with those sea-blue eyes she often found herself getting lost in.

"Hi." The word came out on a soft breath as her body reacted to his presence.

He smiled, making her heart rate kick up a notch. "I was hoping we could grab dinner since we weren't able to have lunch."

She looked around, seeing who may be watching them. "I don't know if that's a good idea."

Jesse frowned and his tone hardened. "Have you changed your mind?"

Her eyes widened and she shook her head. "No. I just…" She glanced around again. "Maybe we shouldn't be seen together at work."

"I told you, Cassie, I'm not hiding. They'll get used to it."

She nodded and stepped out from behind her desk. Walking over to her boss's door, she knocked.

He looked up. "Heading out?"

"Yes, unless there was something else you needed."

"I think I'm good. Enjoy your evening."

"You, too."

Only a handful of people stared at Cassie and Jesse as they made their way to the parking garage together, but that was because the rest had already left. Jesse walked her to her car and waited for her to unlock it. She opened the car door and turned to face him.

His fingers brushed against hers as they stood too close to each other. "Drive home. I'll follow you."

"Okay." She didn't move to get into the vehicle.

Jesse's gaze lowered to her lips. "Get in the car, Cassie."

It took a lot of effort on her part, but she did as he asked, lowering herself into the seat. He gripped the door hard, his knuckles turning white before shutting it, turning around, and striding away.

Cassie closed her eyes and took a moment to center herself before she backed out of the parking space and headed toward her apartment.

Twenty minutes later, she pulled into the parking garage attached to her building. Jesse was right behind her. He got out of his car and met her as she was climbing out of her vehicle.

Her smile disappeared as he pulled her against him. He crushed his mouth over hers, his hands running down her back to cup her ass.

She circled her arms around his waist, kissing him back with all the pent-up tension she was feeling. It wasn't only about not being able to touch each other anytime they wanted. It was also that she felt safe with him. She felt as if he'd catch her if she fell and it was an intoxicating feeling.

He broke the kiss and pressed his lips to her temple. "Baby, we need to stop or I'll lay you out right here on the hood of your car."

Cassie tucked her head into his shoulder as she tried to catch her breath. "I don't think my neighbors would like that very much."

"Right now, I couldn't give a shit about your neighbors."

She chuckled. If she were being honest, she wasn't sure she did either. Which was unusual for her. She'd known Jesse less than two weeks. Normally, she'd never consider sleeping with him this soon, but whenever he kissed her, she lost all sense of reason.

He kissed the top of her head. "How are you doing?"

It took her a moment to realize what he was asking. "I'm better now."

He smiled. "Are you ready to go, or would you like to change first?"

Glancing down at her outfit, Cassie knew she should change. Her three-piece suit didn't exactly scream dinner date. It was more along the lines of a business lunch. "I should probably change."

Jesse took a step back, making sure she was steady on her feet, then took her hand and led her into the building. He waited in the living room while she changed.

When she emerged from her bedroom, Jesse scanned her from head to toe. She'd opted for a spring dress since he'd said they were going somewhere casual. It had spaghetti straps, a low neckline, and it showed off her figure.

His eyes darkened and she felt something low in her belly. Maybe she should tell him she didn't want to go slow, beg him to take her to her bedroom and strip her naked.

The thought was appealing, but then there was the whole dominance and submission thing to consider.

She was still contemplating her options when Jesse groaned. Before she could react, he took her hand and led her out the door.

*　*　*

Jesse blew out a breath to calm himself before opening his door and sliding behind the wheel. He'd never had an issue finding women. Not women to date or women to sleep with. None of them, however, had made him feel as out of control as Cassie did. He wanted to claim her in every way. Screw the consequences.

If it were only sex, that could be dealt with. Sexual attraction came in various forms and intensities. But this was on a whole other level. He both wanted to know everything about her and simultaneously wanted to fuck her and never let her leave his bed. That hadn't happened to him before.

Not wanting to deal with a whole lot of people in a restaurant, Jesse drove to the park. It was a place he liked to come to when he needed to be alone with his thoughts. It had gardens, a lake, and plenty of benches where one could sit and process whatever problem or situation was plaguing them.

"I haven't been here in years," Cassie said as they made their way over to two food trucks parked in the opposite side of the parking lot.

Jesse guided her over to one. "Joe has the best hot dogs."

"Do you come here a lot?"

"I come here when I need to think." Normally, he wouldn't admit that to someone he was dating, but he wanted Cassie to know.

"There was a lake near my dad's house I used to go to sometimes. Especially, in the first couple of years after my parents' divorce."

He noticed Cassie referred to her dad a lot. She'd told him about her family, including her younger brothers, but family wasn't at the top of his mind right now. "How did the rest of your day go?"

Cassie shrugged as she took a bite of her hot dog. "A lot of nosy people, but no one said anything directly to me. I know they were talking behind my back, but I tried to ignore them."

"They'll get over it eventually."

He received no response.

"Cass, I know this will be difficult at first. People like to gossip. They'll move on to other things once they realize it isn't a big deal. We're just two people who happen to be dating."

"I'm not sure some of them will ever see it like that. There's always going to be a question as to whether one of us is getting special treatment because your dad owns the company." She met his gaze. "I knew it was going to happen, but I naively hoped since I'd been there for so long and they all know me that they wouldn't make such a big deal of it."

Jesse took her hand and moved it into his lap. "If it gets to be too much, I want you to tell me."

"There's nothing you can do."

"Cassie." His tone conveyed how he felt about her dismissal. Even though they hadn't discussed the specifics of the power dynamic part of their blooming relationship, he was still a Dominant. Open communication was a critical part of a power exchange. It was best she understood that from the beginning.

She held his gaze for a long moment before looking across the lake. "I've been doing some research." The breeze ruffled her hair, lifting it away from her neck, and she tucked a strand behind her ear. "How long have you"—her gaze took in their surroundings, making sure no one was close by—"been into dominance and submission?"

He was pleased she'd brought up the subject and that she'd caught on to the fact it wasn't her boyfriend who had been insisting on her telling him if things got worse at work. "I began dabbling in college, but I didn't do much besides some basic scenes until I moved to Europe."

The muscles in her neck constricted as she swallowed. She still wasn't looking at him. "What if I can't do it? Will you still want me to be your girlfriend?"

"You're worried you won't be able to submit to me?"

She shrugged. "I'm not sure. I don't have a lot of experience when it comes to men and sex and certainly not"—she lowered the volume of her voice to a whisper—"the type of sex where you do kinky stuff."

Jesse couldn't help but smile. There was no one close enough to hear them. "I quite like the fact I'll be the one introducing you to a world of sexual pleasures." He ran his thumb along the inside of her wrist. "Have you filled out the papers I gave you?"

Cassie nodded.

He decided to test the waters. They couldn't do anything torrid, but he could have some fun teasing her. He gave her arm a gentle tug. "Come here."

Again, she glanced around them. When she spotted no one close by, she scooted closer.

"On my lap."

Her eyes widened. "What if someone sees?"

Jesse raised an eyebrow and waited. He wanted to see if she'd trust him enough to do what he requested.

After several long moments, she stood, took a step to her left, and sat down on his lap. She went to turn so her legs hung off the side of his lap, but he stopped her. "No turning. I want you facing the water."

She swallowed but didn't fight him.

He took the napkin she still held in her hand and stuffed it, along with his own napkin, in his pocket before leaning back against the bench. "Rest your back against my chest."

Cassie leaned back.

Pressing a kiss to the skin at the base of her neck, he circled his arms around her. To the outside observer, they were a young couple cuddling by the water, enjoying the way the evening sun danced across the water.

Jesse positioned his legs between hers and pulled her thighs apart slightly. It wasn't enough to see up her dress, but it would allow the breeze to caress her inner thighs.

He felt her stiffen. "Relax." Then to add to his words, he ran his thumbs along the underside of her breasts. "Watch the water and just feel."

Slowly, Cassie began to let the tension leave her body. If their circumstances were different, if they were in a different place without the wandering eyes of children, he may have pushed things, but they weren't and she wasn't quite ready for that yet, even if his cock was rock hard and begging to thrust into her pussy.

They sat on the bench until the sun began to set, turning the trees brilliant reds and oranges. Most of the families had gone home. Even the animals were starting to settle in for the night.

He sat up, bringing her with him. "I should get you home."

Cassie turned in his arms. Her gaze lingered on his lips, and he knew what was on her mind. It was on his too.

Jesse brushed his lips across hers, and Cassie closed her eyes. He waited until she opened them again. "I promise I'll kiss you properly when I get you home."

"What if I don't want to go home yet?" she whispered.

He rested his forehead against hers and took a steadying breath. She was difficult to resist, but he knew it would be worth it. "Tomorrow, I want you to bring a change of clothes to work with you and let Brie know you won't be home tomorrow night."

Cassie licked her lips and nodded.

Before things could get out of hand, Jesse stood, lifting her. She let out a little squeak, gripping his biceps as he guided her feet to the ground.

Jesse grinned. "Get to the car, Cass."

She turned to walk away, presenting him with her ass, and he couldn't help himself. He gave her behind a swift but firm swat.

Cassie jumped and looked back at him. Their gazes held for a moment before he saw one side of her lips curl up. Something told him she was going to like being his submissive and he couldn't wait to see her kneeling before him, ready, willing, and eager to follow his command. Tomorrow night couldn't come soon enough.

CHAPTER 10

Brie's spoon stopped halfway to her mouth. She stared at Cassie for a long moment, then her mouth curved up into a smile. "Do you need some pointers? I know it's been a while."

Cassie rolled her eyes. "Stop it. I don't even know if we're going to…you know."

Her friend scoffed. "It really has been a long time if you think a guy asking you to spend the night doesn't mean you're going to have sex. Maybe we need to start from the beginning. Go over the basics."

"Very funny."

"Well, I'm here if you need me." Brie's eyes shined with amusement as she ate her cereal.

Shaking her head, Cassie finished her bagel and cleaned up before heading to work with her overnight bag in tow. Stuffed in the side pocket was the limits list Jesse had given her. He hadn't specifically asked her to bring it, but she felt it was better to be safe than sorry.

She tried to keep her mind on work as she scanned through the reports on her desk, but it was difficult to concentrate. All she could think about was what was going to happen later. Or, at least, what might happen later. She was equal parts excited and nervous.

The research she'd done on BDSM varied a lot. Some of it she thought she'd be okay with—maybe even like. But there were other parts she couldn't see herself enjoying. Those were the parts that had her questioning her sanity. That and the fear she couldn't please him. She wasn't exactly the most experienced twenty-seven-year-old.

Of course, when she'd brought her lack of experience up to Jesse, he'd turned it around, saying he liked the idea. Given some of the things she'd seen in her research, that made no sense, but he'd told her to trust him and that's what she was attempting to do. She only hoped she didn't disappoint him.

By the time five o'clock rolled around, Cassie was a ball of nerves. She knew she shouldn't be. This was what she wanted. Or, at least, she was pretty sure she did. But she couldn't stop the worry churning inside her.

Shutting down her computer, Cassie walked to her boss's door and knocked.

"Enter."

She opened the door and stuck her head inside. "Was there anything else you need before I leave for the day?"

Blake Masters looked up from his computer. "I don't believe so. Enjoy your evening, Cassie."

She nodded, closed the door, and took a step back...right into a solid wall of flesh.

Jesse's aftershave permeated the air around her a moment before his low, deep voice sent shivers down her body that settled between her legs. "Are you ready to go?"

Cassie swallowed, trying to control her heart rate. "Yes. I just need to get my purse." She turned to face him and all attempts to regulate her heartbeat failed as she met his gaze.

He lifted his arm and she saw her purse dangling from two of his fingers.

"Thank you." She took her purse and draped it over her shoulder.

"I'll follow you to my place," Jesse said, his voice making her want to beg him to touch her.

But she knew they couldn't. Not here. Not now. There were too many curious eyes, and his father was in the next room.

Jesse smirked, his blue eyes darkening. He knew exactly what she was thinking. "If you keep looking at me like that, I'm going to ask my father if we can borrow his office."

That got her feet moving. She couldn't make it to her car fast enough.

It took them entirely too long to reach his condo. She kept glancing in her rearview mirror to confirm he was still behind her.

Jesse parked his car beside hers in the parking garage before coming to help her out of her vehicle. Tingles moved up her arm when he took her hand and guided her to her feet. He glanced in her back seat. "Where's your bag?"

She licked her lips, desperate for moisture. "In the trunk."

He bent down, his shoulder grazing her hip as he pulled the lever to pop the trunk. How could something so simple send her pulse racing?

Cassie released a steadying breath when he left her side to retrieve her bag. She felt hot all over and he wasn't even touching her.

Jessie reached into the truck and grabbed her bag. He slung her overnight back over his shoulder, then closed the trunk. Their gazes met and his smirk returned.

He held out his hand for her and she took it. Lacing their fingers together, he placed a kiss on her forehead, then guided her toward the elevator.

The reality of the situation began to sink in as they ascended to his floor. The doors opened and the weight of everything seemed to make each step feel heavier than the last. They were really doing this. She was really doing this.

Brie was right. A guy didn't ask you to sleep over if he didn't plan on having sex with you. And Jesse didn't just want sex with her. He wanted kinky sex with her.

Jesse must have felt the change in her mood as they stepped off the elevator. He ran the tips of his fingers over her jaw in a sweet caress. "We're going to talk. Then you can decide if you want anything more."

Talk. She could do that. She was good at talking. Most of the time.

Cassie nodded.

He gave her hand a comforting squeeze as they made their way down the hall to his condo.

His place looked the same as it had when she was there two nights ago down to the book lying on his coffee table. "I'm going to put your bag in the spare room."

She nodded, then caught herself. "Um. The papers…the list…"

He glanced at the bag, then at her. "Dinner first. Then we can discuss the rest."

Dinner? Would she even be able to eat knowing the stuff they'd be talking about after?

As an answer to her question, her stomach growled. She hadn't eaten anything since lunch, and the half of a ham sandwich and chips were long gone.

Jesse returned a few minutes later. "I ordered us Chinese food." He checked his watch. "It should be here any minute."

Feeling the need to say something, she went to the only thing she could think of. "How did you know I like Chinese food?"

He smiled and removed two glasses from the cabinet. "I have my sources."

The only two people who would know her food preferences and would share them with Jesse were her best friend and her boss. She was pretty sure Brie would have mentioned talking to Jesse, which left Jesse's father.

Shock and embarrassment soared through her at the thought that Jesse had discussed their evening plans with the man who signed her paychecks. "You told your dad about tonight?"

"That we're having dinner? Yes. Why wouldn't I?" Jesse asked.

She blanched. "Does he know? About your relationship preferences, I mean?" Flashes of Jesse and his dad discussing the kinky things Jesse wanted to do to her were turning her stomach sour. Would he do that?

Jesse filled the glasses with ice and set them on the counter. "The last conversation I had with my father regarding my sex life was when I was fourteen. It consisted of him handing me a box of condoms and telling me not to get a girl pregnant." He opened the refrigerator and removed a pitcher of what looked to be water with lemon slices in it, then carried it to the table along with the glasses.

As he set everything down, there was a knock on the door.

She'd been so focused on their conversation, the sound startled her, and she let out a squeak.

Jesse cradled her face with his palm in a comforting gesture. "It's just the food."

A few seconds passed before he dropped his hand and went to answer the door.

Cassie was still trying to process everything when he returned with two bags of Chinese food. She could smell the familiar scents of soy sauce and ginger, and it made her stomach growl again. This time, he heard it.

"Have a seat. I'll get us some plates."

Starving, she did as he asked and took a seat at the table next to one of the glasses.

He returned a moment later with two plates and silverware. "I prefer real silverware over plastic. The stuff they give you breaks too easy."

For some reason, her snark decided to make an appearance. "Maybe you're too rough with it."

Again, he grinned. "Maybe."

He seemed to like her snark, although that didn't seem to fall in line with her research. Didn't Dominants want submissives to follow their commands?

Jesse placed two containers in front of her. He opened the flaps, revealing shrimp fried rice and hot and sour soup—her favorites.

"How did you know?" Her words trailed off as she realized she already knew the answer. His dad.

As if reading her mind, he began to talk as he loaded up his plate with his own meal. "Cass, I'd never betray your trust by discussing our private relationship with my father. Little things like what you like to eat for lunch or how you take your coffee are a different matter. Private things. Intimate things. Those are between us and no one else."

She knew he was making sense. And it wasn't a big deal he asked his dad about her favorite Chinese food. The real cause of her emotions was tucked into her overnight bag. "Can I ask you something?"

"Of course. You can ask me anything."

"What happens if we go over my list and we're not compatible?"

He swirled his lo mien noodles around his fork and met her gaze. "We negotiate."

She swallowed. "I'm not good at negotiation."

A wicked gleam in his eye, he responded, "That's better for me, then." Taking a bite, he chewed and went for another. "Eat. Once we're finished, we'll go over our lists. You seem to be anxious to get started."

* * *

Jesse kept an eye on her as he ate his beef lo mien. She was nervous, and he understood that. He was asking her to explore her sexuality in ways she'd never considered before.

The list he'd given her was extensive. He'd explored some kink clubs while he was overseas and one of the nicer ones he'd encountered had the most extensive list of kinks on their website he'd ever seen. It was from that, and viewing other limit lists in the past, that he'd created the list he'd given Cassie.

He didn't want this process to be stressful for her. The list and the play were meant to be mutually beneficial. This wasn't only about his pleasure but hers as well. He was hoping once they got started, she'd understand that.

"How was your day?" he asked, wanting to redirect her focus.

"It was okay."

He waited to see if she'd go on, but she didn't. "Any more problems from your coworkers?"

"I was at my desk most of the day. Everyone seemed to leave me alone unless they needed to drop something off for Mr. Masters." She paused. "It feels strange calling him Mr. Masters when we're talking, but I don't know if I feel comfortable calling him Blake, either."

"It's fine. Call him whatever you're comfortable calling him. I won't be offended either way."

She smiled and continued eating her food.

Jesse wished he could say the same about his day. He'd stopped by the break room to get a refill on coffee and overheard his name as he approached the door. Not one to shy away from confrontation, he strolled inside and met the stares of the two women sitting at the small round table. One of them had looked guilty as hell. The other had met his gaze head-on and given him a big, knowing grin.

He'd greeted them as though he hadn't heard anything and proceeded to get his coffee. They remained quiet while he moved about the room, but he saw the looks they were shooting each other. As he was about to leave, he stopped by their table. "Is there something you ladies needed?"

Again, the one looked ready to dart out of the room and hide under her desk. The other met his stare head-on. "Not at all, Mr. Masters. We're just enjoying our lunch."

He'd wanted to press more, but two other colleagues came in and he lost his opportunity. Besides, what was he going to say? They all knew he and Cassie were an item. Office gossip was to be expected, but the boldness of this woman was rubbing him the wrong way. He was sure, given the opportunity, she'd be one of the ones giving Cassie a hard time.

Jesse and Cassie finished their meals and he stood to clear their dishes. "Why don't you get your list and we'll get started? The spare room is the first door to your left. Your bag's on the bed."

Cassie stood without a word and made her way down the hall. He was beginning to think most of her nerves were from the waiting rather than the prospect of going over their lists together. It was information to remember for future use. His girl didn't like being made to wait and he'd bet that included orgasms as well.

She returned less than a minute later with her papers in hand.

He motioned for her to retake her seat at the table. "I'll be right back."

Not giving her time to respond, he ducked into his study, opened the bottom drawer of his desk, and extracted his list.

When he returned to the dining room, Cassie sat with her back ramrod straight and her palms facing down on the table, her list in front of her. She looked up at his approach and he knew he'd enjoy seeing those hazel eyes of hers beaming up at him as she kneeled before him.

He took a seat next to her. "I know you've never done this before, so I want to be clear on how this works." He waited for her to meet his gaze. "We're going to talk about a lot of things, including our past sexual histories and experiences. There's nothing to be embarrassed about and no need to be shy. I'll learn every inch of you soon enough."

A light pink darkened her cheeks at that. He really did love seeing that flush of her skin and wondered how far down it went.

That, however, was going to have to wait for another time. He placed his list in front of him and met her gaze. "First, let's talk about your sexual experience. How many sexual partners have you had?"

Her eyes went wide and he saw the pulse in her neck pick up its pace. "Do I have to answer that?"

"Yes." Jesse wasn't sure why she was hesitating. He knew she didn't have a lot of sexual experience with men.

She swallowed and looked down. "Two."

That was lower than he'd expected. He knew she hadn't slept with her last boyfriend, but she was twenty-seven.

He tried not to think about all the possibilities and focused on what she was saying. "Tell me about them."

"What do you want to know?" Her voice was soft, barely audible if he hadn't been sitting so close to her. She was clearly uncomfortable.

"Who was the first?" he asked.

"My high school boyfriend. Brian."

"How old were you?" It seemed he was going to have to pull every little detail out of her.

"Sixteen."

"How was the experience?"

She froze and her hands curled into fists. "I don't remember."

He knew she was lying and that irked him, but her body language had all his protective instincts on high alert. "You don't remember your first time?"

"Can we talk about something else?"

Jesse knew she wanted him to drop it, but he refused. Not only did he want to know, he needed to know. Especially if something had happened. And if something had happened, it might explain her hesitation when it came to sex with her last boyfriend. "No."

She met his gaze, then looked across the room before standing and striding toward the door.

He scraped his chair on the hardwood surface and caught her after only a few feet. He turned her to face him, forcing her to meet his gaze. "What happened, Cass? Tell me."

She shook her head.

Placing his forehead against hers, he cupped her face with one hand and tried to comfort her. "Tell me." It wasn't a question, and she knew it.

Cassie closed her eyes and took a deep breath. "We'd been dating for almost six months. He was a star football player and a senior. I was shocked he was even interested in me, but he was. He made me feel beautiful, special."

Something told him he wasn't going to like this, but he kept his thoughts to himself and waited.

"Our team had just won the state championship and he'd wanted me to go to a party with him. Mom said no, so he'd gone to the party alone." She paused. "At two in the morning, he snuck into my room."

"Was he drunk?" Jesse knew what happened at parties after big games. He'd been to a few of them.

"Yes."

Anger for this man he'd never met flared. "Did he rape you, Cassie?"

"No. It wasn't like that. I mean…I was his girlfriend. He…"

"He what?"

"He was a little…rough."

Jesse clenched his jaw. "Did he know you were a virgin?"

She nodded as a tear slid down her cheek.

"Did you tell him no?"

Cassie shook her head. "When he climbed into bed with me, I went to scream and he put his hand over my mouth to keep me quiet."

Jesse had heard all he needed to hear. He scooped Cassie up and carried her over to the couch. Once she was cradled in his arms, he held her tight.

He'd planned to introduce her to his world and explore sensations she had never experienced before tonight. Now he was left wanting to beat the shit out of her first boyfriend.

CHAPTER 11

"Did you ever tell anyone?"

Cassie snuggled against his chest. His arms around her, the scent of him, made her feel safe. "I told Brie when we were in college. She didn't understand why I wasn't interested in sex." Cassie paused. "She told me I should tell my brothers and they'd beat Brian up for me."

"I'd hope so."

She sat up. He was serious. "You agree with her?"

"Yes." His voice was firm. "And if they won't, I will."

Warmth spread through her chest at the thought of him standing up for her. "It was a long time ago."

"No man should ever do that. The fact you were a virgin makes it even worse." He stroked her hair, following it down her shoulder. "I'm sorry that happened to you, Cass."

"Thank you." She paused, not sure how much she should tell him, but she was hoping if she got it all out now, they wouldn't have to talk about this ever again. "He called me the next day and it was like nothing happened. I don't think he remembered coming over." She paused. "Or what happened."

Jesse rubbed his hand along her arm. "Did you ever confront him about it?"

She shook her head. "No. We were only together for another two weeks before he ended things, saying I'd become cold and distant." Cassie sat up, meeting Jesse's gaze. "Every time he'd try to kiss me, I'd freeze up. I couldn't help it. I didn't want to. It just…happened."

"You didn't do anything wrong, Cassie. He did."

When she didn't say anything more, he moved on. "Tell me about your second sexual encounter."

"Do I have to?" she asked, even though she already knew the answer.

"Yes."

"Trent and I had been dating for over a year. He'd been so patient with me. I'd even met his parents." She sighed. "But when I finally had sex with him, it didn't go well."

"Did he—"

"No. No. He was gentle and kind."

Jesse lifted her chin and forced her to look at him. "I'm sensing a but."

"I felt as if I was going through the motions. I knew what I was supposed to do, so that's what I did."

His fingers never left her face as he studied her. "Are you telling me you faked an orgasm?" There was a slight pull at one side of his lips.

Talking about this was weird. She only discussed this kind of stuff with Brie.

"Honesty, remember?" he prompted.

"Yes."

He raised one eyebrow. "Yes, you remember, or yes, you faked an orgasm?"

The look on his face lightened the mood a little. She pressed her lips together. "Yes to both."

"What happened after you faked your orgasm?"

She shook her head. "Nothing. He finished, held me, and fell asleep."

Jesse studied her face. "Was that the only time you had sex with him?"

"No. We were together for another year."

Cassie knew the next question he was going to ask. Or at least, she thought she did.

"Why did you break up?"

She looked at her lap. "He proposed."

"You broke things off because he asked you to marry him?"

She nodded.

"I need you to fill in some gaps for me, Cass."

Releasing a sigh, she met his gaze. "When you kiss me, I feel it all the way to my toes. My heart races and I want you to touch me." She paused. "I never felt that with him. Trent was nice. I felt safe with him. But I didn't love him. Not like I should. Not as a wife should love a husband."

A moment passed before she realized what she'd said and how it must have sounded. She sat up straight and met his gaze. "I didn't mean that like it sounded. I mean, I know we haven't been together long enough to…"

She opened her mouth to continue trying to smooth over what had come out of her runaway mouth, but he stopped her.

"It's okay. I understood what you meant." His fingers brushed the side of her face, sending warmth down to settle in her belly. "There's something special between us, Cassie. I felt it the moment I saw you."

Their gazes held, causing that warmth in her belly to turn into a burning desire to feel his lips on hers again.

As if something was drawing her closer, she leaned in and brushed her lips against his. They were warm and welcoming, and she felt something in her spark as her tongue met his. She shifted to get a better angle, needing to be closer to him.

Before she knew it, she was straddling him, her skirt hiked high on her hips. She could feel his erection pressing against her heat, and she began rocking against it.

Jesse's hands gripped her hips and held her still. "You're a very naughty girl, Cassie. I know what you're trying to do."

The air around them stilled and she felt reality begin creeping in again. "Please."

"Baby, we need to finish talking first."

"I don't want to talk anymore."

He sighed. "Whether you want to or not, we need to have this conversation."

The determination in his voice dashed any hope she had of moving on to more pleasant things. "Why can't we just let things happen?"

Jesse tucked a strand of hair behind her ear and met her gaze. "I don't want to start playing, do something you don't like, and have you either shut down on me, freak out, or worse. I want both of us to enjoy our play and that can't happen if I don't have all the information."

When he said it like that, it made sense. Why did he have to be so logical?

She climbed off him and moved to the opposite side of the couch. Tucking her feet under her, she tried to look casual, but she felt anything but. Sex wasn't something she talked about with anyone but Brie and even then, she kept a lot of it to herself. She wasn't one to overshare and Jesse seemed to want to know everything.

He held her gaze for a long moment, then stood and walked to the dining room table. After retrieving their discarded lists, he returned to his spot on the couch. This time, he handed her his list, then scanned over hers. "Did you ever experiment in the bedroom with Trent or by yourself with toys?"

Heat bloomed on Cassie's cheeks. This all felt very uncomfortable, but she knew he wanted an answer. "Other than my vibrator, no."

Nodding, he went back to reading.

She did the same, but as she looked over his papers, her apprehension grew. He'd tried most of the things listed. When she'd been filling out her list, she'd had to look some of them up.

When she finally glanced up, he was staring at her. "What questions do you have for me?"

"Um." Thoughts raced through her head, but no sound came out.

"Cass, I need you to talk to me."

Talk. She could do that. "Have you really done all these things? With other women?"

He didn't hesitate. "Yes."

She nodded and glanced down at the list again.

"Cassie?"

Her head snapped up. It took her a moment to realize he was waiting for her to ask him a question. Instead, she went with a statement. "I don't know if I can do some of these things."

"You don't need to. That's not how this works. Remember what I said. This is about negotiation. I share with you what I like, and you do the same. From there, we decide what we're both comfortable with." When she didn't say anything, he continued, "Let's take spanking, for example."

The memory of him smacking her backside as she walked away from him the night before flashed in her mind.

"From your response last night, I'd wager you'd enjoy a good erotic spanking."

"An erotic spanking?" For some reason, those two words didn't go together in her brain.

As if he knew what she was thinking, the right side of his mouth tilted up. "Yes. You'd lie across my lap, your ass in the air, and I'd make your ass nice and warm and pink." His eyes darkened as he spoke.

Cassie licked her lips, confused at how her body was reacting to what he was saying. When she'd filled out her list, she'd marked spanking as neutral/unsure. She'd been as torn then as she was now.

But she had to admit she was a little curious. He was correct about the night before. When he'd swatted her butt, she'd felt something zing through her and she'd wanted his hands on her again. What he was describing, however, felt...different. She'd be exposed in a way she'd never been before. "And if I don't like it?"

"After we play, at least at the beginning, we'll talk about what happened, what we liked and didn't like. This arrangement should work for both of us."

That made her feel a little better. "So if I don't like something you do to me, then I use my safeword and you'll stop?"

"You *have* been doing your research." He grinned. "Safewords are to be used when something is wrong. The rope is too tight. You're getting a cramp." Jesse paused. "You're starting to panic because of something that happened in your past."

It didn't take a genius to know what he was referring to. "I've never freaked out during sex before."

He raised an eyebrow. "Did Trent often tie you up? Hold you down? Restrain you in any way?"

"No, but—" Her words died in her throat. Her gaze lowered to his list again. He'd listed bondage and restraint as *love* on his list. She swallowed. "Will you warn me first?"

"How much warning would you prefer?"

"I don't know."

He met her gaze. "If I'm going to restrain you, I'll tell you first. Is that acceptable?"

She nodded.

"Good. Now tell me about your experience when it comes to oral sex, both giving and receiving."

* * *

Cassie stared at him with wide eyes. He was quite enjoying watching her squirm. She wasn't comfortable talking about sex, but she'd get over that soon enough.

"Um. I've done it?"

He chuckled. "I meant, were your experiences positive? Did you enjoy giving your partner oral? Did you like it when he went down on you?"

She squirmed in her seat again and lowered her gaze. "Yes, I liked both. Although, it didn't happen very often."

Jesse nodded, deciding not to press her on the issue. There'd be plenty of time to explore what she liked and didn't like when it came to oral sex. He was a big fan of both giving and receiving.

It took them another hour to get through enough of their lists where he felt confident to move forward. By then, it was almost nine o'clock, too late to do anything elaborate. He removed his list from where she had it resting on her lap, tossed it onto the coffee table, and stood.

Cassie's gaze followed his movement. He held out his hand and waited for her to place hers into it. Given her hesitation to talk about her sexual preferences and her past experiences when it came to sex, he wondered if she'd have second thoughts when he led her to his bedroom.

She didn't. Cassie laced her fingers with his and followed him down the hall to his room.

The thing that sold him on this condo wasn't the view or the spacious living area. It was the master suite. There was plenty of space for a king-sized bed and whatever else he wanted to put in it. Most people would fill the area with dressers and maybe even a reading nook. He, on the other hand, wanted the space so he could have options for play.

Guiding Cassie to the far side of the bed, he turned her to face him. "When we're in this room, you'll address me as Sir. If I tell you to do something, I expect you to do it. If there's a problem, you are to use your safeword, and I'll stop what I'm doing and check in with you. Do you understand?"

"Yes." She paused. "Sir."

That made him smile. "Good girl. You're a fast learner."

The look on her face told him she was happy she'd gotten the response right.

He cupped her jaw and his thumb grazed her cheek. She closed her eyes and leaned into his hand. He wanted to take things slow with her tonight. They'd have other nights to pull out all the toys and play. This first time, he wanted to get to know her.

Moving his hand lower, he traced the curve of her neck down to her collarbone. Her blouse had a slight dip in the center, although it was extremely modest given her position at his father's company. She looked very put together. He was going to enjoy unraveling her.

Cassie's chest moved in a steady rhythm under her blouse as his fingers reached the top button. He slipped his fingers under the fabric, teasing the top swells of her breasts. Her breathing deepened, pushing against his touch.

He popped the top button of her blouse to reveal her lacy bra. For some reason, he thought she'd be a satin bra type of woman, but he wasn't complaining. The visual was something he'd be replaying in his head.

The lace was sheer, barely covering the flesh underneath, and as he continued to unbutton her blouse, he was able to see her dark pink nipples pushing against the fabric. Bending his head, he captured one of her nipples in his mouth and sucked.

Her hands went to his hair. "Keep your hands at your side," he murmured, not releasing her nipple.

She lowered her arms, and he switched to her other breast. When he lifted his head, her bra had wet patches over her very hard nipples and her chest was moving rapidly.

He trailed a finger down the center of her chest to the next button and picked up where he left off. Releasing the last button, he pushed the shirt off her shoulders. It slid to the floor and pooled at her feet.

Without a word, he reached behind her, unzipped her skirt, and let it fall. She wore a matching pair of lace panties, but they were covered by panty hose. "Do you own thigh-high hose?"

"Yes, Sir."

"From now on, that's what I want you to wear. These"—he ran his finger from her waist down between her legs—"are too constricting. I want to have easy access to what is mine." When she didn't answer, he met her gaze. "Is that clear?"

"Yes, Sir. No pantyhose."

Jesse kneeled in front of her and removed the offending hose. He understood why women wore them, but they were too much work to get off when he wanted quick access to her pussy. Thigh-highs would give her the look she needed for work but would allow him to spread her open at a moment's notice, push her panties aside, and be balls deep within a few seconds.

He lifted her feet, one by one, removed the offending material, and tossed them in the trash.

"But…"

Gazing up at her, he raised an eyebrow. "Is there a problem?"

"You threw them away."

"Yes."

She thought about that for a few seconds before responding. "I can't wear them even if you're not around?"

"Our relationship doesn't cease to be just because we're not physically together." He caressed the inside of her leg, traveling up toward the lace panties covering her sex. "I want you thinking of me wherever you are, even if I can't be there with you in person."

She nodded and sucked in a breath as his fingers reached the edge of the lace. He ran the tip of his nose over the fabric, taking in her scent. Her brain was still working, but her body was anticipating what was coming. There was already a damp patch showing him how wet she was. He wanted a taste.

Lifting her leg again, he rested it over his shoulder. He pushed the fabric aside and gave her pussy a long lick.

Cassie released a soft whimper and he saw her hands clench at her sides. She wanted to touch him, but she was trying to be obedient.

He went back in for another taste, but this time he lingered on her clit. Her response wasn't exactly what he'd expected. She arched her back and began tumbling backward.

Jesse wrapped an arm around her back and got to his feet to help brace her fall. Luckily, the bed was at her back, so she didn't go far.

She stared up at him as he braced himself over her. Her face was flushed, but otherwise, she seemed fine. "Are you all right?"

"Yes." She paused. "I'm good if you want to continue, Sir."

He snorted. Something told him she was going to be a handful once she got used to the dynamics of their relationship. "Is that so?"

Then, before she could contemplate an answer, Jesse pushed himself up, sat on the bed, and lifted her legs over his lap. He gave her lace-clad bum a firm swat and she let out a startled squeak.

Jesse ran his hand over her ass several times before pulling her panties down to her knees. "Put your hands behind your back."

She brought her arms down and rested her hands on her lower

back. He knew he'd be taking a chance holding her down this early into their relationship, but he also didn't want to have her arms flailing around and knocking him in the face. "When we're playing, I'm in charge of our play. Do you understand?"

"Yes, Sir." Her voice wasn't as confident now as it had been a moment before.

Raising his hand, he took aim at her right cheek.

CHAPTER 12

CASSIE FLINCHED as his hand made contact with her backside. It felt different than when he'd smacked her the night before, mainly because in the park she'd had clothes on to deaden the blow. Tonight, there was nothing between his hand and her ass.

He repeated the motion on the other cheek. This time, she was expecting it. The hit stung, but it wasn't horrible.

His hand skimmed over her skin before he smacked her ass several more times. It was a weird feeling. There was a part of her brain that told her she shouldn't like this. That being in this position should be humiliating.

On some level, it was, but she wasn't able to concentrate on that. Every time her mind began to wander down that path, his hand would make contact again with her flesh, sending heat and a second of pain.

Jesse took hold of her wrists where they lay on her lower back. "I've got you warmed up. The next are going to be harder."

She swallowed. *Harder?*

He didn't wait for her to respond before another blow came down on her already sensitive flesh. She jerked, trying to get away from the pain, but he held her still. "Stop wiggling." His words were calm as if he were talking about the weather.

Another hit came. Then another and another. Her ass was on fire.

Then his hand was massaging. "Good girl. You did well, Cass."

For some reason, his praise pleased her. She didn't get time to consider why, though, before his fingers were dipping between her legs.

He traced the outside of her lips before circling her entrance. "So wet."

It was only then she realized how aroused she was. *Did him spanking me do that?*

Again, she didn't get the chance to think about it before he was pushing his fingers inside her and drawing her attention to more sensations. As he explored her pussy, he continued to hold her wrists. The whole situation seemed crazy, but her body didn't seem to think so.

Cassie tried to spread her legs to give him better access, but her panties were still around her knees. She was trussed up like a turkey.

Okay, maybe it wasn't that extreme, but her movements were restricted. That shouldn't be something she wanted, and it certainly shouldn't turn her on, but the moisture coating his fingers said otherwise. They slid in and out easily, creating a longing to know what it would feel like having him make love to her.

He removed his fingers and moved them to her clit. It was so sensitive. The desire to come was close to the surface. It wouldn't take much to send her over the edge.

But then his fingers were gone. She let out an irritated groan and he chuckled. "Patience."

"I'm so close."

"I know you are. My girl enjoys being spanked."

She opened her mouth to protest, but before the words were out of her mouth, his hand landed on her bottom again. This time she felt it deep in her core. There seemed to be an electric wire from where he'd hit her to her clit.

He didn't pause between swats. They were fast and firm. And with each one, she felt herself grow wetter, more aroused. All she needed was the right pressure on her clit and she'd explode.

"That's it, baby." His grip on her wrists tightened as he smacked harder. Tears pricked her eyes. It hurt but also made her want him to fuck her until she saw stars.

Her ass was burning by the time he slid his fingers between her legs again and began rubbing her clit. Tears were streaming down her face, but all she wanted was for him to keep going, keep rubbing. She needed to come. Needed that release.

When it finally came, she felt it all the way down to her toes. Cassie had never been a screamer, but she let out a high-pitched noise that could only be described as a scream as she rode the wave of her orgasm.

He kept massaging her clit until the last ripple of her climax. She felt as if she'd run a marathon but in the best way. Her backside was still burning, but she felt more relaxed than she could ever remember being before.

Jesse released her wrists and shifted his weight. She heard a drawer opening and figured he was getting a condom. When he sat back up, he began rubbing something on her ass. "You shouldn't bruise, but this will help just in case."

His hands felt good and she moaned. How could she still be horny?

Cassie had no idea, but she was. That had never happened before. She was usually lucky to orgasm once during sex. Then again, they hadn't had sex. He'd laid her over his lap, spanked her, and made her come.

Once he was finished, he returned whatever he'd been using back in the drawer, then rolled her over. He helped her to sit up, then set her on her feet.

She wabbled a little, so he steadied her.

Jesse stood and reached around her to unclasp her bra. It floated to the floor, leaving her naked in front of him. He was still dressed, his dress shirt now full of wrinkles. For some reason, she hadn't thought about their clothes disparity until now. "You're still dressed."

A smile pulled at his lips. "I am. Why don't you fix that by undressing me."

She began unbuttoning his shirt, soaking in the sight of his chest as she revealed more and more skin. He stood still as she worked, not moving a muscle until she reached the area above his waist. Her fingers brushed his abs and she heard him suck in a breath.

It felt good to know she affected him too—that it wasn't one-sided. She leaned in to press a kiss to his chest before going back to the task she'd been asked to do.

After unbuttoning his cuffs, she pushed the shirt off his shoulders and let it fall to the floor as he'd done with her clothing. She'd never undressed a man before, but she was finding it incredibly erotic. It was no wonder men liked removing a woman's clothes.

The urge to run her tongue along the ridges of his abs was strong, but so was the need to see the rest of him. She unbuckled his belt and pulled it free. As soon as she dropped his belt, she went to work on his pants.

She lowered the zipper and pushed his pants and underwear down his legs. His erection sprang free, pointing straight at her. Big and hard and leaking pre-cum.

Cassie touched the tip, spreading the moisture around. Jesse was bigger than Trent had been. Maybe that should have scared her, but it didn't. She'd never been this turned on with her previous boyfriend.

Jesse placed two fingers beneath her chin and redirected her gaze to his face. She thought he was going to say something, but instead, he lowered his mouth to hers and kissed her. It was slow and deep and made her insides pulse and heat.

His fingers slid into her hair and he crushed her to him—skin against skin—as he held her hip and ground his erection against her. She dug her fingers into his sides, not to steady herself, but in an effort to get closer.

He turned them and the back of her knees bumped the edge of the mattress. Then she fell backward. She landed on the bed and was immediately reminded of the spanking he'd given her.

Before she could focus too much on that, however, her attention was pulled back to Jesse when he hooked one of her legs over his hip, then the other. "Wrap your legs around my waist."

She did so and the movement once again made her acutely aware of her sensitive backside.

Jesse climbed onto the bed and positioned them, so her head was on one of the pillows. He towered over her, his eyes dark and a look on his face that had her pussy aching with need. She wanted him inside her.

He ran his hand down her torso, cupping her breasts on the way up and giving her nipples a firm tug. Her body was humming. "Lift your arms above your head."

She did as he asked and felt something that wasn't wood near her fingers. When she looked up, she saw a rope. Her heart began to pound.

His hand cupped her cheek and drew her attention back to him. "Not tonight. We'll explore bondage soon but not tonight."

Relief flooded through her. She hadn't realized how nervous the thought of being tied down made her, but Jesse obviously had.

"Keep your hands above your head. You can press them on the headboard or hold on to the rope if you want to."

She nodded, waiting to see what he'd do next.

He placed a barely there kiss on her lips, then moved down her jaw to her neck. The kisses were featherlight and before long, she was arching her back, wanting more.

When he reached her beasts, he lingered, circling each breast, then taking her nipple into his mouth and sucking until they were hard and craving more of his attention. She clenched her fists to keep from reaching for him. What he was doing to her felt so good, but it was also torture.

After what felt like an eternity, yet not nearly long enough, he abandoned her breasts and moved lower. He kissed her belly, then trailed his nose down the crease of her leg until he was perched between her thighs, his face level with her pussy.

"I think my girl likes my kisses." As if to prove his point, he pressed a kiss directly to her clit, sending a zap of energy through her sex.

She lifted her hips, silently begging for more.

He chuckled and pressed another soft kiss on her clit.

"Please."

"Please what, baby?"

"Harder. I need more."

He smacked the inside of her thigh, clearing a little of the sexual haze.

She glanced down at him between her legs. He was looking at her, one eyebrow raised.

It took her a moment to realize what he was waiting for. "Please suck my clit harder, Sir. I need more."

Jesse smiled and she realized she must have got it right. Something warmed deep inside her knowing she'd pleased him.

Without saying a word, he dipped his head between her legs. He took her clit between his lips and brought her to the most glorious orgasm in under sixty seconds.

* * *

After Cassie's revelation earlier, Jesse had no idea how the evening would go. He was making sure to watch her reactions, but so far, she was responding in a way that gave him high hopes for the future.

With the taste of her still on his lips, he removed a condom from his bedside drawer and rolled it down his length. His cock was almost painful with his desire to be inside her. She watched him, her eyes fixed on the movement of his hands.

He fell forward, bracing his hands on the bed on either side of her. Her gaze went to his mouth. "Cassie?"

She redirected her gaze to his.

"I'm going to fuck you now."

Her eyes widened a little but not in a way to make him think she was frightened. After the moment of shock at his blunt words, he heard her suck in a breath and felt her hips tilt toward him. His girl was still hungry for more.

Shifting his weight, he positioned the head of his cock at her entrance. Her pussy was wet and engorged from her two orgasms.

Even still, her internal muscles took a few moments to adjust to the intrusion.

He lifted her right leg and rested it on his shoulder, opening her up even more to him. The new position allowed him to slide the rest of the way home. He closed his eyes and relished the feel of her gripping him before he started to move.

Being inside her was better than he'd expected it to be. Deep down, he knew it was because their relationship wasn't only about play. He wanted her around for a long time to come. Maybe even forever.

Cassie braced herself against the headboard as he pounded into her. He hadn't been exaggerating when he said he was going to fuck her. His desire for slow had long passed and if the noises she was making were any indication, she had no issues with the pace he set.

Wanting more leverage, he placed her other leg over his shoulder and rose on his knees. He dug his fingers into her hips and let loose, thrusting hard and deep.

Her tits bounced with every thrust, and he wished he could suck on them, but she wasn't a human pretzel, so that would have to wait. There'd be plenty of time later for him to spend hours worshipping her breasts.

His balls tightened, signaling his orgasm was fast approaching if he kept up this pace. He could have drawn things out, changed angles, or even slowed down his thrusts, but he didn't want that. Jesse had wanted Cassie the moment he saw her standing in his living room. Now that he had her in his bed, he had every intention of possessing her in the most primal way.

He adjusted his hold and placed his thumb so it could brush over her clit. Her sharp intake of breath let him know he was in the right spot. He increased the pressure a little and let the motion of their bodies do the rest.

Cassie's legs tightened around his ears like a vise. She arched her back and began turning her head from side to side. Her lips parted and she flushed the most beautiful shade of pink from her temple all the way down to her breasts. She was close and so was he.

"Come for me, baby." He gave her clit a little pinch and that was all it took. Her body twisted as her pussy clamped down on his cock.

The small bit of control he'd been holding onto unraveled, and a guttural sound tore from his chest. His orgasm was intense, leaving him feeling as if he'd spent several hours in the gym.

He let her legs fall to the bed before collapsing on top of her. While he didn't want to crush her, he wanted her to feel his weight, to feel him.

Cassie gazed up at him, still breathing hard from her climax. He lowered his lips to hers, letting his tongue explore the depths of her mouth. She tangled her tongue with his as their breathing slowed once again to a normal rhythm.

He trailed his hand down her side as he broke the kiss. "I need to clean up. Get under the covers and wait for me."

After another quick peck on the lips, Jesse reached between them and eased out of her. The condom was soaked with her juices. He made his way into the bathroom and disposed of the condom before heading back to the bedroom. Cassie had climbed beneath the covers, the blanket pulled high so all he could see was her head peeking out.

Jesse had to suppress a laugh. Every inch of her had been exposed to him, yet she was hiding under the covers like a virgin on her wedding night.

He strolled to the bed, his now sated cock resting against his thigh, and pulled the covers back. Cassie watched him with a curious gaze but didn't move from her location in the middle of the bed as he got in.

Lying back, he reached for her. "Come here."

Cassie scooted across the bed and rested her head against his shoulder. She went to wrap her arm around his waist, then hesitated.

Jesse placed her hand around his waist, letting her know it was okay to touch him. He pressed his nose to the top of her head, breathing in the lingering scent of her shampoo. Lavender if he had to guess. "How are you feeling?"

"I don't know. Ask me in the morning."

Her response made him smile. "Did I wear you out?"

"Hmm."

He ran his hand along her back, taking in the curve of her spine. "Cass, we need to talk about what we did tonight. Was there anything I did you didn't like? Something you loved?"

She yawned. "No."

His chest vibrated. He really had worn her out. "No, I didn't do anything you didn't like, or no, I didn't do anything you loved?" He paused. "Of course, if you say no to the latter, I'm going to know you're lying. Those three orgasms I gave you don't lie."

It was her turn to chuckle. "No, you didn't do anything I didn't like. I mean, being spanked was weird, but I didn't hate it." Cassie turned her head to look at him. "I thought I would, but…"

"But it turned you on. Made you wet."

She buried her head in his shoulder and nodded.

"There's no need to be embarrassed. I like making you all hot and horny for me."

Cassie pressed her lips to his collarbone. "Will I be able to touch you next time?"

"Did it bother you not being allowed to touch me?"

She shrugged. "A little."

He kissed the top of her head. "I'll take your request under advisement."

"Is that how it works?"

Jesse walked his fingers up her back. "How what works?"

"I tell you the things I want, and you take it under advisement?"

He liked this direct Cassie. "Pretty much. It's my job to make sure your needs are met, but your wants are at my discretion." He lifted her chin so she was looking at him. "But you'll find I can be very generous."

His lips descended, covering her mouth with his in a leisurely kiss. "Close your eyes and try to sleep. We both have a long day tomorrow."

Cassie smiled and met his gaze. "Yes, Sir."

He lay holding her, enjoying the feel of her in his arms and listening to her soft snores before drifting off to sleep.

CHAPTER 13

CASSIE WOKE to the smell of coffee. She lifted her arms above her head to stretch, her fingers encountering something unfamiliar.

Opening her eyes, it took her sleep-muddled brain a moment to remember where she was. Jesse's room. They'd spent the night together.

Her gaze went to his side of the bed. He wasn't there, of course. She was alone in his room. His bed.

She rolled over to look at the clock and was reminded of him spanking her the night before. Her butt was still a little sore. Not to the point of pain, but her skin was more sensitive.

The clock read five thirty in the morning. It was still dark outside, although she could see a hint of light peeking through the curtains.

Throwing off the covers, she scrambled out of the big bed and padded to the bathroom. After taking care of business, she glanced at herself in the mirror. Her hair was all over the place. She'd brought a brush with her, but it was in her bag. As were the change of clothes she'd brought with her.

The hall was empty as she scurried to the spare bedroom. Her bag was on the bed where she'd left it.

Her back was to the door as she removed the items she needed, so she didn't hear him enter. "I was coming to wake you up, but you were missing from my bed."

Cassie jumped at the sound of his voice. Her hand went to her heart, and she took a few deep breaths to settle herself. "I was going to get dressed and come find you."

"Hmm." Jesse was by her side in two strides. He molded her body to his as he kissed her. It wasn't a peck on the lips like she was expecting. Nor was it quick. He took his time. "Good morning."

"Mmm. Good morning."

He smiled. "I'd ask if you slept well, but I already know the answer." His hand cupped her backside. "How's your ass doing this morning."

"It's a little tender."

His smile grew wider.

She didn't want to analyze that too closely. Not when she was standing there naked. "May I use your shower?"

"Of course." He nodded toward his bedroom. "Everything you need should be there. If you can't find something, just ask."

"Thanks." She put her clothes back in her bag and turned to leave the room.

"I like having you naked in my condo."

She ignored his comment and hurried across the hall to take her shower and dress.

Three and a half hours later, she was sitting at her desk, typing up a response to one of the shipping managers, when her phone dinged. She finished what she was doing, then checked her phone. It was her brother.

James is in town this weekend. Mom wants us all over for dinner. 6pm Friday. - Bradley

Crap. She was supposed to have dinner with Jesse's family Friday night.

I can't Friday. I already have plans. - Cassie

Three dots appeared almost immediately, letting her know he was responding.

What plans? - Bradley

She bit her lower lip. Did she want to announce her relationship to her brother? What would he think of Jesse?

??? - Bradley

I'm having dinner with someone. - Cassie

Who? - Bradley

Cassie sighed. **None of your business. – Cassie**

So not Brie or one of your friends from high school. Is it for work? - Bradley

She narrowed her eyes in frustration. **What part of none of your business did you not understand, little brother? - Cassie**

So it's a date. Cancel it. You can go out with this guy another time. Or not. - Bradley

I'm not canceling. - Cassie

There was a brief delay before she saw the three dots appear again. **Who is he? - Bradley**

While she was trying to figure out how to answer him, the man in question strolled off the elevator. Memories of last night and this morning sent heat rushing to her sex. Her butt was still feeling the remnants of the spanking he'd given her when she shifted in her chair, but her body didn't seem to care.

Jesse approached her desk and gave her a knowing smile, like he knew exactly where her mind had gone. "Good morning, Cassie."

She was keenly aware of where they were and that most likely more than one set of eyes were watching them. "Mr. Masters. What can I do for you?"

He raised an eyebrow at her choice of wording.

Cassie hadn't meant it to be sexual, but given the type of relationship he wanted, she should have known. She was going to have to be more careful. "What can I help you with?"

He chuckled, and she realized even that could be taken the wrong way. But he let her off the hook. "Is my father in?"

"He is, but he's on a conference call until lunchtime. Did you want me to have him call you when he's done?" Cassie asked.

"No. Just let him know I won't be able to have lunch with him today. I need to run across town to pick up some paperwork at the bank."

"Sure." It was then she noticed the tension in his forehead. "Is something wrong?"

He shook his head. "Nothing I can't handle."

"Okay."

As he turned to make his way back to the elevator, he stopped to face her again. "I'll call you later. Enjoy your movie night."

He'd asked her to have dinner with him again tonight, but she'd told him Thursday was usually movie night. Between dating and work, her and Brie's schedules were often crazy, so they'd agreed to set aside one day a week to eat pizza, watch a movie, and catch up on life. When she'd told Jesse this morning over breakfast, he'd nodded and commented how he'd have to put taking her to the movies on their list of things he wanted to do with her. It didn't take a genius to know where his mind had gone.

Almost as soon as Jesse left, one of the other executive assistants called, needing her help with a file. Cassie spent the next half hour on the phone with her, walking her through what should have been a five-minute task. By the time she was finished, she'd completely forgotten about her brother's text.

At five o'clock, she shut everything down and headed to the parking garage.

Brie was in the kitchen when Cassie got home. "I already ordered the pizza. Go change and we'll pick out something to watch. Did you want pop or something stronger?"

"I think I'll stick with pop tonight."

Cassie went to her bedroom, removed her work clothes, and dug out her favorite comfy pajamas. She was looking forward to vegging out on the couch with her best friend.

"Comedy, action, or sci-fi?" Brie asked.

"I was thinking sci-fi."

Brie scrolled through the sci-fi options. "*Star Wars. Star Trek, Stargate?*"

"What about *Dune?*"

Her friend scrunched up her nose. "That movie with Patrick Stewart from the eighties?"

Cassie shook her head. "No. The new one. It's supposed to be much better."

It took a moment, but Brie found it and hit play. Things were starting to get good when there was a knock on the door.

"I got it." Brie was on her feet and halfway to the door before Cassie could reach for the remote. Pausing the movie, she waited while Brie paid the delivery guy and brought the large pie back to the couch. Her friend set the box between them, opened the box, and pulled out a slice.

"Hungry?" Cassie removed a slice of her own.

"Starving," Brie said around her bite. Her friend swallowed and picked up her drink. "I'm surprised you aren't scarfing down your dinner. I figured Jesse would have worn you out last night."

Cassie felt heat bloom on her cheeks.

"I knew it!" Brie slapped her own thigh. "So how was it? Is he a sex god? Did he rock your world? He had to be better than Trent, right?"

She took another bite, chewed, and swallowed before responding. "It was good."

"Just good? Or was it goooood?"

Cassie laughed. "The second one."

Brie squealed. "It's about time you had some good sex."

Good didn't begin to cover it. Her fantasies about good sex hadn't come close to what sex had been like with Jesse. He'd made her come three times. Three. She'd struggled to come at all with Trent. Even pleasuring herself, she'd never had an orgasm so intense, let alone three of them.

"Oh wow. That good, huh?"

"What?" Cassie asked.

"Your face. It says it all."

Averting her gaze back to the television, Cassie picked up the remote. "You ready?"

Brie leaned back and propped her feet on the coffee table. "Let's see if Paul can save the spice world."

Cassie shook her head and hit play.

* * *

Jesse stood under the shower, letting the warm water wash away the shit day he'd had. Every time he thought he'd uncovered the last of the previous manager's mistakes, he discovered a new one. And to top things off, it had taken him over two hours at the bank to get all the documents he needed.

He looked up, letting the water hit him in the face, then stepped out of the spray and ran his hands over his face and hair to remove the excess water. His muscles were tight with pent-up energy. He'd already spent an hour at the gym trying to work off his frustration, but it hadn't done much.

Turning off the water, he stepped out of the shower and began drying off. He wished Cassie had been able to come over tonight. She would have been able to relive his tension.

He hung up the towel to dry and exited the bathroom. The cooler air in his bedroom prickled his skin. He sat on the edge of the mattress and flexed his shoulders and neck before checking the clock. It was almost nine thirty. Surely, Cassie and Brie would be done with their movie by now.

Propping himself against the headboard, he reached for his phone. She answered on the second ring. "Hello?"

"Hi, baby." All she'd said was hello and he was already feeling better. "How was your movie night with Brie?"

"It was good. We watched *Dune*. The new version. Not the Patrick Stewart one."

Jesse grinned. "I don't think I've seen the new one."

"It was good. Better than the original."

He heard rustling around in the background. "Did I catch you at a bad time?"

"No." More rustling. "I was just cleaning up the kitchen and starting the dishwasher."

"Did you want me to call you back?" He was hoping she'd say no.

"No. I'm good. Heading to my room now."

The only part of her apartment he'd seen so far was the living room, but that didn't mean he hadn't thought about her bedroom. He heard some more noise, then the sound of a door closing.

She released a contented sigh. "Safely tucked away in my room now."

He chuckled even as his groin tightened at the thought of her in her room and what he'd like to do to her if he were there with her. His cock was already semi-hard. It wouldn't take much to get him fully erect.

"How'd it go at the bank?"

It took a moment for his brain to switch gears. "About as well as could be expected. In the end, I got what I needed."

"That's good." She paused. "Horse hooey!"

Jesse laughed. "Did I miss something?"

"Sorry. I forgot to call my mom today."

"Do you normally call your mom on Thursdays?" He wasn't understanding her obvious distress over not phoning her mother.

"No."

He was missing something. "What is it, Cass?"

"I got a text from my brother today and I sort of let it slip about us. Well, not us, exactly, but he knows I'm seeing someone."

As confessions went, this was rather tame. And he was having trouble figuring out how they'd gone from her not calling her mom to a text from her brother. "Okay. I'm not seeing the issue." From her tone, she clearly thought this was a problem.

"Bradley is..." She paused. "Well, he's a lawyer and he tends to be like a dog with a bone about stuff like this."

Jesse chuckled. "Baby, you're going to need to translate. I'm not understanding why you seem so worried. Our relationship isn't a secret. Your family was going to find out."

"I know."

"So what's the problem?"

"I just don't want him to find out about...you know." She said the last part in a whisper.

Ah. Now the pieces were coming together. At least as far as her brother was concerned. "Cass, it's fine. We're both adults. What we do together is none of his business."

"I know that, too. But that's not what I meant." She paused. "I mean, I guess that's part of what I meant." She blew out a breath. "I'm dating my boss's son. And I'm letting him do kinky stuff to me."

He laughed. "We haven't even scratched the surface on the kinky stuff I want to do to you."

"Jesse!"

He tried to stifle his laugh this time. "I don't think you have anything to worry about. On the kinky front, I mean. As for the other? I can't change who my father is."

"I know." He could almost see her sitting there, her head bowed, her mouth in the cutest pout.

Jesse wished he were there with her. Phones were great for business transactions and quick check-ins. They were not stellar for comforting someone's fears. "If he finds out about the kinky stuff, then we'll deal with it. Until then, there's no reason to spend your energy worrying about it."

She sighed.

When she didn't continue, he decided to redirect the conversation back to her mother. "What does this have to do with forgetting to call your mom?"

"Bradley texted me saying my youngest brother, James, is in town and she wanted us all to come over for dinner tomorrow night. But we're having dinner with your parents, so I can't go. Which is why I needed to call my mom. To let her know I can't be there."

"I can call my parents and reschedule."

"No. Your mom is expecting us. James will be back in town in the next month or two and I can always video chat with him. I don't want your mom to think I'm flighty."

"You're my dad's personal assistant. My mom isn't going to think you're flighty." The suggestion was comical. While his dad wasn't a demanding boss, he did expect his assistant to be competent. There was no way Blake Masters would put up with an assistant who blew off her commitments.

"I want to make a good first impression."

"You've met my mom before, Cass." He was pretty sure she'd met her multiple times. Florence Masters was known to drop in unannounced whenever she felt like it.

"Not as your girlfriend."

"Baby, you have no need to be nervous. My mom likes you. You being my girl isn't going to change that." He needed to change the subject and get her mind off both their families. "Are you in your bed?"

"Yeah…"

"Are you lying down?"

He heard movement.

"Now, I am."

Smiling, he closed his eyes and let his mind picture her lying in her bed. "Are you wearing pajamas?"

"Yes." The word came out in a soft breath.

"Close your eyes. I want you to cup your breast with your free hand. Is your nipple hard?"

"No."

"Well, we're going to make it hard." He wrapped his hand around his cock and began stroking from base to tip. It was early and they weren't in any rush. "Take your thumb and forefinger and tug on your nipple."

"Okay."

"Now, I want you to keep pulling, but I want you to twist it too. Pretend it's my fingers playing with your tits. Don't be gentle. I want those babies nice and hard and sensitive."

He felt her moan in his cock.

"That's it. You know you like a little pain. Can you feel it in your pussy?"

"Yes."

"Are you wet, baby?"

"Yes."

Sometime soon, he was going to recreate this scene, but with him being in the room watching her. The image he was conjuring in his head was hot as hell. He knew the real-life version would be ten times better.

"I want you to touch yourself between your legs. Tell me how wet you are."

The other end of the line was quiet for a few moments, then he heard her suck in a breath. "I wish you were here."

His breath caught in his throat. "So do I, baby. Tell me how wet you are."

"My fingers are covered." She paused. "I want your cock in me, Sir. I want you to fill me up like you did last night."

Where had his shy girl gone? Tonight, she wasn't blushing or being coy. He figured it had to be because they were on the phone, but it made him realize how much of a sex kitten she must be deep inside. Whether she knew it or not, Cassie was a kinky girl.

"Put your fingers inside yourself. Fuck your pussy for me."

Her breathing picked up. "It's not the same."

"I know, baby. My hand isn't the same as having your pussy wrapped around my cock either, but I'll have you in my bed again tomorrow night."

She moaned and he knew it wouldn't take much to get her off. He was close himself.

Jesse reached for the lube in his bedside drawer, coated his hand, and resumed the up and down motion that had him teetering on the edge. "Spread your juices around and lubricate your clit. Make sure it's nice and wet, okay?"

A few moments later, her voice came through the phone sounding as if she were in the middle of a run. "I'm so close."

"Not until I say, Cass. You don't come until I tell you to."

She let out a frustrated whine. It both amused and aroused him.

As a new submissive, he didn't want to test her limits too much. He wanted this to be a positive experience. Something he could build on. "Keep rubbing your clit. Don't stop."

Jesse listened to her moans, the catches in her breath. He was ready to explode himself, but he was holding out. Waiting for her.

He heard a subtle change in the tenor of her moans and knew it was time. "Now, Cass."

She sucked in a breath, then he heard the glorious sound of her release. Cum shot out of his cock, covering his hand as he listened to her climax through the phone. He'd had phone sex before, but with Cassie, it had felt more intimate. This wasn't only about getting each other off.

He carried the phone into the bathroom so he could clean up. She hadn't said a word in several minutes even though her breathing had returned to normal. "You still with me?"

Cassie sighed. "I don't know. I think I may have been transported to another world. You might have to come get me. Orgasms are so much better with you."

"Is that so?"

"Yep." The word was drawn out on a yawn.

"Go to sleep, baby. I'll pick you up in the morning. Oh, and make sure you pack a bag. I plan on bringing you home with me after dinner."

"Okay."

He chuckled. "Good night."

Another yawn. "Night."

CHAPTER 14

Cassie slept like the dead. She hadn't even gotten up to put her phone on the charger before nodding off to sleep.

After taking care of business in the bathroom, she plugged in her phone, hoping it would have enough time to charge before she had to leave, then went to take a shower. Her fingers still had a faint hint of her sex on them, which brought back memories of last night.

She'd never had phone sex before. Trent had tried to initiate it with her once when they were both home with their families over winter break, but she'd felt too self-conscious. She'd listened to him grunt and moan on the other end of the line. The whole thing had been awkward.

Last night was different. Trying to stay quiet so Brie couldn't hear her had made what they were doing hotter. The sound of Jesse's voice, the way he'd told her what to do, where to touch herself, had sent heat rushing to her core. And hearing the strain in his voice as he got closer to his own climax had been a total turn-on.

Cassie wondered why that was. Trent had been a perfectly nice guy. He'd treated her well. But she'd never felt the same spark with him.

Brie was already at the kitchen table when Cassie came in to get breakfast. "Morning."

Her greeting was met with a wicked grin.

"What?"

"Sleep well?"

By the look on Brie's face, Cassie knew she hadn't been as quiet as she thought she'd been last night.

Cassie stuck a bagel in the toaster and went to the refrigerator to get the cream cheese, avoiding looking at her best friend. She was blushing and that was the last thing she wanted Brie to see.

"Come on. It's me."

"I know it's you."

Brie waited for Cassie to bring her bagel to the table before saying anything else. "Sure you don't want to talk about it? I'll just listen. I promise." Brie held up her pinky. "Pinky swear."

"I appreciate it, but I'm good." In truth, Cassie was still trying to wrap her head around the whole thing—what she and Jesse had done together so far and how she'd reacted to it. If someone had told her she'd be turned on by having a guy spank her, she would have told them they were nuts.

Then, last night when he told her she couldn't come until he said so? That should've ticked her off. It was her body after all. But instead, she'd gritted her teeth and held back her orgasm until he'd given her permission to come. Why?

And why had it made her climax that much more intense?

She was trying to come to terms with all of it when her phone rang.

Abandoning her bagel, she ran back to her room to retrieve her phone. She swiped it off the nightstand and answered it without looking at the caller ID. "Hello?"

"Are you avoiding me?"

Cassie carried the phone back to the kitchen as she responded to her brother. "No, I'm not avoiding you. I got busy yesterday and forgot to text you back." She cleaned up what was left of her breakfast and mouthed to Brie it was her brother on the phone. "By the way, did you tell Mom I couldn't make it?"

"I haven't."

Great. That meant she was going to have to call her mom this morning.

She rinsed her plate and loaded it into the dishwasher.

"What are you doing?" Bradley asked.

"Well, it's almost seven in the morning on a workday, which means I'm getting ready to go to work like a normal person."

Bradley ignored her snarky comment. "How long have you known this guy you're seeing?"

"I'm sorry, but since when is who I am or am not dating any of your business?"

There was a long pause on the other end of the phone. "Since Mom gave birth to me and made me your brother."

As irritated as she was that he was grilling her about her love life, his response was rather sweet in an overbearing kind of way. "While I appreciate the sentiment, I don't need your input or your opinion on the men in my life."

"There's more than one?"

She could feel the tension through the phone. "That's not what I meant."

"So is it just sex?"

Cassie turned to see Brie trying hard to hold in her laughter. She was glad her best friend was finding this funny. "Bradley, I'm not discussing this with you. I'm not sure how many ways I can say it."

"Fine. Have it your way." With that, he hung up.

"Well, goodbye to you, too."

Brie burst out laughing.

Cassie stuck out her tongue at her friend.

"Sorry. You know how your brother is."

"Yes, I do. He's an obnoxious pain in the ass."

That only got her more laughter from Brie.

When she narrowed her eyes at her friend, Brie brought it down to a silent chuckle. "Look, Bradley is…protective. You know that. He was like this with Trent, remember? And he was barely out of high school back then."

She didn't need to be reminded. Bradley had shown up at her school one night and waited outside her dorm so he could meet her new boyfriend. Even though Trent had at least six inches on her brother at the time, she had no doubt Bradley would have attempted to kick Trent's ass had he thought the man was messing with Cassie.

Luckily, she was saved from having to go any further down memory lane by the knock on the door.

"I'll get it." Brie was out of her seat and halfway to the door before Cassie could move a muscle. "Good morning, Mr. Masters." Brie glanced over her shoulder. "Cassie, your boyfriend's here."

Cassie rolled her eyes and walked to the door.

Jesse met her gaze and smiled, his blue gaze scanning her body as if to memorize it.

Brie stepped back, allowing Jesse to come inside. "So what brings you by at this time of the morning?"

"I'm taking Cassie to work today."

"Oh?" Brie asked, her gaze shifting to Cassie. "Big plans tonight? Should I expect you home late?"

"We're having dinner with my parents, then Cass is spending the night at my place." He hadn't stopped looking at Cassie since he'd arrived. "Do you have your bag packed?"

She nodded. "It's in my room. I'll run and get it."

The bag was beside her dresser. She scooped it up, turned, and bumped into Brie. "Sorry. I didn't—"

"You're having dinner with his parents?"

Cassie hiked the bag higher on her shoulder. "Yeah."

"Not that I'm not happy for you. I am. But this feels like it's getting serious fast. Are you ready for that?"

It did feel that way. Her brother's question, asking if it was about sex, swirled in her brain. While sex was obviously a part of it, especially considering Jesse wanted her to be his submissive, it didn't encompass the way she felt about the man currently in her living room. He made her feel all the things she'd dreamed about feeling with a guy and then some. "Yeah. I think so."

Brie gave her a long, hard look, then pulled Cassie into her arms for a hug. "Have fun this weekend. Call me if you need anything."

"It's only tonight."

Her friend raised a skeptical eyebrow.

"You're right. I should be prepared."

Cassie went to her drawer and removed another pair of shorts and a T-shirt. She didn't think she had to worry about pajamas if she was staying with Jesse, so she didn't bother packing any. He hadn't mentioned it, but she was guessing naked would be his preferred attire for her while she was in his bed.

"What about work on Monday?"

She took a second to think about it, then went to her closet and grabbed her garment bag. She picked out an outfit for work on Monday, put it in her garment bag, then rolled it so it would fit into her other bag. It felt like overkill, but it was better to be safe than sorry.

Brie followed her back to the living room where Jesse was patiently waiting. "Ready?"

"Ready."

Jesse took her bag and slung it over his shoulder. "It was good seeing you again, Brie."

"You too. Make sure you take good care of my friend."

"Always." Jesse put a hand on the small of Cassie's back and led her into the hallway. "Did you sleep well?"

Heat bloomed on her cheeks. "I did. You?"

"I had an excellent night's sleep."

They made their way to the parking garage. Jesse tossed her bag in the back seat of his Mustang, then opened the passenger door for her.

She slid into the seat and secured her seat belt. When she turned back, Jesse was there, his face inches from hers. "I didn't get to greet you properly upstairs." Then, before she could register what he meant, his mouth was covering hers.

He didn't seem to be in any rush. His tongue played with hers while his hand skimmed up her leg and under her skirt. "Good girl. You remembered."

Cassie opened her eyes, trying to grasp what he was talking about.

Jesse ran the tips of his fingers along the edge of her stockings. "I was wondering if I'd have to punish you."

Visions of her over his lap again came to mind and she was once again shocked at how her body reacted. She licked her lips, hoping his hand would continue upward even knowing they didn't have time to fool around.

He grinned, his eyes sparkling with amusement. "We need to get to work. I promise I'll reward your obedience later."

Removing his hand, he backed away and closed her door.

She tried to put what he'd said out of her mind as they headed toward the office. They had a full day of work ahead of them, then dinner with his parents. It would be a while before they'd have any significant time alone.

Jesse parked his car and helped her from the vehicle. As soon as her feet were on the pavement, he released her, shifting into work mode. "Are you free for lunch?"

"Your dad has a meeting and he's asked me to take notes."

He nodded, resigned, and pushed the button to summon the elevator.

* * *

After seeing Cassie to her desk, Jesse made his way to the third floor. He was passing by the break room on the way to his office when he heard two women talking. "You have to wonder if she's doing both of them."

"I don't know. I've never noticed anything weird with them or anything."

"Things change. I mean it's job security, I suppose."

Even though they didn't say any names, Jesse knew they had to be talking about Cassie. He turned on his heel and made a beeline for the break room.

All the chatter stopped as soon as he entered. The two women looked at him. "Morning, Mr. Masters."

He nodded in acknowledgment. "Christine. Sandy."

Christine looked down at her mug of coffee, but Sandy didn't have any such shame. "Any plans for the weekend?"

Jesse poured himself some coffee and added a packet of sugar. "Not really." He took a sip of his coffee. There was no way he was sharing personal details of his life with these women. "I need to get to my office. You ladies should be heading to your desks, too."

"Of course," Sandy said with a saccharine sweet smile.

He took another drink from his cup and strolled out of the room. He was going to have to keep an eye on those two. This was the second time he'd caught them gossiping about his relationship. Technically, they'd been gossiping about Cassie this time, but their conversation hadn't spoken highly of him or his father.

His assistant was already at her desk when he got there. "Good morning, Mr. Masters."

"Good morning. Could you join me in my office?"

Stephanie stood and followed him inside.

"Close the door."

Stephanie did as he asked, then turned to face him.

"What can you tell me about Christine and Sandy."

"Christine Johnson?"

"Tall. Dark Hair. Wears red lipstick all the time."

Stephanie nodded. "Christine Johnson. She's been working here for about a year. Decent worker. Doesn't call off much. Her team lead seems to think highly of her. Why? Is there a problem?"

Instead of answering her, he asked another question. "What about Sandy? I think her last name is Green. Around my age. Blond hair. Usually wears it in a bun."

"Um. She's been here a while. At least three years. She's quiet. I don't know much about her to be honest."

She hadn't been quiet this morning in the break room. "Let me know if you hear anything, okay?"

"Sure." Stephanie paused. "Did you need anything else?"

"Yeah. Can you bring me the Campbell files? I want to look over them again."

"Will do."

As soon as he was alone, Jesse logged into human resources and searched for Sandy Green and Christine Johnson. One of the advantages of his position was he had full access to all employee files.

It didn't take him long to read over their files. There wasn't much beyond the basics found in any employee file. Name, date of birth, hire date, work history. There weren't any write-ups for either of them. On paper, they seemed to come to work, do their jobs, and go home. They didn't excel, but they did their jobs without much supervision.

Jesse logged out of HR and pulled up his email. He was clearing out his inbox when there was a knock on his office door. "Enter."

Stephanie walked in with a stack of papers in her hand. "The files you asked for."

"Thanks." He took the papers and placed them on his desk. "I think that's all I need for now."

She smiled and left his office, closing the door behind her even though he hadn't asked her to. Stephanie was a good assistant, and he was lucky to have her. He hadn't discussed the mess he'd found in one of their biggest accounts files, but she'd picked up on the fact something was wrong.

It only took him an hour to find what he was looking for in the Campbell files. He cross-referenced them with what had been processed for payment and sure enough, they were different. Not by a lot, but enough that if the same error occurred repeatedly, it would add up to a significant amount of money.

This was the fifth account where he'd found a similar error, and he still had at least twenty more he wanted to go over. He scanned the relevant documents and printed off the corresponding report, then tucked them in a file in the bottom drawer of his desk.

His father needed to know about this as soon as possible. He'd found too many inconsistencies for it to be a coincidence. The whole reason the previous manager and his assistant had been let go was due to accounting errors, but this didn't feel like an accounting error to him. This felt deliberate.

After spending the rest of his day crunching numbers and rechecking the work of his managers, Jesse was ready for a more relaxing evening. He would have loved to spend a quiet night at home with Cassie, but his mother would have his head if he called and canceled.

Cassie was at her desk when he walked off the elevator. Her head came up when she heard his footsteps, and a smile graced her face when she saw him.

Warmth spread through his chest as he came to a stop in front of her desk. "Hi."

"Hi." She pressed her lips together as if she were trying to keep a secret.

"Ready for tonight?" His dad's voice startled him. He'd been so focused on Cassie, he hadn't noticed his dad coming out of his office.

"For dinner?" he asked.

His dad chuckled. "Yeah."

"Sure. We'll see you at the house."

Blake Masters nodded, fixing the collar on his jacket before picking up his briefcase. "Don't be late."

They watched as his dad strolled toward the elevator, leaving them alone.

He waited for Cassie to gather her things. They walked to the elevator, encountering a few sideways glances, but it was less than before.

She glanced up at him as they waited. "How was your day?"

"Long."

She chuckled. "That bad, huh?"

"T.G.I.F."

The elevator stopped on every floor, gaining riders each time. By the time they reached the parking garage, the elevator was full. They were pressed together like sardines. Cassie kept brushing the back of her hand against his and it took discipline to keep his hands to himself. After the day he'd had, there was nothing he wanted more than to touch her.

When the doors opened, everyone flooded out, scattering to their cars. For once, no one spared them any glances. Their coworkers were in too much of a hurry to get home.

As soon as they were in his vehicle, he reached for her hand. "Were you able to talk to your mom?"

"Yeah." Her response wasn't encouraging.

"What did you end up telling her?"

"That I'd been invited to dinner at my boss's house."

He glanced over at her, raising a questioning eyebrow. "So she thinks you have a business engagement tonight at your boss's house?"

"Kinda." She looked guilty.

"You know you're going to have to tell them sooner or later. Why wait?"

She sighed. "I don't know." She bit the side of her lip. "Okay. I do know. My brother can be a royal pain in the ass. He doesn't really do relationships, but yet always has to be up in mine. My mom will ask a ton of questions and insist I invite you over for dinner. And my dad… well, he'll want to see if you're good enough for his little girl even though I'm twenty-seven."

He took in what she said. And what she didn't say. "What about your youngest brother. James?"

Cassie shrugged. "James is focused on college. He doesn't tend to get involved in my personal life. That, and he's more laid back than Bradley. Well, at least with most things."

This was interesting. "What sort of things isn't he laid back about?"

"He's a big fitness buff. Goes to competitions. He takes working out and nutrition very seriously. And school, of course."

"Well, if we survive tonight, why don't we plan to have dinner with your family the next time your brother is in town?"

She opened her mouth, then closed it again.

"Something the matter?" Jesse was beginning to think she may not want him to meet her family and that would be a problem.

"No."

Jesse turned into his parents' driveway and stopped at the gate. After entering his code, the iron gate opened, allowing them to pass. "Do you not see our relationship lasting long term?"

His parents' house came into view. He'd been looking forward to introducing Cassie to his mom as his girlfriend, but now he was beginning to have second thoughts. Did she see him as temporary?

He pulled up in front of the house and put the car in park before turning to face her.

Cassie unbuckled her seat belt and shifted so she was looking at him. She brought a hand up to trace the outline of his lips. "I wouldn't have slept with you if I didn't."

Bringing her hand to his lips, he kissed her palm. He wanted to ask her more questions, get to the bottom of why she didn't want him to meet her family, but he knew they wouldn't be alone for long. "I want to talk more about this later, but if we don't get inside soon, my mom will come out."

She nodded, seeming to accept that they'd be revisiting the subject.

He kissed her palm again and opened his door. His parents were waiting. Everything else would have to be put on hold.

CHAPTER 15

CASSIE TRIED NOT to let her nerves get the better of her as Jesse walked her into the large estate. She knew Blake and Florence Masters. She saw Blake five days a week. This was no big deal.

The foyer was as big as her apartment, the sound of their footsteps echoing as they walked down the hall toward the dining room. For some reason, it felt larger, more encompassing, than it had the last time she was there. She knew it was all in her head, that the house hadn't magically morphed into something new, but that wasn't doing anything to help her perception of the grandness of it all.

Her dad's house was big by most standards. It was possible for two people to be in the house at the same time and not realize it. But the Masters's house was on a whole different level. It made her feel small.

Blake and Florence liked to host dinner parties. They were both very active in their community and several charities. Rubbing elbows with other business moguls and politicians was part of the norm. Her dad was more of a home body and so was she. While she could hold polite conversation when she needed to, she'd much rather be home reading a book or vegging out in front of the television.

Jesse placed a hand on the small of her back and guided her past the kitchen. The smell of food tickled her senses and made her realize how hungry she was. It had been hours since she'd eaten lunch.

They entered the large formal dining room to find his dad and Beks seated at the table scrolling through their phones. Blake was most likely checking emails. She had no idea about Beks. Social media probably. His mom was rearranging some of the flowers in the centerpiece.

Florence noticed Jesse and Cassie. "There you are."

She embraced Jesse, and he placed a kiss on her cheek. "We're not late, are we?"

His dad put his phone away. "No, but your mom has been crawling the walls, waiting for you to get here."

Jesse chuckled. "Mom, you know Cassie."

Florence turned her attention to Cassie. "How have you been? My husband isn't working you to death, is he?"

Cassie smiled. "No, ma'am."

Beks tucked her phone into her pocket before addressing Cassie. "Hello again."

Robert, the Masters's personal chef, strolled into the dining room. He was pushing a cart full of food.

Florence took a seat beside her husband and Jesse held out a chair for Cassie. Once she was seated, he lowered himself into the seat beside her. The atmosphere felt formal and not at the same time.

Robert served everyone a plate, the food arranged beautifully. Everyone was silent as the food and drinks were served. Robert made sure everyone had what they needed, then discreetly disappeared into the kitchen.

Cassie followed Jesse's lead and began eating her food. She'd never had roasted duck before, but it was good. Not as gamey as she'd expected.

"My big brother charmed you, huh?" The grin on Beks's face told Cassie she wasn't upset with this. "I was wondering when I found you two snuggled up together at the party."

His dad raised an eyebrow, but he was looking at Jesse, not Cassie.

She wasn't sure how to respond, and luckily, she didn't have to.

Jesse spoke up and answered his sister. "I didn't charm her. I wore down her defenses." He sent Cassie a sly smile and she felt her insides melt a little.

"At least your brother has found a nice girl he wants to date," Florence said.

Beks rolled her eyes. "Jesse's thirty. If we're going by age alone, I have time."

"You're not getting any younger and I want grandchildren before I'm too old to enjoy them." Florence picked up her wine glass and took a sip.

Cassie averted her eyes, keeping them on her food. This conversation sounded a lot like ones she'd at with her own mother. Jessica Rourke was all about becoming a grandmother. She wanted grandbabies and lots of them. And she wasn't shy about bringing up the subject any chance she got.

"See, this is why it needs to work between the two of you." Beks looked at Cassie as if it were solely up to her as to whether the relationship between her and Jesse would last. "If you two stay together, then you can give Mom the grandchildren she wants, and the pressure's off me."

Jesse spoke before Cassie could figure out how to respond. "I think we need to cool it on the baby talk. Cassie and I have only been together for a week. We're not rushing into anything."

Blake cleared his throat. "Your mother and I are hosting a dinner party next month. My college roommate is in town and I'd like for you to attend."

It wasn't clear to Cassie if the invitation included her or not. She'd never been to one of the Masters's dinner parties, but she'd helped organize several.

"Send me the date and I'll check my calendar." Jesse took a sip of his water. "How long is he staying?"

"He's taking over his uncle's law firm, so he'll be in Kansas City for the foreseeable future."

Jesse smiled. "That's great. You'll have a golf partner now and won't be trying to drag me along."

Blake chuckled. "Yes, well, he has great timing. It will be good to have him close by again."

It took a moment for Cassie to realize what her boss was referring to, but when she did, she glanced over at Jesse. His expression told her he knew exactly what his father was talking about, and she made a note to ask him about it later.

The conversation soon turned to Beks. She was planning to follow in her brother's footsteps and spend some time in Europe. Unlike her brother, however, she was headed to Milan to study fashion.

After dinner, Blake asked Jesse to join him in his study. Beks disappeared upstairs, and Cassie and Florence watched the sun as it set behind the trees.

"You're good for him," Florence said, taking a sip of her coffee.

The compliment brought a smile to Cassie's lips. "Thanks."

"Has there been any trouble at work? I know how office gossips can be."

Cassie was a little surprised at that. While Florence stopped by the office on occasion, she wasn't a regular fixture.

The look on Cassie's face prompted a smile from the older woman. "I'm guessing you don't know how Blake and I met."

"No." While her boss was friendly and respectful, he didn't tend to overshare.

Florence took another drink before speaking again. "Blake hired me as his secretary when he first started the company. We worked together for three years before he got up the courage to ask me out."

"He was your boss?"

Jesse's mom chuckled. "He was. And when it got out that he and I were an item, there was quite a lot of talk."

Cassie nodded. "I've gotten looks more than anything. I think the worst is said behind my back."

"I have no doubt." Florence finished off her coffee and looked Cassie in the eye. "I know I'm Jesse's mom, but if you ever need someone to talk to, I'm here to listen."

"Thank you." The gesture was appreciated.

A few moments later, Jesse reappeared with his father. Both had rather stern looks on their faces, but Jesse's expression lightened when he met Cassie's gaze. He came to stand beside her and wrapped his arm around her waist. When he spoke, however, it was to his parents. "We're going to head out. Thank you for dinner."

Florence gave her son a hug, then turned to Cassie. She took her right hand and gave it a brief squeeze. "You're both welcome anytime."

A few minutes later, Jesse was helping her into his car. It had cooled off quite a bit since they'd arrived, and Cassie had forgotten to bring a jacket. She ran her hands up and down her arms, trying to ward off the chill.

Jesse removed his suit jacket before sliding into the driver's seat. Before turning on the engine, he draped the jacket over her, tucking in the sides on either side of her arms. It warmed her almost instantly. "Thank you."

"Can't let you catch a cold. I have plans for us this weekend." His sly grin sent a completely different type of heat coursing through her.

"What did you have in mind?" she asked, feeling bold.

His only answer was a mischievous grin as he started the car and made his way down the long driveway toward the road.

* * *

Jesse was trying to put the conversation with this dad out of his mind. He wanted to enjoy his weekend with Cassie and that wasn't going to happen if he continued to dwell on the shit show he was uncovering. That, and he needed to get to the bottom of Cassie's hesitation regarding her family. He couldn't fix something he didn't understand.

He opened the passenger door and offered her his hand. She took it and stood. Her heels brought her head to his eye level, so she didn't need to raise her gaze very far to meet his. She'd turned his jacket so it hung from her shoulders and wrapped around her like a blanket.

Her pupils darkened and the air around them began to spark. She swayed toward him as if drawn by some unseen force. It was always like this with her. He felt this pull deep in his gut, the urge to possess every part of her surging through his veins.

They were alone in the parking garage, and it had been more than twelve hours since he'd felt her mouth on his. He closed the distance between them and kissed her.

Cassie melted into him, her fingers gripping the front of his dress shirt as his tongue played with hers. He wanted to forget all sense and bury himself deep inside her. But he didn't want someone to catch them. Or worse yet, for it to be caught on surveillance video and be leaked to the press.

While his family wasn't known for making headlines outside of the occasional mention in the business section, the last thing they needed right now was any type of focused attention. If Jesse's instincts were right, and he had no reason to doubt them, someone had been skimming off profits from the company. Once he found out the source and how deep the corruption went, it would be hard to keep it under wraps.

"What's wrong?" Cassie's whispered words brought him back to the present.

"We should get upstairs before we do something indecent."

She frowned.

Jesse sighed and began moving them toward the elevator. "It's nothing to worry about. Not yet, at least."

"Does it have to do with work?"

"Yes."

She circled her arms around his waist and hugged him as they rode the elevator to his floor. Having her with him, knowing she provided refuge from the piles of paperwork that never seemed to end, had him wanting to forgo the conversation he knew they needed to have. All he wanted to do was take her to his bed, strip her down, and lay her out on his mattress.

But the logical part of his brain knew better.

Once they were inside his condo, she removed his jacket and went to hand it to him. She froze. "We forgot my bag in the car."

He'd been so focused on getting her upstairs that he'd forgotten her overnight bag. "Make yourself comfortable. I'll get it."

Giving her a quick kiss, Jesse headed downstairs. He grabbed her bag from the car and hopped back on the elevator.

The living room was empty when he reentered the condo, and the only light was coming from the large windows on the far wall. He dropped her bag on the couch and went to find her.

Jesse was halfway down the hall when the door to the bathroom opened. Cassie walked out in nothing but her bra, panties, and stockings. His cock responded without any consideration of his intentions.

She saw him and smiled. "You're back."

Jesse stalked toward her. His only thought was to get his hands on her. He backed her against the wall and kissed her.

Cassie didn't miss a beat. She kissed him back, meeting every stroke of his tongue with one of her own. Her hands went to his hair as she tried to climb his body.

A low growl emerged from deep in his chest as he positioned her leg around his waist, opening her to him. He dug his fingers into her ass as he ground his erection against her pussy. "So fucking sexy."

He dipped a finger beneath the hem of her panties, seeking the wetness he knew he would find. She was swollen and oh so wet. He slipped a finger inside. By the way she was responding, he knew it wouldn't take much to get her off. Hell, it wouldn't take much to get him off.

A little voice in the back of his head was attempting to remind him they needed to talk, but he couldn't, for the life of him, remember what about. The only thing dominating his thoughts was figuring out how many times he wanted to make her come before he found his own release.

Cassie lifted herself up on her toes, shifting their position and causing his finger to brush against her clit. She sucked in a breath, and he felt a vibration go through her.

Deciding he didn't want to wait, he used his free hand to unbuckle his belt and unfasten his slacks. She was his all weekend. He'd have time to play with her later.

Once his erection was free, he lifted her. He used the wall as support and impaled her on his cock.

She didn't miss a beat, kissing him back with fierce passion. He wanted to devour her and from her response, she wanted to do the same to him.

He fucked her hard against the wall, driving his cock into her until they were both breathless.

When he knew he wasn't going to be able to last much longer, he adjusted his hold on her hips and dipped his thumb above where they were joined.

Less than thirty seconds later, she was going off like a rocket. Her fingers scrapped his scalp to the point of pain as her climax racked her body.

Jesse felt his release surge a moment before it dawned on him he'd forgotten a condom.

"Fuck!"

He tried to separate them enough to pull out of her, but she was holding on to him. His orgasm ended up coating her, the wall, and the floor.

Cassie lowered her legs to the floor and he rested his forehead on her shoulder, trying to catch his breath. How could he have been so irresponsible? She wasn't on birth control. He'd planned on broaching the subject this weekend.

His hands tightened on her hips and released.

"Are you okay?" she asked.

Jesse laughed without humor. "I think I should be the one asking you that question." He lifted his head to meet her gaze. "I forgot to use a condom."

"Oh." It was only then she seemed to realize his cum was streaming down her leg.

He waited for her to say more, but she didn't. "Let's get cleaned up, and we should talk."

Leading her into the bathroom, he removed a washcloth from the cabinet and wet it with warm water. He kneeled in front of her and cleaned the remnants of their lovemaking from her legs and pussy. "I left your bag on the couch. Why don't you take it into the bedroom and get yourself settled. I'll be in as soon as I get things cleaned up."

She nodded and left him to his task.

Jesse had no idea what he was going to say. He'd lost his head, which had never happened with a woman before. This was new territory for him. He was nervous, but more for her reaction than anything else.

With the last of the mess removed from the hall, he washed his hands, then went to find Cassie. It was time to face the consequences of his actions. Whatever they may be.

Cassie was already in bed when he walked into the room. The covers were pulled up to her neck, but she turned to look at him when he entered.

He sat on the edge of the bed next to her. "We should talk about what happened."

"Okay." She paused. "I'm not upset."

That surprised him. "You're not?"

She shook her head. "No."

"Why not? You should be. I screwed up. It's my job to protect you and I didn't."

"I'm not ready for a baby right now, but I can't be mad at you without being mad at myself."

He furrowed his brow, confused. "That makes no sense."

"I could have told you to stop, but it didn't even cross my mind. All I could think about was how much I wanted you."

"But—"

Cassie scooted closer to him, the blanket she'd had covering her falling to her waist, revealing she'd removed the bra she'd been wearing. Her nipples stood proud on breasts he wanted to taste. Despite having been inside her less than twenty minutes ago, he felt his body responding.

She placed a finger on his lips. "There's two of us in this relationship. I can always say no. Or use my safeword." She gave him a little smile, referencing that aspect of their relationship.

He removed her finger from his lips and turned her palm over to kiss it. That feeling of warmth deep in his chest was back, making him want to keep her with him forever.

Instead of going down that road of thought, he refocused the conversation on the topic at hand. "I think you should look into birth control. As much as I'd like to assure you something like that will never happen again, I lose all common sense when it comes to you sometimes."

That seemed to please her. "I lose all common sense when it comes to you, too, sometimes."

He brought both her hands to his lips, pressing them against his mouth and giving them a squeeze. "So you'll make an appointment with your doctor?"

Cassie nodded.

Releasing a breath, he lowered her hands to her lap. "Okay. I only have one more question for you, then, for tonight." He paused. "Are you completely naked under those blankets?"

She giggled. "You'll have to find out for yourself."

Standing, he lifted the covers and sure enough, she was naked from head to toe.

CHAPTER 16

CASSIE SNUGGLED into the covers as the memories of last night flooded back to her. She smiled, remembering how Jesse had reacted to her being naked in his bed. The way his body felt pressing her into the mattress.

He'd kissed every inch of her before pinning her to the bed and filling her. Sex had never been like this before for her. She'd never been so...overwhelmed by sensations flooding her senses.

The space beside her was empty, but it was still warm from where he'd been. She ran her hand over the sheets, letting her memory of the night play out in vivid color. Cassie didn't want to forget any of it. Ever.

The shower was running in the bathroom. Cassie imagined the water flowing over his body, caressing his muscles, begging to be licked, and felt heat build between her legs. She wanted him again. She wanted to join him in the shower and let their bodies take over.

But was that something he'd want?

Cassie hated the fact she was second-guessing herself. She didn't want to screw this up.

Before she could decide, the water shut off. She'd missed her chance.

A few minutes later, the door opened, and Jesse walked out, rubbing a towel over his hair. He wasn't wearing a stitch of clothing. Her gaze trailed over his body, taking in the dips and planes she was becoming familiar with.

She must have made a noise because he turned and caught her staring. One side of his mouth quirked up. "Enjoying the view?"

Heat bloomed on her cheeks. A denial was on the tip of her tongue, but she decided against it.

When she didn't respond, his smile grew. He crossed to the bed, leaned over, and captured her lips with his. The kiss was soft and slow but lingering. By the time he backed away, she was aching for more.

She had no idea when she'd become a sex fiend. It must have been somewhere between him fingering her and him taking her up against the wall. Or maybe it was when he'd explored her pussy with his tongue as if he'd never tasted anything better.

Jesse stood to his full height beside the bed. It brought his now not so flaccid cock within inches of her face. She had a sudden desire to know what he tasted like.

He grazed his thumb along her jaw and tilted her chin up to meet his gaze. "There'll be time for that later. This morning, there are things we need to talk about."

A strange disappointment mixed with trepidation filled her belly. "Talk?"

He nodded and released her. "Shower and dress while I make us breakfast. Then, we can talk."

Without waiting for a response from her, he went to the closet to get dressed.

Cassie flipped off the covers, padded to the bathroom, and closed the door before he reemerged from the closet. She tried to figure out what he wanted to talk about, then she recalled the discussion they had in the car before dinner. Her family. He thought she didn't want him to meet them.

To be honest, it had nothing to do with him and everything to do with her mom. Jessica Rourke was a lot to deal with sometimes. She loved her mom, she really did, but since she'd divorced Cassie's dad and remarried David, she'd changed.

Mom was great for the fun stuff. She and David loved to party. Not in the get drunk and do drugs sort of way, but in the carefree, don't worry about tomorrow way. At one time, Cassie thought she wanted to be that way, too.

She still remembered her dad's reaction to her sneaking out of his house when she was seventeen to go to a party. Let's just say, Cassie had never done that again. Not even at her mom's. She'd been too afraid her dad would find out somehow and she hadn't wanted to chance it.

Then, of course, there was her brother, Bradley. While he was great at being a pain in her ass and would insert himself into her private life if he took the notion to, she was confident Jesse could handle him.

No, it was her mom who had her dreading the eventual meeting. She liked Jesse. A lot. She wasn't sure how to be a good submissive, but she was trying. What if her mom said something to mess things up between them?

Cassie took her time in the shower and got dressed. She knew she was dragging her feet, but she couldn't bring herself to rush.

The condo was quiet when she made her way into the main living area. She could smell food, but Jesse wasn't in the kitchen or the living room.

Her stomach rumbled, pulling her attention back to the food. At least, that's what she told herself. The truth was, Cassie wasn't looking forward to the conversation ahead. She was beginning to realize Jesse and her dad had something in common. When they decided it was time to discuss something, it was impossible to deter them. But that didn't mean she couldn't try to delay it as long as possible.

She followed the smell of food to the oven. It was turned off, but she could feel heat radiating off it. She opened the door to peek inside.

"Sneaking around?"

Cassie jumped as if she'd been caught with her hand in the cookie jar. Clutching her chest, she turned to face Jesse. "You scared me."

"I noticed." He strolled over to the counter, picked up two oven mitts, and opened the oven door Cassie had let slam closed when he'd startled her.

The casserole dish he removed bubbled with cheese and had her mouth watering. "Take a seat at the table. I'll get this dished up and bring it over."

She waited while he carried the food to the table, then placed a large scoop onto her plate. "Thanks."

"You're welcome," he said, then served himself.

He let her get a few bites in before getting directly to the point. "Why is it you don't want me to meet your family? Or do you not want your family to meet me?"

"Neither?"

His only response was to raise a questioning eyebrow.

Cassie blew out a breath. "It's not that I don't want you to meet them. I mean, I'm nervous about it, but I know if we stay together, then you'll have to meet them eventually."

He waited for her to go on.

"My brother, Bradley, is a royal pain in the ass. He's stubborn like my dad, but unlike my dad, he always seems to think the worst of people. I think being a lawyer has jaded him."

There was no response from Jesse.

"Then here's my mom. As soon as she meets you, she's going to be planning our wedding. She's a romantic and gets caught up in the idea of love. I introduced her to Trent, and a month later, he was proposing."

"You believe he proposed because of your mom?" Jesse asked.

She shrugged. "I don't know. She was all over him, talking about the perfect wedding venues and how she wanted to meet his parents. Get to know her daughter's future in-laws."

Her revelation was met with silence. He chewed his food and swallowed, then took another bite.

Several minutes passed before he spoke. "Anything else?"

"Isn't that enough?"

To her surprise, he chuckled. "Cass, neither your mother nor your brother is going to push me into something I'm not ready to do. Nor are they going to scare me away. If that's what you're worried about, then you don't need to be. I have no issue with your mother discussing wedding venues or even wanting to meet my parents."

Cassie opened her mouth, then closed it again. What did he mean by that?

She tried not to read too much into it, but her mind began to wonder. They'd both said they wanted this relationship to be more than a casual fling. He'd been very clear about that. But they'd only known each other for a couple of weeks. She wasn't even sure if she could be the submissive he wanted her to be.

"I can see your mind working overtime. You're worried about something. Tell me what it is."

She met his gaze across the table and tried to put how she was feeling, her uncertainty, into words. "I'm not sure how to do this."

He cocked his head to the side. "Eat breakfast together?"

That made her laugh. "No."

"What, then?"

"I'm not sure how to be your submissive. I'm supposed to do what you tell me to do, but then I get so caught up when you touch me that I forget everything but how it feels when I'm with you." Cassie lowered her gaze. "I don't want to screw this up."

* * *

Now they were getting to the heart of the issue. Her family. His family. All of that was a smoke screen to what was really bothering her.

"Cassie, do you feel you can't be yourself around me?"

She lifted her head to meet his gaze. "Sometimes."

He put his fork down and held her gaze. "Why do you feel you can't be yourself?"

"You want me to be submissive."

"Did you like it when I put you over my knee and spanked you?"

She started to speak, then stopped herself. Then, she began again, only to again remain silent. He waited her out, deciding to resume eating his breakfast while she gathered her thoughts.

Several minutes later, she sighed, and he returned his fork to his plate. "I shouldn't have."

He understood her confusion. It had been years since he'd played with a submissive who was new to the lifestyle. Sometimes, they had problems reconciling themselves to enjoying submission. The modern world screams women should be aggressive and go after what they want. Letting a man dominate them, and liking it, seems like something they should run away from.

But he had no doubt in his mind Cassie was submissive. Her reaction to his spanking was proof of that. Not to mention how she'd responded to his other dominant behaviors in the bedroom.

He knew he was going to have to push her out of her comfort zone. The sooner she admitted her needs to herself, her desires, the better off they'd both be. "We all have needs, Cass. It's not something to be ashamed of."

"But it's embarrassing."

Jesse raised his eyebrows in question. "Why is it embarrassing?"

"Things aren't supposed to be that way. Women aren't supposed to want that anymore."

"Do you think I'd ever force you to do something you truly didn't want to do?"

She thought about it for a moment before answering. "No."

"What we do isn't something you should be embarrassed about as long as it's something we both want and enjoy. Most people don't venture outside of the norm when it comes to relationships and sex and to me that's a pity. Learning your partner's needs can be extremely fulfilling. It can also bring them closer. We've only been together for two nights and already I know how your skin flushes as you near orgasm. I know the way your body shakes right before you come. And I know how to make you shiver with need just from running my lips along your neck."

He watched a shiver ripple through her body and knew she was turned on. That hadn't been his intention, but he'd take it.

"I don't want you to ever feel like you can't come to me with what you need. My job as your Dominant is to make sure your needs are met. But I can't fix something I don't know about. So if there's something bothering you, I need you to come to me."

She took a calming breath and nodded. "All right."

"Good." He picked up his fork again. "Now eat your breakfast before it gets cold."

He finished eating and waited for her, not wanting to rush her or pull her into another discussion. Once they were both done eating, they cleaned up their dishes and moved to the living room. They had no real plans for the day and that was perfect, in his opinion. He needed time to decompress after the week he'd had at the office.

Settling onto the couch, he pulled her against him, tucking her into his side. They needed to talk, but he was willing to do this at her pace. For now. He was hoping, however, she'd understand the importance of communication and push the conversation forward herself.

Several minutes passed before she twisted into the cutest little pout. "If there's something I want to try, then I can tell you, right?"

"Of course." He paused. "It doesn't mean we'll do it, or maybe not immediately, but I always want to know what you're thinking."

Cassie nodded. "When I was doing research on BDSM, I noticed the Doms tended to use a lot of...toys on their submissives."

She paused as if she were expecting him to answer a question she hadn't asked. Instead, he let her statement hang in the air, waiting.

"You've never used any toys on me." She paused again but seemed to realize he was going to sit there until she put words to her question. "Why is that?"

Instead of answering, he asked a question of his own. "Is there a particular toy or implement you wanted me to use on you?"

"No." She paused. "Maybe." She paused again. "I don't know."

He pressed his lips together, trying not to chuckle. She was so cute when she was flustered. "The reason I haven't used any toys on you is because you're new to this. I wanted you to get comfortable with our dynamic before I introduced you to toys."

"Oh." He was hoping she'd go on, but she didn't.

"Tell me what you're thinking."

"Do you already have the toys?"

"Yes."

She inhaled.

He ran the tips of his fingers down her arm, then up to her shoulder. She leaned her head against him, letting her eyes flitter shut. He continued to brush his fingers up and down her skin, letting her think and feel. This was new to her, and he was okay taking things slow. He planned on them being together for a long time. There was no need to rush.

"What toy is your favorite?" Her voice was soft, but it rang clear in the quiet room.

"I have several favorites, but if I had to choose one, I'd go with a flogger."

"That's the things with all the long leather strings, right?"

He grinned. "Yes. The long leather strings are called falls."

"Why's it your favorite?"

Jesse liked this inquisitive side of her. "A flogger has a lot of versatility. It can be used in a more traditional way for flogging or spanking, but it can also be used to create a soothing sensation by running the falls over the skin."

"Does it hurt?" He heard a note of unease in her voice.

"That depends on the flogger and the one using it. Some floggers are heavier than others."

"And the heavier ones hurt." She said it as though she was stating a fact.

"No. The lighter ones tend to sting whereas the heavier ones have more of a thud to them."

She turned in his arms, bringing their noses within inches of each other. "I don't think I'd like the stinging ones."

"I don't know. You seemed to like the sting of my palm on your ass."

Cassie didn't answer right away, but he saw her pupils darken. She really enjoyed her spanking the other night. He was going to have to remember that. Something told him she'd be spending a lot of time across his lap in the future.

Her eyes drifted closed again and she brought her hands to rest on his chest. "Why am I equally curious and scared?"

"Because it's new and you have no point of reference. For what it's worth, I think you'll like floggers." He lifted her and placed her onto his lap, putting her in the same position she'd been in when they were at the lake. This time, however, they didn't have anyone watching.

She tilted her head back, resting it on his shoulder. "Why's that?"

Jesse ran his hands along the inseam of her jeans. He would have preferred her to be wearing a skirt, but he could adapt. "Because you like impact play." He grazed his fingers over her denim-covered pussy and continued upward, dipping under her shirt.

Her only response was a low hum.

Tilting her head to the side, he ran the tip of his nose along her neck, then captured her earlobe with his teeth. She was putty in his hands, even if she didn't realize it.

He cupped her breasts, kneading them in his palms, the lacy fabric scratching his fingers. Her nipples hardened as the pressure in his own jeans began to build. He wanted to suck on her tits, but that would come in time. They had all day. There was no need to rush.

She arched her back, pushing her breasts into his hands, silently begging for him to increase the pressure, to give her more.

Instead of giving her what she wanted, he removed one of his hands and popped the button on her jeans. The zipper released as he slid his hand inside, burrowing beneath her panties until he found her wet heat.

CHAPTER 17

CASSIE WANTED his hands everywhere all at once. And his mouth.

His finger circled her clit as his other hand continued to massage her breast. The fabric from her bra added to the sensation, but she wanted it out of the way. That went double for her jeans. Why had she packed jeans anyway?

"Do you want more?" Jesse asked, whispering in her ear.

"Yes." The word came out more as a breath, but she knew he'd heard her.

Instead of giving her more, though, his hands stopped moving. "Yes, what?"

It took her a moment to realize what he was talking about. "Yes, Sir. Please, more. Touch me more."

The next thing she knew, she was lying flat on her back on the couch, and he was hovering over her. She blinked up at him, trying to get her bearings.

Cool air teased her heated flesh as he removed her jeans and threw them to the floor. She was naked from the waist down in a matter of seconds.

In the past, she would have been looking for something to cover up with, but now, with Jesse, she felt the opposite. She spread her legs, giving him a clear view of her sex. He rewarded her by placing a kiss on her clit, then giving it a slow lick with the tip of his tongue.

She threaded her fingers through his hair, wanting to keep him there, but he had other plans.

"You're still wearing too many clothes, baby." Jesse crawled up her torso, pushing her shirt up as he went.

Cassie lifted her arms as he maneuvered her shirt over her shoulders and head. The only stitch of clothing she had left was her bra and she had a feeling it would be gone soon, too.

His lips captured hers in a searing kiss that left her toes curling. He lifted her leg, securing it around his waist. The fabric of his jeans scraped against her sensitive skin, sending tingles of need coursing through her. She could feel his hard length pressing against her and she wanted his jeans out of the way. She didn't want anything separating them.

But she couldn't say anything. He had her mouth occupied. She tried to convey what she wanted with her body, but he either didn't understand or was choosing to ignore it.

Jesse pulled the straps of her bra down her arms, restricting her movement. She dug her fingers into his sides since that was the only place she could reach.

His tongue continued to dominate her mouth, demanding she kiss him back with as much passion. She was so hot.

He finally broke the kiss and stared down at her for a long moment. Then, he got up from the couch and removed his clothing. His erection stood straight and proud. She wanted to taste him.

"May I taste you, Sir?"

Jesse paused, then took a pillow from a nearby chair and dropped it on the floor in front of him. "Kneel on the pillow."

Cassie rolled off the couch and kneeled on the pillow. She knew from her research that kneeling before your dominant was a common thing in this lifestyle, but before today, Jesse had never asked her to do it.

He combed his fingers through her hair, cupping the back of her head. "You want to suck my cock, baby?"

The body part in question was inches away from her face and her need to take him into her mouth increased. Her sex pulsed with desire, a primal urge she didn't understand. "Yes, Sir."

Jesse knew from when they'd gone over their lists that she'd only done this a few times before. She didn't hate it, but it wasn't something she'd ever thought she'd crave. Yet, here she was, the need to suck his cock so strong she was almost willing to beg.

He ran his thumb along the base of her jaw a few times before taking a small step forward and bringing his erection to her mouth. His thumb pulled at her lower lip, and she opened her mouth. His cock slid inside.

It was warm and had a hint of saltiness. But it was more than that. She couldn't explain it. A rush of heat surged between her legs as she took more of him in.

Both of Jesse's hands settled on her head as she moved up and down over his length. She experimented using her tongue to lick, then sucking like she would on a straw. Every now and then, she'd feel his fingers flex against her scalp. At first, she'd thought she'd done something wrong, but then she'd hear his breath hitch in the same way he did when she'd kissed her way up his chest the night before.

As Cassie continued, she gained more confidence in what she was doing. Her movements became more bold. He liked that, too.

Then, he was gone. Jesse ripped his cock out of her mouth.

She thought she'd done something wrong, but then she saw him reach for a condom she hadn't noticed on the coffee table. He rolled it down his length, then turned to face her again.

Cassie had no idea what he was going to do. Okay, that wasn't true. She knew he was going to fuck her.

Before she could contemplate the hows, he took hold of her bicep and turned her to face the couch. She was still on her knees, but that didn't seem to matter. He pushed on her back until her face was against the couch.

Jesse kneeled behind her and lined himself up. He thrust forward, his cock filling her pussy.

A feeling of rightness came over her as he moved inside her, pulling out, then plunging forward again. Over and over, he thrust, bringing every emotion she felt since meeting him to the surface.

He brushed her hair away from her neck and leaned forward until his chest was against her back. She could feel his harsh breaths against her skin, only adding to everything she was feeling. Cassie loved that she could do this to him. That this wasn't only one-sided. She felt powerful, yet taken care of at the same time. She didn't want this feeling to ever end.

His hands were everywhere, on her breasts, her hips, her belly. She was so hot, yet she didn't want him to stop. She never wanted him to stop.

One of Jesse's hands cupped her still cloth-covered breast while the other found its way between her legs. His fingers plucked at her nipple, the sensation almost painful, while the digits of his other hand worked her clit. She was pressed against the couch, his body holding her down.

He began kissing her shoulder, her neck, anywhere his mouth could reach. "Are you ready to come, Cass?"

She tried to nod, but she couldn't move all that much. "Yes. Yes, Sir."

He did something with his hips, and she gasped. Then she felt his teeth scrape against her shoulder and his fingers pinch her nipple. That, combined with what he was doing to her clit, was too much.

Her orgasm hit her hard. She released a strangled cry as her climax rocked her body.

Jesse picked up his pace, sucking on the skin at the base of her neck as if demons were chasing him. He released a grunt from deep in his belly as he surged forward once more and held himself deep inside her.

Neither of them moved for several long moments. She could feel his heart pounding against his chest as their breathing came back to normal. He kissed along her spine, keeping his arms around her.

As her pulse returned to normal, their position registered. She was trapped. She couldn't move.

Cassie shifted and Jesse must have felt the change in her mood. He sat up, pulling out of her.

She straightened immediately and readjusted her bra straps so they were on her shoulders again and didn't restrict the movement of her arms.

Jesse brushed the back of his fingers along her cheek. It was only then she realized she was crying. "Cass?"

She wiped the tears away.

"Did I hurt you?"

"No."

He waited for her to go on. When she didn't, he stood, helped her up, and grabbed a blanket from inside an ottoman a few feet away. He wrapped the blanket around her, making sure it was secure. "Wait here. I need to clean up." He kissed the top of her head. "I won't be long."

Cassie hugged the blanket, feeling so many emotions she was having trouble naming them. How had she gone from feeling on top of the world, to crying, to utter panic?

She glanced at the door, then disregarded the notion of fleeing. Jesse would follow her. Even if she went to her mom's for the rest of the weekend, there would be no avoiding him come Monday, and the last thing she wanted to do was have a confrontation at work.

No, she was going to have to suck it up and deal with this like an adult. She didn't want to lose Jesse. In fact, she was pretty sure she was falling in love with him. Taking a seat on the couch, she snuggled into her blanket and waited.

* * *

She'd been fine. Jesse knew he was pushing her boundaries, so he'd paid close attention to how she was reacting to having her movement restricted, to being held down by his weight. She'd shown no signs of distress. In fact, it was the opposite.

He threw the condom away, washed his hands, and hurried back to the living room. Cassie was huddled in the corner of his couch, still wrapped in the throw blanket he'd put around her.

Disregarding both their clothes, he sat beside her on the couch and pulled her into his arms. She snuggled into him, burrowing her face into his neck. A shiver ran through her, but this time it had nothing to do with arousal. "Cass, I need you to tell me what happened."

Jesse felt something wet trickle down his chest. She was crying again.

He was about to ask her again, when she brought a hand up through the blanket and wiped the moisture away from her cheeks. "I don't know, exactly. One minute everything was great. Then, it wasn't."

That didn't tell him anything useful. "Did something change?"

She was quiet for a long moment. "I realized I was trapped. I couldn't move. And I..."

When she didn't finish her sentence, he filled in the blanks. "Got scared."

Cassie nodded. "Yeah."

Jesse held her tighter. He kissed the top of her head before lifting her chin so she could look him in the eyes. "It's okay to be scared. You don't have to be the strong one. If you fall, I'll catch you." He brushed the fresh tears from her cheeks and one side of his mouth lifted in a half smile. "That's sort of my job as your Dom."

"You're not mad?"

"Of course not." He tucked a strand of hair behind her ear. "Why would I be mad?"

"I ruined the moment."

Lifting her onto his lap, he repositioned the blanket so it encompassed them both. Not only did this keep them both warm given neither of them had any clothes on, but it also meant her naked body was pressed against his. "Baby, you didn't ruin anything. This is just growing pains. We're learning about each other. The important thing is we talk through the things that worked and those that didn't."

She thought about that for a long moment. "I liked when you were lying on top of me while we were having sex. I don't know what changed for me. I was okay, then I wasn't. It makes no sense."

"It makes more sense than you might think." He caressed her hip, keeping his hands in more neutral areas. "During sexual arousal, your mind processes things differently. Pain. Pleasure. It all gets jumbled. Things you wouldn't normally be okay with can suddenly be okay when combined with sexual stimulation."

"You think once I wasn't sexually stimulated anymore, my brain processed you lying on top of me differently?"

"Me holding you down. Yes."

Cassie was quiet for a long moment. "Does that mean you won't hold me down anymore?"

He couldn't stop the snort that escaped, nor his smile. "No."

"No, you won't hold me down anymore, or no, it doesn't mean you won't hold me down anymore?" Cassie's lips twisted and her brow furrowed. "That didn't even make sense to me."

Jesse laughed, then answered her question. "This won't be the last time I restrict your movement. Whether that's by holding you down, as I did today, or by securing your limbs to my bed, or by trussing you up and hanging you from the ceiling."

Her eyes grew wide. "Truss me up? Like a turkey?"

Again, he couldn't help but chuckle. "Trust me, you'll look much better than any turkey."

Cassie swallowed. "I'm not sure I'm ready for something like that."

He sobered. "No, you're not. Not yet. But that doesn't mean you won't be in the future. What happened today, this is a learning experience, nothing more."

She sighed. "What do we do now?"

"I'll pay more attention to your emotional state as you come down from your climax and I need you to communicate to me when you feel that panic beginning to take hold."

"You mean use my safeword."

Jesse nodded. "Say yellow if you feel it coming on." He cupped her cheek and rested his forehead against hers. "I don't like seeing you in distress like that."

She closed the distance between them and pressed a soft kiss to his lips. "Thank you."

He gave her a soft kiss in return. "I'm thinking a movie might be a nice way to continue our day. Do you have any suggestions?"

"Have you seen *Outlander?*"

Jesse had watched a lot of movies over the years, but he didn't recall one called *Outlander*. "Do you mean the television show?"

She nodded.

"No. I've heard about it, but I haven't seen it."

"It's soooo good. Jamie is just…" Cassie sighed.

The dreamy look in her eyes amused him. "Do I need to be jealous?" He'd never been jealous before, and it felt strange to think it might happen over a fictional character.

Cassie ran her hand over Jesse's chest. "He's not real. Or his character isn't. You, on the other hand…"

She gazed up at him with a glint in her eye that had his cock twitching.

He kissed the tip of her nose and reached for the remote. It took him several minutes to locate *Outlander* on the screen. He clicked on it and was shocked to see there were multiple seasons. "What season are you on?"

"No, we have to start from the beginning. You won't understand the story otherwise," she said. "I don't mind watching it again."

Nodding, he clicked on season one, episode one, and hit play.

Three hours later, Jesse found himself as enchanted by the story as she was. He was realizing what all the hype was about. It had everything. Action. Adventure. Romance. Time travel. And so many twists and turns he was trying to keep up with them all.

Cassie was tucked against him, her naked body warm against his. He'd draped the blanket over them, creating a cozy bubble as they binged on the show. It was the most relaxed he could ever remember being and he could see himself repeating this day with her for the rest of their lives.

He glanced at the clock and was shocked to see it was after one. "Are you getting hungry?"

"A little." She tore her gaze away from the screen to look at him. "I can wait, though."

Hitting pause on the show, Jesse climbed off the couch and went to get his phone. While he enjoyed cooking, he was also a foodie. He loved trying new restaurants, which meant he had an extensive knowledge of what was good in the area.

It took him all of five minutes to order their lunch and arrange for it to be delivered. Once that was done, he returned to his position on the couch. He picked up the remote and pressed play.

Cassie continued to stare at him.

He pressed pause again and raised his eyebrows in question.

"You didn't ask me what I wanted."

"No."

"What if I don't like what you ordered?" she asked.

"I ordered a variety of options. I'm confident you'll find something." He'd ordered enough food for the entire weekend, should they need it. If he were honest, he wanted to stay in the condo and block out the outside world for as long as possible.

She looked at him for several more moments, then rolled to face the television.

"Is that a problem?"

"No." She paused for a long moment. "I'm not used to people ordering for me without asking me first."

This didn't have anything to do with their sexual relationship, so it didn't necessarily fall under the Dominant/submissive arrangement. He liked taking care of her, and making sure she was fed was part of that, but he could see where it might be an adjustment for her.

"Do you not want me to order for you in the future?" He was hoping she wouldn't say yes because he wasn't sure he could agree to that.

She rolled back to face him. "You like ordering for me."

"I do."

The crease in Cassie's brow became more pronounced as she considered the situation. "How about this, when we're here, you can order for me." She paused. "As long as I don't have to eat anything I don't like." She scrunched up her nose. "No crazy stuff."

"And when we're not here?" he asked.

"If we're on a date, then I get to choose, but you can do the ordering. If you want. But if we're at work, or it's not a date, then I do my own ordering."

Cassie had told him she wasn't good at negotiation. She was better than she thought.

"I think I can agree to those terms."

The smile she sent him was worth the concession he'd made.

He brushed his lips against hers before capturing them in a leisurely kiss. "Ready to finish watching this episode?"

She nodded and turned around to face the screen. Her ass was pressed against his groin, and it took all his self-control not to line her up and slip inside.

But there would be plenty of time for that later. The food would be there soon, and the last thing he wanted was to be interrupted.

CHAPTER 18

JESSE thew his jeans on to answer the door and left them on until after they finished their lunch. Cassie had remained naked.

She had to admit, she kind of liked not wearing clothes. And from the way he kept touching her, she knew he liked it too.

After lunch, they moved to the bedroom. He stripped back down to his birthday suit, and they cuddled on the bed while continuing to watch the first season of *Outlander*.

When they got to the episode of Jamie and Claire's wedding night, Cassie was sitting between Jesse's legs. She wasn't quite sure how she'd gotten into that position, but she wasn't complaining. She could feel his heart beating against her back, his chest rising and falling with every breath.

As the couple on the screen moved to the more physical part of the evening, Jesse's touches became more purposeful. He guided his hands down her side, over her hips and thighs. Dipping his hands between her legs, he skimmed the sensitive flesh before shifting his attention upward until he cupped her breasts.

Cassie sighed, pressing back against him as his fingers continued to wonder. She closed her eyes, taking in the feeling of his hands ghosting over her body. Over and over, he ran his hands up and down, sliding over her hips, skimming her inner thighs, and then traveled back up to her breasts…every time skipping over the good stuff.

The next time he caressed her inner thighs, she tried to spread her legs wider. Her body was humming, needing more.

But he ignored her silent pleas and continued at his leisurely pace. She didn't know how much more torture she could take. And it was torture. Torture of the most wonderful kind but torture all the same.

Cassie decided she needed to do something to try and encourage him to speed things up, so she snaked her hand behind her back until she found his hard cock. Wrapping her fingers around his length, she began moving her hand up and down.

"What do you think you're doing?"

"Touching you." Why was he asking her so many questions? It was hard enough to concentrate on what she was doing.

"Why?" Again, his fingers came so close to her sex, but instead of going where she most wanted them to, he bypassed it altogether and began heading north again.

Cassie lifted her hips, trying to get his fingers to touch her on their way by, but it didn't work. She let out a soft whine.

Jesse's chest rumbled behind her. "Are you getting impatient, baby?"

There was no reason to deny it. "Yes."

One of his hands came up to pinch her nipple and she squeaked.

It took a moment for her brain to catch up and realize why he'd gone from caressing her with a feather-like touch to sending pain coursing through her nipple. "Sorry, Sir. I forgot."

"The next time you forget to address me properly, I'll turn you over my knee and give you a reminder."

That sobered her a little. She was going to have to do better. "Yes, Sir."

He went back to what he was doing. She was so wet, her pussy aching for his touch. Her hand was still on his cock, but it was no longer moving. The only thing she could focus on was the need for him to touch her.

Cassie relaxed back into him, letting her hand fall away from his length. She spread her legs open as far as they would go, letting him do whatever it was he wanted and hoping he'd touch her the way she desired.

Every cell in her body was primed. Her nipples were hard, her clit was pulsing with desire, and still he continued. She was wondering if it was possible to die from sexual frustration.

His fingers trailed down her stomach and smoothed over her hips before grazing her inner thighs. It was the same path his hands had taken before, but this time on his way back up, his digits brushed her clit.

Electricity shot through her core. Her breath caught in her throat, and her pussy clenched, seeking to be filled.

She thought having him touch her would ease the ache in her belly, but if anything, it made it worse. The next time his fingers came near her clit, she held her breath, hoping he'd touch her again.

He did. This time, he lingered for a fraction of a second longer, making a light circle around her clit before continuing his journey upward. It really was torture. She didn't know how much more she could take.

The next time he made his way down, she lifted her hips, encouraging him to linger, but it didn't work. He did no more than circle her clit again. She let out a desperate whimper.

"Something wrong?" His voice was sure and steady. If not for his rock-hard cock pressing against her back, she'd think he was completely unaffected.

"I need more. I need you to touch me, Sir."

"I am touching you." As if to prove his point, he skimmed his palms along her sides to the outside of her hips.

He was being intentionally obtuse. She was beginning to realize he enjoyed playing with her like this—making her wait—making her beg. "Please, Sir. Please touch my clit and make me come."

His teeth scraped the flesh of her ear. "See, now, that wasn't too hard, was it?"

Jesse brought both hands between her legs and spread her open.

She thought he was going to touch her clit, but instead, he slid two fingers inside her pussy. He moved them in and out several times before bringing them up to where she wanted his touch most.

His fingers were slippery as they rubbed her clit. She fisted the sheets, trying to ground herself. She was going to go off any second, it wouldn't take much. She was primed and ready.

But before she could come, his fingers were gone. She wanted to cry. Her body was shaking with all the pent-up energy.

He shifted behind her, and she heard a drawer opening. She looked over to see him extracting a condom. A mix of relief and excitement filled her as she watched him roll the condom down his erection.

As soon as he had the condom in place, Jesse grasped her by the hips and lifted her onto his cock. There were no pleasantries. There was no need. She was wet and beyond ready for him.

He filled her and began thrusting his hips upward while driving her down onto his cock. She wasn't in a position to help, her legs still spread over his thighs.

"Touch yourself," he grunted out against her ear, his breath harsh as he drove into her.

She let go of the sheet and slipped her hand between her legs. Her fingers brushed against where they were joined before zeroing in on her clit.

Two circles around her clit was all it took for her orgasm to take over. She yelled out her climax, feeling her breath leave her as all the pent-up sexual energy surged out of her.

But he didn't stop. He continued to move as she rode out her orgasm. Before she knew what was happening, Cassie felt her climax building again.

"That's it, baby. You like it when I fuck you, don't you?" As if to prove that point, he rammed his cock deep inside her, making her cry out. "I want you to come again. I want to feel your pussy squeeze my cock."

Jesse brushed her hair away with his nose and began sucking on the back of her neck. He wasn't being gentle about it either. She could feel his teeth nibbling on her skin. Nothing about this was gentle. If anything, it was animalistic.

She began rubbing her clit again, faster this time. Her orgasm was so close. She could feel it.

This time when it hit her, it was a rush of waves one right after another. Her pussy clamped down on his cock as it was buried insider her, trying to hold onto it before he ripped it away again.

Jesse's teeth bit into her shoulder as he stilled, his own climax taking over. He held her against him, keeping their bodies locked together. "You okay, Cass?"

His question struck her as funny for some reason and she started to laugh.

"Cass?"

* * *

Jesse slipped out and turned her so he could see her face. He hadn't been sure if she was laughing or crying, but once he was sure it was laughter, he smiled back at her. "I'll take that as a yes."

She nodded.

He cupped her cheeks and brought her in for a kiss. He was falling hard for this woman.

Cassie went limp against the pillow when he released her. Her chest was still vibrating with her laughter, causing her tits to jiggle. If he wasn't already spent, he'd be tempted to get things going again. But there'd be more time for that later. They had nowhere to be for the rest of the weekend.

He gave her another brief kiss before climbing out of bed and making his way to the bathroom to clean up. His cock was limp against his leg as he washed his hands and headed back to the bedroom, but it twitched at the sight of her lying naked in his bed.

She hadn't bothered to pull the covers up and he was enjoying the view. Her arms were stretched above her head, and her legs were bent. If he walked to the end of the mattress, he'd have a clear view of her pussy.

He'd always had a strong sex drive, but he couldn't remember the last time he'd wanted to take a woman again so soon. Cassie was different. He'd known it from the start.

As if sensing him staring, she turned her head and met his gaze. "Hi."

Jesse strolled toward her, putting a knee on the bed. He lowered himself down, his body covering her. "Hi."

She circled her arms around his neck and when he lowered his mouth to meet hers, she kissed him back.

He took his time, not in any rush. This wasn't about getting her libido going. It was about comfort and affection. "Are you thirsty?"

"A little."

Rolling off her, Jesse retrieved their drinks from earlier. He waited until she'd propped herself up against the headboard, then handed her the glass.

"Thanks." Cassie brought the water to her lips and drank.

He followed suit. They both needed to stay hydrated.

She looked toward the television. It was still playing *Outlander*, but he had no idea what was going on in the story. Jamie and Claire had been in their room the last time he'd looked at the screen. They were now back at the castle.

"I think we've skipped an entire episode," Cassie said.

"That's the great thing about streaming. You can always go back." He picked up the remote and found the episode they'd been watching when he'd begun playing with her. They'd missed the last half of that episode and the next.

They ended up watching the rest of the first season. It wasn't what he'd expected, but he'd enjoyed it.

For dinner, they'd eaten the remainder of the food he'd ordered earlier in the day. He hadn't bothered to get dressed again and he'd made sure she stayed naked as well.

Before they headed to bed for the night, he drew them a bath in his large tub. It was big enough for two and he planned to take advantage of it.

Jesse turned the lights down and lit a few candles. When everything was ready, he led her into the bathroom. Her eyes lit up when she saw the setup and he thought he saw the beginning of tears.

He kissed the top of her head. "What's wrong?"

"Nothing. It's perfect."

Sometimes he didn't understand women, but he was starting to understand Cassie. He was willing to bet none of her past lovers had done anything like this for her. A part of him was upset she'd never been pampered before, but another part—a larger part—was happy he could be the one to treat her the way she deserved.

He helped her into the bathtub, then climbed in behind her. Once he was settled against the porcelain, he gathered her against him. Cassie leaned back and sighed.

"Comfortable?"

She nodded.

He kissed the exposed skin at the top of her shoulder.

"Thank you."

"For?"

Cassie released a contented sigh. "This. It's very romantic."

Jesse smiled and reached for the soap. "Are you trying to tell me you're a romantic?"

"I shouldn't be."

He dunked the soap beneath the water, getting it wet before rubbing it between his hands. Once a good lather had formed, he began massaging her shoulders and chest. He kissed the side of her head, right above her ear. "If things like this mean I get to see you naked more, I'll make sure to keep the romance coming."

His comment was meant to make her laugh, and it did. Her tits bobbed up and down in the water, temping him. His younger self would have forgotten the plans he had for their bath and lifted her onto his cock. But he wasn't a teenager anymore, and he had more self-control than that.

The water sloshed at the sides of the tub as he moved down her body with the soap, getting her arms and legs before changing his focus to her chest once more. This time, after lathering his hands, he covered her breasts with his palms and cleaned them.

Cassie was lying limp against him. If not for her breathing, he'd think she was asleep.

Nothing he'd done in their bath so far had been overly sexual. He'd kept everything tame. This wasn't about sex, although his semi-hard cock pressed against her back might dispute that. Then again, he always wanted Cassie. That had been the case from the beginning, and he doubted it would ever change.

She released a soft moan of pleasure as he caressed her nipples and skimmed over her torso down to her belly. The bubbles in the water obscured his view, but he could still see the patch of hair covering her sex.

Normally, he preferred his women to have nothing more than a landing strip, but for some reason, Cassie's pubic hair didn't bother him. It was trimmed and she either had it waxed on the edges or kept it shaved.

He threaded his fingers through the hair in question, pulling the curls taut before letting them spring back into place. Everything about Cassie turned him on. Her body, for sure, but he also liked that he could have a conversation with her without it turning into an argument, or worse, having her just agree to whatever he said.

Yes, he was a Dominant. He liked to be in control, especially when it came to sex, but that didn't mean he wanted a doormat. He wanted a partner. Someone who could fit with him like a matching puzzle piece.

Jesse ran his fingers down her sides before settling his hands on her hips. The water was cooling off.

He rinsed any of the residual soap from her body, then slid her forward so he could get out. The moment he stood, Cassie turned, her eyes twinkling in the candlelight. She looked like an angel. His angel.

Before his libido took over, he stepped out of the bathtub and pulled the plug so the water could drain. He helped Cassie out, grabbed a towel, and began drying her off.

She never took her gaze off him.

Once he finished drying her off, he got another towel for himself. Before he could use it, however, Cassie stopped him. "May I dry you off, Sir."

That was all it took for his cock to go from half-mast to rock-hard.

CHAPTER 19

Was it possible to die from too many orgasms? Cassie wasn't sure, but she was thinking if it was, then it was a good way to go. She'd lost count of how many orgasms she'd had over the last two days.

Unfortunately, the weekend couldn't last forever and on Monday morning, she found herself standing in front of his bathroom mirror doing her hair and makeup. Jesse had made them both breakfast and had left her alone to dress, saying he needed to check his messages.

It felt strange to wear clothes again, which she found a little odd. How could she have gotten used to running around naked so fast?

With a final look in the mirror, Cassie returned everything to her toiletry bag and headed across the hall to the spare room where she'd left her things. She was zipping up her overnight bag when Jesse popped his head into the room. He scanned her from head to toe, assessing. "I prefer you naked."

Cassie chuckled. "Yes, well, I can't go to work naked."

"Hmm." Jesse strolled across the room and pulled her against him. He palmed her ass, giving it a squeeze, then lowered his mouth to hers.

She opened her mouth, letting his tongue slip inside. He tasted of mint toothpaste and coffee. Within moments, she felt her sex heating, readying itself for him.

He gave her a peck on the lips and released her. "You have no idea how much I want to chain you to my bed right now and refuse to let you leave."

Her pussy clenched at his words and not in a bad way. She really had become a sex addict. "I think your dad might have a problem with that."

His only response was to raise one eyebrow.

Instead of commenting or trying to argue why chaining her to his bed would be a bad idea, she grabbed her overnight bag.

Before she could sling it over her shoulder, Jesse took it from her. With the bag in one hand, he reached for her with the other, threading his fingers through hers. "Come on. Let's get going before I change my mind."

Cassie pressed her lips together and let him lead her out.

Jesse kissed her before they got out of his vehicle and escorted her up to her floor. He didn't follow her to her desk, although she had a feeling he wanted to. Instead, he stayed in the elevator while she exited on the executive floor, then he took the elevator back down to the accounting level.

It was almost lunchtime when the cell rang. She debated letting it go to voicemail, but then she saw the name on the screen. "Dad?"

"Did I catch you at a bad time?"

"No. Of course not. Is something wrong?" Her dad never called her at work. Okay, almost never. The last time he'd called was to tell her James had been taken to the hospital after throwing his back out at a competition.

"I'm hoping you can tell me."

She was confused. "Huh?"

"I received a very long email from your brother suggesting I run a background check on a man you're apparently dating. Then I got a frantic call from your mom demanding I find out everything I can about the man you're seeing."

Cassie covered her face with her free hand. "I'm going to kill them."

Her dad laughed. "Don't be too hard on them. They're doing it because they love you."

She blew out a loud breath. "I know. But they need to mind their own business."

"Good luck with that."

As much as she hated to admit it, she knew he was right.

"I'm calling to ask if you'd like me to run a background check on your new man." He paused. "I'm surprised Bradley didn't do it himself, but he was going on about how it would look better coming from me."

Cassie snorted, then looked around to make sure no one had heard her. Mr. Masters was in a meeting with some of the other executives at the other end of the building, but that didn't mean there weren't other people within earshot.

Confident no one overheard, she answered her dad. "I'd appreciate it if you didn't."

There was silence on the other end of the line.

"Dad?"

"I'm here."

She blew out a breath. "You've already run a background check on him, haven't you?"

"I may have done a little digging."

Cassie huffed. "Dad."

He ignored her protest. "Is it serious?"

She knew she could downplay her relationship with Jesse, but she didn't want to. "Yes."

Again, she was met with a long moment of silence.

If her dad had done any digging, then he already knew who Jesse's father was. Daniel Ross had resources. More resources than her brother.

"Does he treat you right?" her dad asked.

"He does." The man they were discussing strolled toward her with a bag in his hand. Her heart rate kicked up a notch at the sight of him.

"I expect to meet him soon."

She nodded even though she knew her dad couldn't see her. "Okay."

Her dad didn't seem overly thrilled with her short response, but she was having trouble focusing on the conversation with Jesse standing right in front of her. His blue eyes roamed over her, sending beads of awareness darting to all her girly bits. Not exactly something she wanted to be feeling while talking to her father.

"Dad, I need to let you go. I have a lunch…appointment."

Jesse sent her a questioning look.

"All right. I'll let you go. But you need to call your mother." He paused. "And, Cassie, be careful. Office romances can implode on you."

Any doubt she had about her dad knowing who Jesse was went out the window. But before she could say anything back, her dad disconnected. She lowered the phone from her ear and tucked it in her purse.

"Everything okay?"

Cassie sighed. "Yeah."

He gave her a once-over, then tilted his head toward the bag he was holding. "I ordered us lunch. I don't have much time today, but with Dad in a meeting until three, I asked him if we could use his office."

"I thought I was doing the ordering during working hours."

"Are you saying you don't want what I brought you?"

She made sure no one was listening to their conversation before answering. "No, but I would have appreciated it if you'd consulted me before ordering for both of us."

"Noted." The smirk on his face didn't give her much hope this wouldn't be repeated.

Grabbing her purse, she stood. "Do you think it's a good idea for us to have lunch in your dad's office?"

"Are you afraid I'll ravish you on my father's desk?"

Heat flooded her cheeks. "No."

She eased around him and went directly to the small table in the corner Blake used when he needed to go over paperwork with someone. He rarely used it for eating. If he had lunch in his office, he typically ate at his desk.

Taking a seat, she waited for him to join her. She noticed he left the door open, which made her feel a little better.

Cassie hadn't been lying when she told him she wasn't worried he'd ravish her on his dad's desk, but that didn't mean there weren't busybodies in the office who wouldn't imagine that's what he was doing. She didn't need to add fuel to the fire. The sly glances she got from people were bad enough as it was.

Jesse removed two bags of chips, two bottles of water, and two sandwiches from the bag. "Turkey or ham?"

"Turkey, please."

He nodded, handed her the sandwich marked turkey, then took a seat opposite her.

Cassie took a bite and chewed. The sandwich was good. She didn't recognize the bag, so she had no idea where the food had come from. Where she tended to go to the same tried and true places over and over again, Jesse liked to try new places.

As she ate her lunch, she replayed the conversation with her dad. She wasn't looking forward to talking to her mom, especially since Bradley had obviously spilled the beans that she was seeing someone. But she could handle her mom. She was more concerned with what her dad had found out about Jesse. It wasn't so much she was worried he'd found out something he shouldn't, but was it wrong of her to be curious about the man she was falling in love with?

If her dad had found out something bad, he would have gotten on a plane and been waiting for her at her apartment. Or Jesse's. Either way, he would have found her.

Her dad was just as relentless as her brother, but he was more calculated. Maybe it was because he was older, but her dad protected his family. It wouldn't matter who Jesse's dad was.

"Are you going to sit over there in silence the entire time, or are you going to tell me what's bothering you?"

Cassie froze with a chip halfway to her mouth. It took her a moment to realize what he'd asked. "No. Sorry. I was just...thinking."

"I noticed." He picked up his water and took a drink. "Did something your dad say upset you?"

"Not really." She paused. "He told me I need to call my mom."

"And you don't want to call your mom?"

"No." Again, she hesitated. "I mean, I'm not looking forward to the conversation, but my mom is who she is."

"Then what has that crease in your forehead growing by the second?"

She touched the crease in question, rubbing it as though that would make it somehow go away. "Nothing, really. Bradley told Dad about you, and he did some digging. I have no idea how deep he went, but he obviously didn't find anything too bad."

"Why do you say that?" He didn't seem bothered by the topic of conversation, but given some of their previous talks along the same lines, she wasn't surprised by his reaction.

"Because if he had, he wouldn't have delivered the message over the phone."

* * *

This was getting out of hand. Jesse had done everything he could to reassure her of his intentions. He wasn't going to be frightened away by her mom, her brothers, or her father. But it seemed it was going to take more than words to get her over this hump. "I want you to call your mom and set up a time for us to come to dinner this week. She can invite your brothers as well if she wants. I'd suggest inviting your father as well, but I think that might need to be a separate event."

Cassie's eyes were as wide as saucers. She'd stopped eating and was looking at him as if he'd lost his mind.

He finished off his sandwich and waited until she'd found her voice again. "Why?"

Not the response he'd been hoping for, but one he could work with. "We're getting you over this aversion you have of me meeting your family. You've created this nightmare scenario in your head and the only way to dispel it is to tackle it head-on. Call your mom."

"Now?"

"Now."

She stared at him for a long moment, then retrieved her phone from her purse. Reluctantly, she punched in her mom's number.

Before Cassie could say a word, he heard a woman's voice coming through the phone. He couldn't make out what she was saying, but she sounded agitated.

"Mom, that's why I'm calling. Yes. Yes. Um…Wednesday?"

Cassie met his gaze and he nodded. He'd planned to work late on Wednesday, but plans could be changed.

"Sounds good."

There was more talking from the other end of the line.

"Okay. We'll see you then. Love you, too." Cassie lowered the phone from her ear and placed it in her lap. "Dinner's at six on Wednesday. We'll have to leave from here to get there on time. They live outside the city."

"That isn't a problem." He gathered his trash and stuffed it in the bag. "Now you can relax and finish your sandwich."

"You're not nervous at all about meeting my family, are you?"

"No." That wasn't completely true. He was nervous about meeting her dad. Her mom, he could handle.

Cassie sighed and resumed eating.

They spent the rest of their lunch break talking about *Outlander*. They'd finished the first two seasons over the weekend, and he had to admit, he was hooked. He'd thought it would be all about the romance, and while the relationship between the two main characters was front and center, there was so much more to the story.

At the end of their time, Jesse stole a quick kiss before they left his dad's office, then headed back to his own. Cassie was going home tonight, which meant he had free time to fill. Time he was going to spend digging through years' worth of accounts.

Stephanie knocked on his door at five o'clock. "Come in."

"Hey, I wanted to see if you needed anything before I go."

"No. I think I'm good. Thanks." Stephanie had been his eyes and ears on the office floor while he'd been spending hours combing through accounting sheets and contracts.

She nodded but stepped into the office and closed the door. "Are you making any sense of things?"

"Some. It's just a lot."

"Do you want any help?" she asked.

As much as he'd love her help, he needed to do this himself. It wasn't that he didn't trust her. It was more he didn't have a clear enough picture of what he was looking for. "I appreciate the offer, but I'm okay for now."

Without another word, Stephanie turned on her heel and headed out, leaving his office door open.

The office was quiet except for the humming of the air conditioning blowing through the vents. Everyone else had gone home. He was the only one crazy enough to still be there on a Monday night.

Numbers were starting to blur on the page when something caught his eye. He looked over the sheet again and reached for his calculator.

Seven minutes later, he'd rerun the numbers five times and had come out with the same result. The customer had pre-purchased inventory for the year, then when they didn't use it, had been credited for the remaining balance.

But that's where everything fell apart. Instead of crediting them back for the dollar amount the pre-paid inventory had cost them that was supposed to happen, someone had credited them for the actual inventory.

He searched his desk for the rest of the customers' files and flipped through the next three years. The same credit had been applied.

While this explained the discrepancy, at least part of it, these files only showed the credits being applied to the customer's accounts. The money, and therefore the inventory, should still be with the company. Right?

Jesse picked up the next contract in the customer's file, but instead of being for the next year, it was for the year after—last year. He went through the entire folder, but the contract for two years ago was missing.

Curious, he reviewed the contract from last year and it looked normal. No credit had rolled over. Not inventory. Not money. The contract started with a credit balance of zero.

It was already eight o'clock and he had no idea where to start looking for this missing contract. He'd have to wait till tomorrow and see if Stephanie had any ideas.

He was logging off his computer when he heard what sounded like a door closing. They had security in the building, but the guard had made his rounds an hour ago and Jesse didn't expect him to be around again so soon. As far as he knew, they were the only two in the building.

Crossing the room, he poked his head outside the door, taking in the room full of empty cubicles. Everything was quiet. There was no sign of anyone else in the area and the only door in the vicinity led to the stairwell and it was closed.

Jesse returned to his desk, finished closing everything down, and donned his suit jacket. He stored the folder in the bottom drawer of his desk and locked it. Maybe he was being paranoid, but he'd spent too much time looking for the elusive file to take the chance.

For extra measure, he locked his office door behind him before walking to the door that led to the staircase. He glanced inside the rectangular window but didn't see any movement or anything out of place.

Before leaving, he took a detour to the lobby. The security guard looked up from behind the reception desk as he exited the elevator.

"Wanted to let you know I'm heading out," Jesse said. "Do you know if anyone else is in the building besides you and me?"

"Not that I know of, sir. The cleaning crew usually doesn't get here until after nine, but sometimes they're early. They come through the service entrance, so I don't always see them right away."

"Do they typically use the stairwell?"

The guard frowned, realizing Jesse's inquiry wasn't random. "They dust and mop the staircase some nights."

Jesse nodded. That must be what he'd heard. "Okay. Well, have a good night."

"You, too, sir."

Jesse waited for the doors of the elevator to close again, then pushed the button for the parking garage.

The parking garage was empty except for his vehicle. He hit the button on his key fob to unlock the doors, and the lights flashed against the concrete.

As he slid into the driver seat, he got a whiff of Cassie's perfume. He'd driven her to work this morning, then had a car service take her home. The desire to drive to her apartment and spend the night with her wrapped in his arms was almost too much to resist, but instead of doing what he wanted, he maneuvered out of the garage and turned his vehicle toward his condo.

The entire drive home, he was thinking over the contracts, trying to figure out why the credit had been rolled over in inventory and not in monetary credit. It meant the company was holding inventory for the client for years. From a business standpoint, it made no sense.

Every one of the contracts had been signed off on by the previous manager. His signature had been there in black ink. Did he have ties to the client? Or was he using the account to scam the company?

Jesse didn't know and that bothered him.

Needing to get his head off work, he dialed the one person he knew could distract him.

"Are you still at work?" Cassie's voice purred across the line as he parked his car in his assigned parking spot at his condo building.

"No. I'm just getting home."

"It's after eight."

He chuckled. "I'm aware." He exited his vehicle, locked it, then headed upstairs. "How was your evening? More exciting than mine, I'd venture."

"I'm not sure how exciting it was. Brie and I cleaned the apartment, then cooked spaghetti and meatballs for dinner."

The image of her cleaning his condo in nothing but a French maid's apron flashed through his mind.

He must have made a noise because she giggled. "You're picturing me naked, aren't you?"

Jesse unlocked the door to his condo and let himself inside. "Yes. Tell me you're alone."

"I'm in my room."

"Are you by yourself?" he asked.

"Yes."

"Good. Take off your clothes."

CHAPTER 20

CASSIE'S BREATH caught in her throat at the low growl that came through the phone. The sound went directly to her pussy.

She'd been wearing a long T-shirt and some panties, so getting naked wasn't difficult.

There was a lot of rustling through the phone, and she imagined him removing his shirt and pants. She wished she could be there to see. Her fingers itched to touch him. As much as she'd missed spending time with Brie, her need to be close to Jesse defied logic.

Was it all hormones? Maybe. She'd never experienced a relationship like this. Brie said it was normal at this stage for her to want to be with Jesse all the time, and she might be right.

"Are you naked?"

She kicked her blanket off and lay back on the bed. "Yes, Sir.

"Good girl. Now I want you to tell me about your toys."

Cassie froze. Her toys? "My toys?"

"Don't be shy, baby. Tell me about your sex toys. Do you have a dildo? A vibrator? Some anal beads?"

Her body heated thinking of the vibrator she had in her bedside drawer and the dildo Brie had given her after she broke up with Trent. She'd never used the dildo, but she couldn't bring herself to get rid of it either. "I have a vibrator." She paused, knowing lying to him probably wasn't a good idea. "And a dildo."

"Go get them."

She knew he was going to say that.

Getting up, she went to her closet and found the tote where she kept her seasonal clothes. She opened the lid and dug to the bottom until she felt the outline of the box she was looking for and pulled it out.

"I've never used the dildo. It's still in the box."

"Why haven't you used it?" he asked as if they were talking about a restaurant she'd never tried.

"I don't know. It was a gift from Brie."

He was quiet for a moment, and she wondered if he was smiling again. "Take it out of the box."

Cassie closed her eyes, then ripped open the box.

She may have been a little too aggressive, however, because the silicone phallus flew from the box and landed on her bed. Her gaze went to the door. For some reason, she expected Brie to rush in, asking what had happened.

Logically, she knew that was unlikely given the noise had been almost nonexistent outside of her opening the box. Still, it only added to her discomfort.

Once she was sure her best friend wasn't going to barge in, Cassie stuffed the now empty box in the trash can, making sure to cover it up with an empty bag as best as she could. Then, she turned to stare at the fake penis lying on her mattress, its mushroomed head pointed in her direction.

"Cass?"

His voice pulled her back to the present. "I'm here."

"Good. Did you remove it from the package?"

"Yes." She took a deep breath and gave herself a pep talk. She could do this. It was Jesse. He'd done things to her she'd only read about in books. "It's on my bed."

"Take it and your vibrator and lie on your bed."

She went to climb on the bed, but then detoured to lock her door.

While she didn't think Brie would come in, she didn't want to take the chance.

Confident no one was going to walk in on her, Cassie got onto the mattress. She opened the drawer on her nightstand and found her vibrator. It wasn't big, but it got the job done.

The dildo, on the other hand, was another story. It was huge and she knew it would fill her. Before she'd been with Jesse, its size had scared her. Now, thinking about it had her pussy pulsing with anticipation.

She held the vibrator in one hand and the dildo in the other, then lay on the bed. "I'm ready, Sir."

"Good girl. Keep both toys where you can reach them, but I want you to start massaging your tits for me."

Letting the toys fall to the bed on either side of her, Cassie then cupped her breasts and began massaging them.

"Don't be gentle. You know how I like to twist and tug on your nipples."

Yes, she did know. The first time he'd pinched her nipple and twisted it, she'd gasped with shock at the pain that had zinged through her breast. But that pain had morphed into something more. She couldn't explain it if she tried, but the pain had heightened her arousal.

Cassie brought her hands up to her nipples, pinched them, then twisted and pulled. She moaned as pain shot through her nipples.

"That's it, baby. Does it feel good?"

"Yes, Sir. But it's not the same as when you do it."

His breathing stuttered for a moment before returning to normal. "Don't worry, I plan to spend a lot of time playing with those beautiful tits of yours very soon."

The thought of his hands on her, his mouth, his teeth…

Heat rushed to her pussy. "Yes, please."

"Are your nipples hard, baby?"

"Yes, Sir."

"Good. Now, I want you to take your vibrator and put it between your legs. I want you to tease your clit, but you're not to make yourself come."

Cassie patted the bed beside her until she found her vibrator. She turned it on and placed it between her legs, directly on her clit.

Her body reacted to the stimulation immediately. She moaned and spread her legs wider.

"I wish I could see you, baby. I'm sure you look amazing right now."

"I wish you were here, too," she whispered through the phone. She wanted his hands on her.

"Soon." His breathing sounded harsher through the phone and that turned her on even more.

She felt her orgasm building. If she were doing this on her own, she'd have increased the pressure and let things happen, but he'd told her not to come. Still, she wasn't sure she was going to last much longer if she kept the vibrator on her clit. "Sir?"

"Are you getting close to coming?" It was as if he could read her mind.

"Yes, Sir."

"Have you ever tried to delay orgasm before?"

She was almost afraid to answer. "No, Sir."

"Hmm. Maybe we should work on that. Do you have a clock by your bed?"

"Yes, Sir." She was afraid she knew where he was going with this.

"What time does it say?"

"Nine fifty-two."

She held her breath as she waited for his next words. "You may come at ten o'clock."

Eight minutes. While that didn't sound like a lot of time, Cassie knew better. When she was going solo, she could come in less than two minutes. Not always. But if she was really turned on like she was now, it didn't take much to send her over the edge.

"Did you hear me, Cass?"

"Yes, Sir. Ten o'clock." She paused and asked the burning question. "What if I can't hold off that long?"

"Then I'll have to punish you."

She had no idea what that meant, but she wasn't sure she wanted to find out.

A few moments passed before Jesse spoke again. "Pick up the dildo and put it in your mouth."

That surprised her a little, but she did what he told her to do. Her lips wrapped around the fake penis, and she pushed it inside her mouth with her free hand. The silicone didn't have too much of a taste, which she was grateful for. She'd never had a fake cock in her mouth before.

"I want you to pretend you're sucking on my cock."

Cassie closed her eyes and tried to imagine it was him in her mouth. She thought of Saturday when she'd been in his living room on her knees before him, feeling his taste against her tongue.

"Get it nice and wet. I want to be all lubricated before I fuck your pussy."

His words went straight to her sex. She hummed around the fake cock, making sure to get it nice and wet.

"Remove the cock from your mouth and put it between your legs. I want you to shove it deep in your pussy. Fuck yourself like it was me fucking you."

She positioned the fake penis at the entrance of her sex and pushed it inside. All the lubrication from her own juices and her saliva on the dildo had it sliding in with ease. It filled her, but she felt empty at the same time. She didn't want the dildo. She wanted him.

* * *

Cassie released a whimper.

"What's wrong, baby?" He thought maybe she hadn't gotten it lubricated enough, although he was pretty sure her pussy would be wet enough on its own.

"Nothing."

He stopped rubbing his cock, needing her to tell him what was wrong. "It's not nothing. Tell me."

"It doesn't feel like you."

Something squeezed in his chest. He liked that she was feeling the same way he was. "I know. My hand is a poor substitute for your pussy as well."

He knew it was late when he left work, but maybe he should have gone to her place anyway. Things were moving fast, or at least it felt like they were. They'd only known each other for a little over two weeks, and yet he wanted her in his bed every night.

"Close your eyes and think about this morning. Remember how I woke you up?"

That got a hum out of her. "Yes, Sir. I remember."

Jesse smiled. He remembered too. After feasting on her pussy and making her come twice, he'd kissed his way up her body and thrust his cock into her hard until he'd come.

He'd almost forgotten a condom again. She needed to get on another form of birth control soon. He didn't like having to stop to dig out a condom every time he wanted to fuck his girl.

Glancing at the clock, Jesse noticed it was almost ten. "Do you still have the vibrator on your clit?"

"Yes, Sir."

"Turn it up on high. No holding back. I'll tell you when you can come. Understand?"

He heard a slight buzzing sound in the background, one he hadn't heard prior. "Yes, Sir." Her breath hitched a little on the 'sir' and his cock twitched at the sound.

Jesse moved his hand faster along his length, trying to catch up to her as her breathing became faster in his ear. He felt the energy building and his gaze went to the clock. "Not yet."

She was breathing hard, and she let another whine. He was right there with her, sweat rolling down his temple as he tried to keep his own climax at bay.

The clock changed, and he gave her permission to let go.

A sound he was becoming familiar with filled his ears as Cassie's orgasm washed over her. He gave himself a firm tug and grunted as cum shot from his cock and covered his hand and stomach.

Neither one of them said anything for several moments. Jesse needed a shower and sleep. He also needed her beside him in his bed, but he wasn't going to get that tonight.

"You still with me, Cass?" he asked when she still hadn't said anything.

"Yeah, I think so."

He chuckled. "Go clean up and get some sleep. I'll pick you up a little after seven in the morning."

She didn't argue with him, which spoke volumes.

"Good night, baby."

"Good night."

After disconnecting the call, he made his way to the bathroom to clean up. He was beyond tired, but when he lay down in bed twenty minutes later, his mind wouldn't shut off. The missing contract was bugging him, as was the noise he'd heard.

Sure, it could have been the cleaning crew, but something told him it wasn't. But then the question was who would be lingering in the office so late and why. The entire floor had been quiet for at least two hours before he'd heard what sounded like a door closing.

At midnight, he gave up and walked down the hall to his study. He booted up his computer and answered some emails before settling on the couch to watch a movie.

He ended up dozing off somewhere around two thirty. Luckily, he set the alarm on his phone or else he would have overslept.

With every mile he drove toward Cassie's apartment, he felt a sense of rightness. This whole business with the messed-up accounting was putting him in a bad mood. Seeing Cassie was bound to improve it.

The ride up to her floor felt like it took forever. Jesse stepped off the elevator and headed down the hall. He knocked and waited.

A few seconds passed before he heard footsteps coming from inside. The door opened and he came face to face with Brie. "Hey."

"Hey." He gave Brie a smile, but she wasn't who he wanted to see.

"She's in her room. She'll be out in a few." Brie disappeared into the kitchen. "Did you want anything to drink?"

"No, thank you."

Brie moved about the kitchen, loading the dishwasher. "So you and Cassie seem to be getting serious. I hear you're meeting her family tomorrow night."

"Yes." He didn't specify whether he was replying to her about him and Cassie getting serious or him meeting her family. Not that it mattered. The answer was yes to both.

"Her mom's nice. She'll ask you a million questions but given you're…" Brie came around the corner and gave him a throughout once-over. "You. You'll be fine. Her stepdad's cool. He worships the ground her mom walks on. Her brother…well, you're dating his sister, so…" Brie put an earring in one ear, tilting her head to the side as she did so.

Jesse had no doubt he could handle Cassie's brothers. He was his father's son after all. "Thanks for the heads-up."

"Sure. No problem." Brie tilted her head to the other side to put another earring on. "Just a reminder that if you're playing a game, or if you end up hurting her, I'll be right there beside them to make sure you pay."

He nodded. "Noted."

Finished putting her earrings in, Brie slid into her jacket and grabbed her purse. "Her bedroom's down the hall to the left." Then she winked and headed out the door.

Jesse walked down the hallway. The apartment wasn't that big, so finding Cassie's room was easy.

He'd imagined her room many times, but his visual images tended to hover around her bed. There'd really been no need to contemplate anything else.

Her bed was made up, nice and neat, with several smaller pillows. The bedspread was gray and purple. The rest of the room was clean and organized, but it felt lived in.

Cassie was dressed in a business suit, her hair pulled back away from her face and twisted into a clip behind her head. She was looking in a mirror, putting on a necklace.

A slow smile graced her lips when she saw him. "You're early."

"Am I?" he asked, propping himself against the doorjamb. She looked polished and professional and all he wanted to do was see her flushed and rumpled.

She finished fastening the clasp to the necklace, then crossed to where he stood leaning against the doorjamb. Tilting her head up, she met his gaze.

Neither of them said anything as his body began heating up. It would be so easy to pick her up, toss her on the bed, and take her, but he knew that would make them late. The last thing he wanted to do was cause more office gossip. He could take it, but he didn't want to make things more difficult for Cassie.

Shifting them both, he backed her against the doorframe. He could see the pulse in her neck beating faster in anticipation. "Did you sleep well last night?"

"Yes, Sir." Her answer came out sounding breathy and his cock twitched at her use of his title.

He brushed his nose against hers before dipping his mouth down to capture her lips. She tasted like strawberries and coffee. He loved being able to tell what she had for breakfast with a kiss.

Cassie circled her arms around his neck and met his tongue stroke for stroke.

He'd meant to keep the kiss short and sweet, but the woman drove him crazy. Cupping her ass, he lifted her feet off the floor, making sure she could feel how hard she made him. "Tonight, you're coming home with me."

CHAPTER 21

CASSIE HAD THOUGHT for sure they were going to be late for work, but he'd ended the kiss and dragged her out of her apartment like the house was on fire. They made it with a few minutes to spare.

She'd had to reapply her lipstick in the car, but it was well worth it. He'd ridden up to the executive floor with her before promising to bring her lunch.

"Good morning, Mr. Masters," Cassie said when her boss approached her desk a little before eight.

"Good morning, Cassie." He smiled and disappeared into his office.

She spent the rest of the morning responding to emails and setting up next month's calendar. At noon, Jesse brought her a sandwich and a salad from yet another restaurant she'd never heard of. They ended up in the conference room.

"How was your morning?" she asked before taking a bite of her sandwich.

"Still doing research." He'd told her a little about what he was working on, but she understood he couldn't go into too much detail. Not until he fleshed out exactly what was going on and who was involved.

Being Blake Masters's assistant gave her access to a lot of things.

She knew something was wrong with the accounting. She'd been the first one to notice and bring it to her boss's attention. "Let me know if there's anything I can do to help. I'm sure your dad wouldn't mind."

Jesse studied her for a long moment. "There might be something you could do." He paused, glanced at the door, then back at her. "There's a file missing."

She lowered her voice and sat forward. "A client file?"

He nodded. "A contract."

Cassie's eyes widened. It didn't take a genius to know that wasn't good. "It's not in the archives?"

"No. Or at least, not where it should be in the archives. Stephanie and I have spent the morning going through every file in the surrounding area, hoping it was just misplaced."

"What can I do?"

"We need to go through all the files, one at a time."

The company had been in business for over twenty years, and they had thousands of clients. It could take weeks or even months to go through every paper in every file. "I can stay late."

"While I appreciate that, what I need is a way to narrow down our search. Assuming someone isn't deliberately trying to hide it."

Cassie thought about it. "Who's the client?"

"Campbell Industries."

She'd never heard of them, which meant they were probably a smaller client. "I'll look into it. I should have some time this afternoon."

* * *

There was a note on Cassie's desk when she got back from lunch.

I know it was you.

Cassie looked around, but no one was lurking. She turned her attention to the note. It didn't give her a whole lot to go on. What did they know?

She racked her brain, trying to figure out who may have left the message. It wasn't exactly threatening. More of a warning. But a warning of what she had no idea.

Blake Masters strolled out of his office, suit jacket on. He had a meeting across town at two thirty. He closed his door then turned to her. "Everything all right?"

Her confusion must have been written on her face. "Did you happen to see anyone at my desk while I was away?"

"No. I was on a call most of the last hour with Bree Reynolds." He paused. "Was something taken?"

"The opposite. They left me a rather cryptic note." She knew some people would have kept the note to themselves, but Cassie knew she hadn't done anything wrong. The only thing even questionable she was doing was dating Jesse and that wasn't a secret.

"I wouldn't worry too much about it. If it's important, they'll stop by again."

"You're probably right." Cassie forced a smile. "Should I expect you back after your meeting?"

Her boss shook his head. "No. I'll see you in the morning."

Cassie nodded.

She was still thinking about the note when Jesse came to pick her up at five. Gathering her things, she let him lead her to his vehicle. He didn't press her on why she was being so reserved until they were both in the car. "Tell me what's wrong."

"There was a strange note on my desk when I got back from lunch. I've been trying to figure out who it came from, but I'm drawing a blank." Of course it would help if she had a clue what the note was referring to, but she didn't.

He weaved through the parking garage and turned onto the road, heading toward her apartment.

"I thought we were going to your place."

Jesse took the turn onto the highway. "I figured you might want clothes to wear into the office tomorrow."

"Oh." Yeah, that would be good. Needing clothes hadn't crossed her mind. "Yeah. Good idea."

He chuckled. "As much as I love seeing you running around

without clothes on, I don't think you showing up naked tomorrow would be well received." He paused. "Now back to the note. What did it say?"

Cassie told him. "I have no idea what they're talking about. What do they know I did?"

He frowned. "Maybe it was someone's idea of a joke. They know you had lunch with me or something."

She shrugged. "The whole office knows I'm dating you. Why would us eating lunch together be a secret?"

"I don't know." He found a parking spot at her apartment complex. "I'd ignore it. There's nothing you can do about it one way or another given you don't know what they're talking about, nor do you know who left it."

"I know you're right."

Jesse got out of the Mustang and went around to open the passenger door for her. He helped her out and placed a hand on her lower back as they walked inside.

The apartment was quiet. Brie worked until six on Tuesdays, so she wouldn't be home for another hour, at least.

Cassie went to her room and packed an outfit for Wednesday, as well as one for Thursday. She had a feeling Jesse would want her to spend the night after they had dinner with her family. And if not, she would have something for the next time she stayed over.

She found him thumbing through the bookcase when she returned to the living room. He ran his hands along one of the shelves. "You have quite the eclectic collection."

"The thrillers are Brie's. She loves them."

"And are these yours?" Jesse picked up one of the romance novels on the third shelf.

"Yes."

He returned the book to its place, then ran his finger along the spines until he came to one that had lots of creases. Pulling it out, he flipped through it, scanning the pages. "Is this your favorite one?"

She didn't answer as heat crept up her cheeks.

Jesse met her gaze and waited.

Words wouldn't come, so she nodded.

That seemed to be enough for him. But instead of putting the book back, he tucked it under his arm. "Do you have everything you need?"

Finally, she found her words. "Are you taking that with you?" She was referring to her book and he knew it.

"Yes. I thought I might do a little light reading tonight before bed."

"No."

"No?" He seemed amused she was telling him no.

"You have plenty of books at your house. Surely you can find something to read there."

He took her bag from her, then reached for her hand as if she hadn't said anything. Before she knew it, he was leading her out of the apartment. "Give me your keys so I can lock up."

She gave them to him without a second thought. Her mind was still on the book. "Why do you want to read it?"

"I want to see what you like." He pushed the button to take them to the parking lot.

"I don't think it's your type of story."

The side of Jesse's mouth pulled up into a smile, but that was his only response.

* * *

Jesse was enjoying her discomfort. He knew the book was a romance. And from the cover, he was guessing it had a fair amount of sex in it. He didn't understand why him knowing what she was reading would make her uneasy given his sexual proclivities.

"Do you have a preference for dinner?"

She looked at him with a hint of surprise. "You mean I get to pick tonight?"

He smiled. "I wouldn't go that far."

Closing the passenger door, he made his way around the car and slid into the driver's seat. He tucked the book into the center console and put on his seat belt before starting the engine and backing out of the parking spot.

"A nice salad sounds good."

For some reason, that made him laugh.

"What?"

He shook his head. "I just wasn't expecting you to say a salad, that's all. I figured you'd want Italian or Thai."

"I haven't had a lot of greens this week." She paused. "What's wrong with a salad?"

"Nothing at all." They'd been eating a lot of carbs lately. Not that they hadn't burned them off, but he did see the point. "Salad it is."

Jesse headed to the south end of the city. Cassie didn't bother asking him where he was going.

He found a place to park along the street and leaned in to give her a kiss. "I'll be right back."

"Guess that means I don't get to pick which salad I want?"

He grinned, pressed another quick kiss to her lips, then reached for the door.

The restaurant wasn't busy, so he didn't have to wait long for their salads. He ordered extra meat on his, knowing he'd need the protein boost for later tonight.

Food in hand, Jesse made his way out to the vehicle. Cassie was on her cell phone, talking to someone. He opened the back door, placed the bag of food inside, then slipped behind the wheel.

"That's not my problem."

Jesse's eyebrows rose at Cassie's tone. It wasn't directed at him, but she was agitated about something. Or someone.

"Again, not my issue." She paused. "Fine."

She disconnected the call and blew out a loud breath.

"Everything good?"

"Yeah. Just my pain in the ass brother."

Jesse started the car and pulled away from the curb. "I'm going to take a guess here. Bradley?"

"Of course. James doesn't care about my love life."

"And Bradley does."

She nodded. "Apparently, he can't fathom the notion I may have found a good man who treats me right."

Jesse's chest warmed at the compliment. He reached for her hand and brought it to his lips, kissing the tips of her fingers. "Is he coming to dinner tomorrow night?"

"I don't know. He's working on a case and doesn't know if he'll be able to make it or not. That's why he called. To see if we could reschedule." She huffed. "He thinks the world revolves around him."

He chuckled. "I'm sure that's not the case. He's probably just worried about you."

"I know that, too. I've not exactly had the best luck with boyfriends, but he needs to trust me."

Jesse had to admit, he was curious about Cassie's brother. He understood being protective of your sister, he was of Beks, but this seemed excessive. Her dad's response was more in line with what he'd expect. He would have done the same if it were his daughter. But Bradley was bordering on obnoxious.

"Try to forget about your brother and let's enjoy our evening."

She took what he assumed to be a cleansing breath. Then another.

"Is that helping?"

"Not really, but it isn't hurting."

Jesse laughed. "Why don't I try to distract you, then?"

"I'm not sure you're supposed to be doing that while you're driving."

He glanced in her direction as a wicked smile formed. "You naughty girl. That's not exactly what I had in mind." He gave her leg a squeeze. "Stephanie and I spent all afternoon going through files. No luck yet, although she says we might have some luck in the dead files." He paused. "I didn't know there was such a thing."

"Your dad's supposed to be in the office all day tomorrow. I can probably get in there and look," she said.

"I don't want to take you away from your work."

Cassie shook her head. "Your dad won't mind. He wants to get to the bottom of this as much as you do."

That was true enough. And when it came down to it, he'd take all the help he could get.

They ended up curled up on the couch, watching more of

Outlander. Every time he thought he had the season figured out, there was a new twist. He was hoping his own mystery of the missing file didn't send him on a wild goose chase.

Even if he did locate it, there was no way to know what it would show, if anything. He could be scouring the files for something that could simply be a mathematical error.

At nine, they headed into the bedroom. He let her use the bathroom first, then took his turn.

She was already in bed when he emerged from the bathroom. The covers pulled up, covering her chest, but he knew she was naked underneath.

Jesse turned off the lights and walked to the other side of the bed. He pulled back the covers, slid in next to her, and opened his arms in invitation.

Cassie moved into his embrace. She pressed against him, her soft skin sending awareness through every nerve ending he had.

He ran his hand down her back, over her hip, to the curve of her ass. She had a great ass. It was round and firm and perfect for when he needed to get a good grip on her.

She arched her back, pressing her tits into him, telling him without words she liked his touch. That was good because he liked touching her. A lot.

Not having her in his bed last night had affected him more than he thought it would. He'd missed her, sure, but it was more than that. His bed felt empty without her in it. When he woke up in the morning, the first thing he did was look for her beside him and felt a pang deep in his chest when she wasn't there.

He traced circles on her hip, letting himself enjoy the moment. "I like having you in my bed."

She kissed his pec and met his gaze. "I like it, too." There was a pause before she continued. "Is that weird?"

"That you like being in my bed?" He cupped her ass and gave it a squeeze. "I hope not. That would mean I'm not doing my job very well."

Cassie grinned. "That's not exactly what I meant. Brie says it's normal to feel this way, but it feels…"

"What does it feel like, Cass?"

She pressed her lips together, then took a deep breath as if she were about to reveal something big. "I think I'm falling in love with you."

Jesse brought his free hand up to brush the side of her face. "I know I'm falling in love with you. In fact, I think I've already fallen."

Her eyes went wide. "But isn't it too soon? I mean, we haven't been dating for a month yet. Don't we have to be seeing each other for at least three months or something?"

He laughed, causing their bodies to rub against each other. The movement was doing nothing to help the growing ache in his cock. "I don't think there's a prerequisite time limit on when you fall in love with someone."

She shifted, moving half her body on top of him. "But is this normal? To feel this way, so soon?"

"I wouldn't say it's normal." She frowned. "But I won't say it's unusual either. Sometimes you just know."

"And you just know?"

He picked her up and moved her the rest of the way on top of him. "I just know."

His cock grazed against her heat. He needed to be inside her. "I don't like wearing a condom to be inside you. I want to feel all of you surrounding me without any barrier between us."

She blinked at the change in subject. "Um. But I'm not on anything."

"I know. We need to address that. Have you called your doctor yet?"

"No. I—" She paused. "With everything that's been happening at work, I forgot."

He reached into the bedside drawer to get a condom. As much as he didn't want to wear one, it was a necessary evil until they figured something else out. "I want to be able to take your pussy whenever I want. No waiting."

Cassie sucked in a breath.

"I want you to make an appointment with your doctor as soon as possible."

He lifted her into a sitting position, the blanket falling on his legs behind him. Then he rolled the condom down his hard length.

Once he was sheathed, he reached for her. "Understood?"

"Yes, Sir."

His cock pulsed with anticipation as he lined her up, needing to be inside her like he needed his next breath. The moment he felt her muscles flex around him, he knew he was where he was meant to be.

CHAPTER 22

By the time lunch arrived the next day, Cassie knew something was wrong. People got quiet when she entered a room, and the looks they were giving her were a lot like the ones she'd gotten the day after everyone found out she was dating Jesse.

Nothing new had happened, though. Not really. They'd spent the night together at his condo, then came in together this morning. The same as they had almost every day since they'd started seeing each other. It shouldn't be news.

Jesse stepped off the elevator at noon and she was filled with a mixture of relief and anxiety. Would him bringing her lunch add to the gossip wheel?

He took one look at her and picked up on her unease. "What happened?"

Cassie looked over her shoulder and caught the eye of one of the other executive assistants. As soon as they locked gazes, the other woman looked away. What the hell was going on?

"Can we go out for lunch?"

He paused for a moment, then nodded.

She grabbed her purse and hurried out from behind her desk. "I need to let your dad know I'm going."

Jesse waited for her to knock on his father's office door and let him know she'd be away from her desk. Blake gave her a concerned look but nodded. "Enjoy your lunch."

Once that was taken care of, she let Jesse lead her to the elevator. He didn't say anything as they made their way to the lobby and out of the building, onto the street. It was a nice day, which was good. She hadn't even thought to grab her jacket.

He guided her down two blocks to a bus stop. Still, he didn't say anything.

The bus came and they climbed on board. Six blocks later, they got off the bus across from Washington Square Park. There were a few people in the park, but it wasn't crowded. Most people didn't come to the park during their lunch hour.

They found a park bench and Jesse began unpacking the bag of food. He handed her a sandwich, took one for himself, then motioned for her to eat. He didn't ask her what was wrong again until after she had finished eating. "Tell me what's wrong."

"I don't know if I'm being paranoid or not."

"You're going to have to give me more than that."

She blew out a frustrated breath. "People are acting weird around me. Kind of like they did when it came out we were an item. But we've been seeing each other for a couple of weeks now and the looks and the quiet whispers were getting less. Now they've started up again and I don't know why."

"I'm going to talk to my dad and Craig about putting up some cameras."

His change of topic threw her as did his mention of his dad's head of security. "What are you talking about? Cameras?"

"There are cameras in the main traffic areas, the lobby, the main hallways, and in front of the elevators. That leaves too many blind spots."

She was still confused. "Jesse, I'm not following you."

"Monday night, I thought I heard the stairwell door closing. No one else was in the building except for me and the security guard. When I asked him about it, he thought it might have been the cleaning crew, but I have my doubts."

"What does that have to do with the office gossip mill?" she asked.

"Someone left a note on your desk yesterday."

Maybe his change in subject hadn't been so random after all. "We don't know if what's going on today has anything to do with the other two things." They didn't know it didn't, either.

Jesse stood and she followed suit. He found a nearby trash can, threw what was left of their lunch away, then returned to her side, taking her hand in his. "I'd been thinking about the need for more cameras anyway. This just accelerates the timeline."

They made their way across the grass toward the bus stop. "What are you hoping to find?"

"I'm not sure, but if we can at least narrow down who's been hanging about your desk and roaming the stairwells after hours, that would be a start."

Cassie thought about that during their bus ride back to the office. She wasn't sure finding out who was leaving her notes would accomplish much. Sure, they could report them to Human Resources, but there was no real way to prove they were leaving her anything inappropriate. Not unless there was a camera pointed directly over her desk with a resolution that allowed them to read whatever note was left. That seemed like overkill. Not to mention, an invasion of her privacy.

Blake was still in his office when they returned. Jesse gave her a pointed look and headed into his dad's office.

* * *

Jesse gave a brief knock before walking into his father's office. His dad looked up. He started to smile, then he saw the look on Jesse's face.

"Close the door." Blake waited until Jesse took a seat before saying anything. "What's going on?"

As a rule, Jesse had tried to keep things professional between him and his dad at work. He didn't barge into his office unannounced, nor did he regale him with tales of office gossip. "We need to discuss increasing security in the building."

One of his dad's eyebrows rose in question. "Is there a security threat I'm unaware of?"

"That's yet to be determined." Then he told him about Monday night.

"Do you have any reason to believe it wasn't the cleaning crew?" his dad asked.

"No. But something about that doesn't feel right. Even if the cleaning crew were in the stairwell, why would they come to the floor only to turn around and leave again?"

His dad nodded. "I see what you mean. And they have supplies and equipment. I doubt they're hauling them up the stairs when they have access to the elevator." It was one of those little things that didn't add up and Jesse liked things to add up.

"There's also something else I think you need to be aware of." Jesse considered not telling his dad about Cassie's note, but after thinking about it, he felt compelled to give his dad the whole picture. "Someone left a note on Cassie's desk yesterday while we were at lunch."

"People leave Cassie notes all the time."

Jesse knew that. "The note was...ominous."

This time both his dad's eyes narrowed. Blake was protective of things and people he viewed as his. Cassie fell under that umbrella as his assistant. "Did someone threaten her?"

"That's open for interpretation."

He could see his dad's temper rising. "Why didn't she come to me?"

"She told me about it last night. The note was vague, saying something along the lines of knowing what she'd done." Jesse leaned forward in his chair, resting his elbows on his knees and steepling his fingers. "Cassie says she has no idea what they're referring to. She also says the gossip mill has been hard at work today."

His dad leaned back in his chair, listening, taking in everything Jesse was telling him.

"And the more I think about it, I'm seeing it myself as well.

Nothing major, but I've noticed conversations abruptly stopping as I walk past. I hadn't given it much thought until Cassie pointed it out today at lunch."

"You think the note and the gossip are related." It wasn't a question.

"While I have no proof of that, I'd say the timing is suspicious. Cassie and I have been discreet while at the office. We don't even touch until we're out of the building."

"You had lunch in my office the other day."

It was Jesse's turn to raise his eyebrows.

The corners of Blake's lips turned up into a tiny smile. "I have my sources."

"Do your sources have any information on this?" Jesse asked, sitting back again in his chair.

Blake's mouth tightened. "No." His dad picked up his phone and punched in several numbers. "Could you come to my office? Yes."

Jesse waited. He had no idea who his father had called.

His father hung up the phone. "Craig's on his way up."

Less than five minutes later, Cassie's voice came through the speaker on his dad's phone. "Craig Allen is here to see you, Mr. Masters."

"Send him in."

Craig Allen was six-foot-three and weighed over two hundred pounds. He was in his late forties and ex-military. He ran security for the building and for his dad's personal protection. He closed the door behind him and faced Blake. "You wanted to see me?"

"Yes. Have a seat."

For the next twenty minutes, the three of them discussed the building's security. By the end of the meeting, they'd hashed out a plan not only for more cameras but also for some additional security in the building after hours.

Cassie's gaze met his when he left his father's office. He shook Craig's hand, then crossed to her desk. "I'll be back to pick you up at five. We don't want to be late to your mom's."

She grimaced. "I'll be here."

Jesse smiled. He knew she was worried about dinner with her family. "With bells on?"

That made her chuckle. "Are you providing the bells?"

His only answer was a wink, then he headed back to his office. He still had a contract to find.

Not long after Jesse exited his dad's office, Blake called her in. Her boss asked her to close the door behind her and take a seat. He got straight to the point. "Jesse told me about the note that was left on your desk. He tells me you don't know what the note is referring to."

"No, I don't. I've racked my brain trying to come up with something, but there's nothing I can think of." She paused. "Nothing work related anyway."

Blake held her gaze for a long moment, then nodded. "My son has suggested we install additional cameras. Craig agrees."

"Is there something you need me to do?" Why else would he be telling her?

"The cameras are going to be installed after hours. If someone's doing something they aren't supposed to, I don't want to give them a heads-up. However, there will be some aesthetic changes in certain areas. I doubt anyone will mention them to me, but they might approach you." He paused. "Tell them we're prepping for an upgrade to our internet. That will explain any wiring they see."

Cassie nodded.

"One more thing." Blake's gaze softened. "If you get any more strange notes, I want to know about them."

"Yes, sir."

Back at her desk, Cassie struggled to focus on her work. Before meeting Jesse, her days were rather boring.

Not that she didn't like her job. She did. She was treated well and respected. The pay wasn't horrible either.

Her thoughts drifted to the missing file Jesse was trying to find. So much had happened since she'd met him, but that hadn't been the start of the office drama. Not really.

It started with the former accounting manager, Zac Travers. She still remembered finding the error on the end of month sheets. The numbers didn't add up. Or they did, kind of, but only if one didn't go through everything line by line.

The numbers had been manipulated, adjusted by pennies to make them all add up at the bottom of the page. It was unlike anything she'd ever seen before. The amount of time it would take to make so many tweaks baffled her mind. She'd thought she had to be reading it wrong.

So, she'd checked, and checked again, rerunning the numbers a dozen times before bringing it to Blake's attention. They'd spent an entire weekend in his office with papers spread out over the last year trying to make sense of it.

By the end of the weekend, they'd found more evidence of tampering with the numbers. It was subtle, but over time it had added up to a substantial amount.

She hadn't been in on the meeting with Zac Travers, but she'd witnessed the aftermath. The meeting had lasted less than twenty minutes, and it had ended with security escorting him down to get his things, then out of the building.

The look on his face was one she'd never forget. It wasn't remorseful or defiant. More shell-shocked.

Blake had also let Travers's assistant, Crystal, go. Again, she hadn't been privy to the details, but she got the impression Travers had blamed the errors on Crystal.

When everything was all said and done, Blake had wanted to make sure they had all the documents locked away. Not the originals, mind you, but duplicates in case Zac tried to sue or cause trouble. They'd stashed the documentation in a storage room on the sixth floor.

There wasn't anything up there, really. Most of the space was ventilation and piping, but there were two decent-sized rooms where old promotional materials and signage were stored.

The more Cassie thought about it, the more she felt she needed to go upstairs. Jesse said he and Stephanie had combed through most of the archives already. What if the contract he was looking for had been one of the ones they'd made a copy of and put in storage?

It was worth a shot, right?

* * *

At four fifty-five, Jesse logged off his computer, made sure his office was locked, and said goodbye to his assistant before heading upstairs to get Cassie. On his way to the elevator, he passed by Christine's cubicle. She was on the phone and didn't notice him, but he heard her say something about someone getting what they deserved.

He stopped. "Ms. Johnson?"

Christine jumped. She fumbled with the phone, then mumbled she had to go into it. "Mr. Masters. Sorry, I didn't see you there."

"It's almost five o'clock. I'm sure you can wait five minutes before making a personal call."

"Yes, sir." She looked at her computer screen, then at him. "I was just." She paused. "It won't happen again."

Jesse considered his options. He could let it go or he could push. With everything that had gone on today, he wasn't in the mood to let it go. "I don't approve of office gossip, Ms. Johnson. What you do on your own time is your business, but while you're on company time, I expect you to do your job and be respectful of others."

"I would never—"

"I have ears, Ms. Johnson. Remember that." He turned on his heel and continued toward the elevator. Cassie was waiting for him.

Only she wasn't. Cassie wasn't at her desk.

He went to the break room to see if she was there, but there was no sign of her. His dad's office was empty as well, so he couldn't ask him.

Figuring she must have gone to the ladies' room, he decided to wait.

Ten minutes later, he was still waiting. He tried her phone on the off chance she might have it with her, but he wasn't in luck. The sound of her phone ringing came from inside her desk.

He was about to start going from room to room when the door to the stairwell opened and Cassie appeared. She saw him and visibly took a breath as if she were relieved to see him.

"What—"

She shook her head and tilted her head, indicating he should follow her.

While he wanted to demand she tell him what was going on, curiosity got the better of him. There were too many eyes and ears around. He was willing to give her a little leeway.

Cassie led him into the stairwell and up the stairs to the sixth floor. He hadn't been up there since he was a kid.

There was a single door with a sign marked maintenance. Cassie inserted a key into the lock and turned. The door opened and she stepped inside.

Jesse followed, wanting to know why she was being so cautious but willing to give her the benefit of the doubt. He knew what was up here for the most part. Besides all the ductwork and plumbing for the building, there were also a couple of rooms full of marketing materials that should have been thrown away years ago. He had no idea why his father insisted on keeping them.

Instead of going to the storage rooms, she took a left, following a large pipe. They'd gone about thirty feet before something caught his eye. He placed a hand on Cassie's arm, halting her movement.

She looked back at him, then stepped to the side, allowing him an unobstructed view. Tucked in a corner in between several air ducts were some blankets. That's what had caught his attention.

He turned to look at Cassie and he could tell she was as perplexed as he was. Why were there blankets laid out like a makeshift bed?

Needing to investigate, Jesse moved closer.

Jesse felt a hand on his arm. He met Cassie's gaze. "Wait here."

She stared at him wide-eyed.

He gave her hand a squeeze, then continued moving toward the blankets.

It took a little maneuvering around the equipment, but he got close enough to see the area in question. It wasn't only blankets. It was a pillow, what looked like a pile of clothes, and what he assumed were toiletries. Someone was living up here.

CHAPTER 23

NEITHER OF THEM said a word as they left the sixth floor. They made their way back to Cassie's desk. Jesse went to her desk, got her purse, and ushered her toward the elevator. She wanted to question him, but his body language told her to keep her thoughts to herself for now.

They were the only ones in the elevator, but still, he remained quiet. Jesse hurried her into the passenger seat of his Mustang before taking his place in the driver's seat. She was about to say something when he pulled out his phone and dialed, putting it on speaker while he backed out of his parking spot.

It rang twice before Craig answered. "Allen."

Jesse got straight to the point. "Someone's living on the sixth floor. Cassie and I were up there looking for files and discovered blankets, a pillow, and some clothes. We didn't stick around to see if there was more."

"Hold on."

There was some noise in the background as they waited on the line. Jesse drove toward her mom's while they waited.

She heard more noise through the phone, the sound of a door closing, then Craig came back on the line. "I'm putting you on speaker."

"Jesse, what's going on?" Blake Master's asked.

"Cassie's with me. I'm going to let her tell you, since she's the one who stumbled upon it." Jesse gave her a nod of encouragement.

She decided to jump in with both feet. "Remember I said I was going to look upstairs for the contract Jesse's been looking for?"

He didn't comment, so she continued.

"I haven't been up there for a while, and I forgot how confusing it can be." And creepy. She didn't mention that, though. "I was coming out of the first storage room, on my way to the second when I thought I saw something, so I went to check it out."

She hadn't told Jesse how she'd found the sleeping area, so this was the first time he'd heard about it as well. "At first, I thought maybe some animals had gotten in there or something. Dragged some garbage in. But as I got closer, I realized it was a blanket." She paused. "Then I saw the pillow and I decided I should get out of there."

"Jesse, you saw this, too?"

"I did." He paused. "I didn't see anyone up there at the time, but there are a lot of hiding places. The person could have heard us and took cover." Jesse took the exit off the highway, and she realized they were almost at her mom's. "We didn't stay long, but it looked as if whoever it is has been there for a while. They've been careful, though. Cassie was lucky to see the blanket. It's tucked between two HVAC ducts."

"I'll go check it out as soon as we hang up here," Craig said.

Jesse shook his head even though Craig and his dad couldn't see him. "I'm not sure that's a great idea."

"We can't have someone living up there, son. Not only is it a security risk but a safety one as well."

"If Craig rushes over there, he might get lucky and catch the person in the act. But he might not," Jesse said. "I think we should continue with the original plan. Put the cameras up as discreetly as possible and see what they tell us."

Blake was quiet for a long time. Her mom's house came into view by the time he broke the silence. "We'll do it your way. Craig, let's get those cameras up. Tonight."

"I think that's best," Jesse said as he pulled into her mom's driveway.

"I'm on it," Craig said.

"Cassie?" Blake's voice was softer this time.

"Yes, Mr. Masters?"

"I don't want you going up there alone anymore. At least, not until we get this figured out."

Jesse answered before she did. "Not to worry. She won't be."

Cassie stared at Jesse. She wasn't sure if she should be happy he was acting so protective or upset he was speaking for her.

"Good. We'll talk about this more tomorrow in my office." With that parting comment, Blake and Craig disconnected.

Jesse turned off the vehicle, returned the phone to his pocket, and climbed out of the car. He opened her door and offered her a hand to help her out.

Cassie was still trying to wrap her head around everything that had happened in the last hour. Was the person homeless? Or were they there to cause trouble? Did the person have anything to do with the missing file? And what about the crazy accounting?

But what if it was all a coincidence and none of it was related? Someone could just be down on their luck, needing a place to stay, and it had nothing to do with the other issues going on.

She was so lost in thought, she was startled when Jesse's lips brushed against hers. The feel of his mouth on hers brought her back to the present.

"There she is," he whispered against her lips. "Stop worrying about what we found. Craig and my dad will take care of it. We have more important things to do tonight." Jesse motioned toward her mom's front door.

Right. Dinner with her mom and David.

Cassie nodded.

Jesse pressed another brief kiss to her lips, then wrapped an arm around her waist and guided her to the door.

Her mom must have been hovering. They didn't even get a chance to knock before the door was flung open. Jessica Rourke stood, framed in the doorway, smiling. She extended her hand to Jesse. "You must be the man I've heard so little about. I can see why my daughter's been keeping you hidden."

"Mom."

Jessica ignored her.

Jesse shook her hand. "Jesse Masters. It's a pleasure to meet you."

Cassie could almost see the hearts in her mother's eyes. Jesse was winning her over and he hadn't even stepped inside the house.

"Come in, come in. David's putting the finishing touches on dinner. It should only be a few more minutes. I do hope you're both hungry."

"Starving," Jesse said.

Cassie met his gaze, and she could see his eyes were full of amusement. He was getting a kick out of her mom's reaction to him.

He gave her side a little squeeze as they followed her mom into the formal dining room.

She was surprised to find the room was empty. Well, not empty. But there was no sign of either of her brothers. She'd been sure Bradley would insert himself into the evening whether she wanted him to be there or not.

"That's good," David said, coming in from the kitchen carrying a large platter. "I think we have enough food here to feed an army." He placed the food on the table, then turned to Jesse, offering his hand. "I'm Cassie's stepdad, David."

"Jesse Masters."

After the introductions were over, they all took a seat at the table.

"So, Jesse, how did you two meet?" Jessica asked as they began to dig into the meal.

"I saw her across the room at a party and knew I had to introduce myself."

"Oh, how romantic." Her mom paused, her gaze drifting to Cassie. The grin on her mom's face said it all.

"Your brother mentioned you work together?" David asked.

Of course Bradley had gotten his digs in even if he wasn't there in person.

Cassie opened her mouth to reply, but Jesse beat her to it. "We work in the same building, but my office is on the third floor. Cassie's is on the fifth."

Jessica scrunched her nose. "Isn't your boss's last name Masters?"

Cassie swallowed. She knew this would come out sooner or later. "Yes. Blake Masters is Jesse's father."

* * *

Jesse watched as Jessica's eyes went wide. He'd seen that look on Cassie's face many times. Although her mom's had an added element of calculation. Jessica Rourke was assessing him.

He wasn't sure if she was focused on what him being related to the man who wrote her daughter's paychecks meant, or if she was trying to calculate the balance of his bank account. Being Blake Masters's son, he'd encountered both types of people. He didn't know Cassie's mom well enough yet to determine which camp she fell into.

"So you work for your dad?" Jessica asked.

"Yes. I'm running the accounting department."

David nodded. "A numbers guy."

"I have degrees in both finance and business administration."

"Impressive," David said. "Isn't that impressive?" He looked at his wife, who had gone quiet.

Jessica nodded. "Yes, very impressive."

When Jessica didn't pick up the thread of the conversation, David continued. "So what do you like to do outside of work? Are you a big sports fan?"

Jesse let David lead the conversation in a different direction. They ended up debating whether Kansas City needed another professional sports team. Personally, he didn't care. Sure, he enjoyed watching sports, but he wasn't obsessed with it like some guys were. He'd rather play basketball than watch it.

Not that he had a lot of time to dedicate to sports. He worked out at least three times a week and tried to get a couple of runs in, as well. Other than that, he kept busy with work…and Cassie.

Jessica asked Cassie to help her carry the dishes into the kitchen. He started to gather up some of the plates as well, but Jessica stopped him. "We've got it. You're a guest. Why don't you and David head into the living room. We'll be in shortly."

Cassie gave him a guarded smile and followed her mom into the next room.

"Come on," David said. "Let's see what's on the television."

Jesse followed the other man into a modest living room. Everything was clean and well kept, but it wasn't anything like his parents' formal living room with its high ceilings and massive bookshelves.

"I don't think my wife knows what to make of you." David had turned on the sports commentary, his comment not matching his actions.

"In what way?" Jesse asked.

"Jessica wants Cassie to find someone who'll make her happy. Who'll take care of her." David glanced over at Jesse. "She's trying to decide whether you might be that guy, but she's not sure."

Before Jesse could decide how to respond to that, David continued. "Cassie's been hurt in the past. I'm not sure how much she's told you…"

He let the sentence hang and Jesse knew he was being tested. David may be Cassie's stepfather, but he seemed to care about her. "I'm aware."

David nodded. "She deserves someone who will cherish her."

"Yes, she does."

The other man held his gaze for a long moment. "What do your parents think of the two of you dating?"

Somehow Jesse wasn't expecting this level of questioning from Cassie's stepfather. Especially when he'd been so laid-back during dinner. "My parents like Cassie. While my dad's aware of the potential pitfalls of perusing a relationship given our positions, he understands some things, despite the obstacles, are worth perusing."

"Is that how you see it? An obstacle?"

Jesse wasn't a teenager, and he knew a trap was being laid when he saw it. "Anything in life worth your time and energy has challenges one must overcome. Being the son of the man Cassie works for does present some interesting situations at work, but it can be navigated. I'm not one to shy away from something I want."

He received another long, pensive look from David. "Did Cassie tell you how I met her mother?"

"Not the details, no. I know she was still rather young when her dad and mom divorced."

David nodded. "Jessica worked for my best friend. I knew the moment I saw her that she was the one. The problem was, she was married to someone else."

Cassie had implied her mom had started seeing David not long after her parents had separated, but he hadn't realized something had been going on before that.

"I know what you're thinking," David said, pulling Jesse out of his thoughts. "Jessica was faithful to Cassie's father until their divorce was final." He paused. "As much as it frustrated me at the time, looking back, I understand her reasons."

"Why are you telling me this?" Jesse was genuinely curious. David didn't know him.

"I want you to understand where Jessica and I are coming from. We both believe love is worth fighting for, but we also understand that sometimes it isn't easy. Cassie's worked hard to make her way in life. She's had her own setbacks."

Did David know about Cassie being raped as a teenager? He had no idea. Cassie didn't think anyone but Brie knew, but the way David said it, the look in his eyes, communicated to Jesse that David might know more than Cassie thought he did. And if David knew, then did that mean the other men in her family did as well?

Before Jesse could decide what to say next, David turned back to the television. Apparently, he'd said his piece, and he was ready to move on.

The sport's commentator broke down the last game between the two teams and Jesse let his mind wander. He imagined Craig was already on site and hopefully installing the cameras. His dad was no doubt going through the footage they already had, and his urge to join in on the research was making his palms itch.

Then there was Cassie. He knew she'd been shaken today. She wanted answers as much as the rest of them.

Jesse's gaze landed on the door that led to the kitchen. He couldn't hear anything.

The commentators on the television droned on until they switched over to the game. Jesse was about to excuse himself to go find Cassie when the two women strolled into the room.

He met Cassie's gaze, but it was unreadable. She sat beside him on the couch, and he reached for her hand, lacing their fingers together.

Jessica had brought cookies with her and offered them to him. He took one. "Thanks."

Once they all had a cookie, Jessica sat down across from her husband. She ignored what was on the television and focused all her attention on Jesse. "How old are you, Jesse?"

"I'm thirty."

She nodded. "And do you want kids?"

Cassie groaned.

Thanks to Cassie's heads-up about her mother, he'd been prepared for this. "Eventually, yes."

"Well, you know, it's better to have kids while you're young and can enjoy them, so I wouldn't wait too long."

He watched as all the color drained from Cassie's face.

"I'll keep that in mind."

CHAPTER 24

Cassie couldn't get out of her mom's house fast enough. She couldn't believe her mother had said that.

Okay, yes, she could. Her mom had basically said the same thing to her in the kitchen, but Cassie couldn't believe she'd said it to Jesse.

They'd been dating for less than a month. Couldn't her mom give them at least six months or so before bringing up kids?

She ran a hand over her face as Jesse slid into the driver's seat beside her. He'd been good about it, letting her mom's comments pass without much reaction, but he had to be bothered by it. Right?

Jesse backed out of her mom's driveway and drove toward his condo. "What's going on in that pretty head of yours?"

"I can't believe she said that to you."

"Your mom. And David, for that matter. Want to see you happy."

Cassie blew out a breath. "And that requires me to have children?"

"In their view? Yes."

She groaned. "I'm so sorry."

"Don't be. The vision of you pregnant with my child doesn't scare me."

Her breath caught in her throat. "What?"

Jesse chuckled. "Maybe I'll find us a homestead and keep you barefoot and pregnant."

"You would not."

That only made him laugh harder. "No. Probably not. I don't really see myself as a homesteading type of guy."

"But the barefoot and pregnant part?"

"I'd let you wear shoes. No need to be barefoot. You might catch a cold." The amusement in his voice was evident. He was having fun with this.

Cassie rolled her eyes. "Very funny."

"I thought so."

Silence filled the car for a few moments. "I'm still sorry. Mom tends to be very focused when she wants something."

He nodded. "She's worried about you. I'm okay with that."

"You'd think I was still a teenager."

"I think that's normal behavior for parents. The last time I spent the night at my parents', my mom brought me breakfast in bed."

"My dad did that the last time I visited him. It was nice."

Jesse smiled. "See." He took the ramp off the highway. "Don't stress so much about your mom. What she says has no bearing on my feelings toward you. Or what I plan to do to you once we're inside my condo."

The shift in topic took her a moment, but once she registered what he'd said, her body began to warm. All his teasing about keeping her pregnant, having to listen to her mom grill her about Jesse, and even finding the makeshift bed on the sixth floor fell by the wayside with images of him doing all sorts of wicked things to her body.

His fingers caressed the soft skin on the inside of her wrist as they took the elevator up to his condo. It was crazy. She shouldn't be this turned on from such a simple touch, but she was. He could play her body like a well-tuned instrument without even trying. She could already feel herself getting wet.

Cassie was expecting him to pounce on her as soon as the door closed, but instead, he took her purse, tossed it onto the couch, then led her toward his bedroom.

He didn't bother to turn on any lights once they were in his room and for some reason, that only added to the anticipation. "We're going to push your limits tonight."

A jolt of fear hit her belly, but it was short-lived. Jesse pulled her against him, covering her mouth with his. His tongue forced its way between her parted lips, leaving no doubt as to who was in charge of the kiss.

She clung to him, her fingers digging into his biceps as she lifted her toes to get closer.

Jesse was having none of it, though. He kept his hands firmly on her hips, holding her where he wanted her. It was both frustrating and exciting at the same time.

He backed her up against the wall before reaching for her hands. She was expecting him to lift them over her head as he had before, but instead, he brought them down to her side, then pushed them behind her back.

The next thing she knew, she was facing the wall, her breasts flat against the vertical surface and her forearms tucked against her lower back. "What—"

"Shhh. No talking unless you're using your safeword. Nod if you understand."

She hesitated, then nodded. What did he mean he was going to push her boundaries?

Cassie didn't speak the words out loud, though.

"Don't move." He released her wrist, leaving her standing against the wall.

She held her breath and waited for what came next. Her mind raced through the possibilities. Was he going to take her from behind? But if that was it, then where had he gone?

Jesse didn't make her wait too long. He was back in a matter of seconds. "I'm going to bind your wrists." That was the only warning she got before she felt his fingers curling around her wrists and wrapping them with what felt like silk.

Her reaction was automatic. She tugged at the restraints, unease pooling in the pit of her stomach.

"Breathe. You're doing fine, baby."

She did what he said, trying to calm her nerves. He wouldn't hurt her. She knew that. Everything he'd done to her had given her more pleasure than she'd ever thought possible.

For that reason, she was forcing herself to keep quiet. She could do this. A part of her wanted to do this if for no other reason than to prove she could. Other women did kinky things with their men. Why couldn't she?

Jesse pressed his chest against her back, flattening her against the wall again. His warm breath caressed her ear. She expected him to say something, give her instructions, but he didn't.

For the longest time, he stayed there, locked against her, their bodies pressed together. Cassie began to relax, her muscles softening to the familiar feel of being surrounded by his scent, his heat.

"Good girl." His whispered praise sent a shiver of pleasure through her.

Jesse skimmed his hands down her sides, over her hips, and around her ass until he reached the zipper at the back. He pulled the tab, and the fabric began to pull away from her body. It slid down her legs, landing at her feet.

She was wearing knee-high stockings and a pair of panties, as per his instructions. They weren't anything fancy, really, but she did like the way the satin felt against her skin.

He traced a finger along the edge of her underwear starting at her hip and moved downward. She opened her legs to give him better access and she could almost see him smile.

The tips of his fingers played with her wet folds as they spread her moisture around. She lifted her hips, trying to get him to touch her clit, but he was having none of it.

"Patience. I promise it'll be worth it."

Cassie bit her lower lip, trying to keep herself in check. The more he touched her, the more frustrated she became.

Right when she thought she wouldn't be able to take it anymore, he grazed his thumb over her clit. She felt a zing go through her and her knees nearly buckled with the sensation.

Jesse's chest vibrated against her back. "So sensitive. I'll have to remember that."

Before she could decide if that was a good thing or not, he used her bound wrists to rip her away from the wall and turn her toward the bed. She was barely able to resister what was happening before he pushed her down onto the bed.

He took hold of both sides of her panties and shimmied them down her legs. Cool air brushed against her pussy as he repositioned her so her knees were on the mattress and her ass was in the air.

His hand connected to her bare flesh, making a loud slapping sound. Cassie jerked at the unexpected assault to her ass.

Another two blows landed on her backside. The burning began to grow, but so did her arousal. She was getting wetter, something she would have never thought possible before being with Jesse.

He spanked her several more times until her ass felt warm and tingly, then dipped his fingers into her pussy. "Hm. You're so wet for me, baby."

She strained toward his fingers, needing more as he circled her clit. But instead of giving her more, he removed his hand.

Cassie must have made a sound because he landed another firm smack on her ass. "You'll learn to be patient and accept what I give you."

Stifling a groan, she buried her face in the comforter.

Something pressed against her entrance, but it didn't feel like him. Not exactly. It felt…harder, more rigid.

Whatever it was, he pushed it inside her. The next thing she knew, the thing started buzzing. She wasn't able to keep a moan from escaping.

Jesse hummed. "Such a pretty sight."

He ran a hand over her ass before giving the base of the vibrator a couple taps. She was trying not to make a sound, then he found her clit and began rubbing it with firm pressure. Her internal muscles clenched against the invading object.

Cassie felt her orgasm coming seconds before it happened. Jesse pressed the base of the vibrator, keeping it inside her as she rode out her climax.

She came down from her high and slumped on the bed, her legs feeling heavy. The intense energy that had been coiling inside her had released, but the vibrator didn't stop. It continued to hum, and within minutes, she felt the energy beginning to build once more.

Jesse ran his hand over her ass and up the length of her spine. "Did you enjoy your orgasm?"

He'd told her not to speak, so she nodded.

She heard more movement. Then the bed dipped as he kneeled behind her. He opened her legs wider and the hair on the back of his thighs brushed against her.

Cassie didn't move. She waited to see what he'd do next.

He didn't make her wait long. Running his hand along her spine, he came to where he had her wrists bound together and traced the material circling her wrists. "I like seeing you like this. Helpless and completely at my mercy, waiting to see how I'll pleasure you."

A shiver ran down her spine, but this time it wasn't because she was nervous or afraid. No, this was from pure anticipation. She wanted to see what he'd do next. This wasn't like what happened with her first boyfriend. She wanted this, wanted everything from Jesse.

His lips pressed against her back as he kissed and licked at her skin. By the time he stopped, her skin was tingling. She wanted him inside her. She wanted to feel him warm and hard filling her. The vibrator was nice, but it wasn't him.

Jesse's grip on her wrists tightened. And as if he could read her mind, he pulled out the vibrator and replaced it with something much better. Him.

She tried to push back against him, but she could barely move. He had her legs so far apart and her hands were useless. She didn't have anything to push against.

His cock stretched her, and it felt so good, but she needed more. She needed him to move. To fuck her.

He didn't make her wait too long. Once he was balls deep inside her, he began to pull out. When he thrust forward, it wasn't gentle. If not for his hold on her wrists, she would have found herself flat on the bed with her face buried in the mattress.

He continued to pound into her and there was nothing she could do. Sweat prickled her skin as the tension in her body coiled tighter. All she needed was some stimulation to her clit and she'd explode.

But he wasn't touching her clit. He hadn't gone near it since he'd made her come the last time.

The urge to beg was building with every second that passed. She bit her lip, trying to keep the words from escaping, but she didn't know how much longer she could hold on.

A whimper left her as he pulled out of her. Cool air rushed over her hot pussy leaving her feeling raw and empty.

She gasped, startled, as Jesse lifted her and moved her like a rag doll. He climbed onto the bed, and before she knew it, he was lying beside her—only it wasn't his face she was staring at. It was his cock.

The smell of her own sex filled her nostrils and for some reason that only added to her arousal. She leaned forward, took his cock into her mouth, and began to suck as if her life depended on it.

Jesse rewarded her by burying his face in her pussy. As he licked and sucked her very sensitive flesh, she tried to take him deeper. She'd never sixty-nined before with a guy. It was hotter than she'd thought it would be.

He began pumping his hips, driving himself deeper. She had to concentrate on her breathing so she didn't choke, but something inside her wanted that too. She wanted whatever he was willing to give her.

His focus moved to her clit and Cassie clamped her thighs down on his head, trying to hold him in place. He didn't seem to mind as he didn't miss a beat.

Her climax hit her hard. She screamed around his cock as he continued to pump in and out of her mouth until his own orgasm shot down her throat.

Cassie tried to swallow as fast as she could, but there was so much, and he was still filling her mouth. She felt some escape her lips and drip down the side of her face.

Jesse pulled away and the cool air in the bedroom hit her once again. She opened her eyes, finding his form in shadow, looking down at her.

He held her gaze for a long moment, then bent to untie her wrists. As he gathered the material in his hands, she realized it was the tie he'd been wearing. She wasn't sure she'd ever be able to look at that tie in the same way again.

After placing the tie on the back of a nearby chair, he returned to the bed and helped her up. Her legs wobbled as she stood. He steadied her, then picked her up and carried her into the bathroom.

Cassie wrapped her arms around his neck and rested her head against his chest. His heart beat strong under her ear and she breathed in the scent of him mixed with sex.

He carried her to the shower and placed her on the bench along the back before turning the water on. She braced herself for the cold, knowing how showers were when you first turned them on, but it never hit her. Jesse stood between her and the stream of water, blocking it until it had warmed.

It was probably a simple thing, him shielding her from the cold water, but it had her heart melting. He brought her to her feet, pressing their bodies together as the water, now the perfect temperature, cascaded from the showerhead.

He pressed his lips to hers in a soft kiss. "Are you all right? Are your shoulders sore?"

She brushed her fingers against his lips and looked up to meet his gaze. "I love you."

The look in his eyes went from concerned to tender. He kissed her again. This time, his lips lingered on hers. She felt it all the way down to her toes.

When he broke their kiss, he turned her toward the wall so his chest was at her back. He brushed her hair to one side and pressed his mouth right below her ear. "I think I've loved you since that first night when I saw you across the room. You captivated me. Grabbed hold of my heart and you haven't let go."

Cassie sucked in a breath. She turned in his arms, meeting his gaze. "I feel the same."

He brushed the back of his hand along her jaw to her hair and threaded his fingers through her long locks. "I want you in my bed every night."

Something very feminine clenched low in her belly. "I—"

"I know we haven't been together that long, so I won't ask you to move in with me. Not yet. Not officially, anyway. But I don't like not having you in my bed. If that means I need to spend the night at your apartment sometimes, I'm willing to do that until you feel comfortable."

She didn't know what to say. Her heart was screaming *yes*, while her brain was telling her all the reasons she shouldn't be rushing into anything with him. But one look into Jesse's blue eyes and her heart won. "I think I can live with that."

The side of Jesse's mouth pulled up into a smile before he kissed her again. Something told her it wouldn't be long before he wore down her defenses.

CHAPTER 25

JESSE WAITED for Cassie to fall asleep before easing out of bed to check his phone. He was hoping to have a message from Craig, but there was nothing.

Update? - Jesse

Cameras in place. Now we wait. - Craig

While he knew this would be a process, he'd been hoping for more. He didn't like knowing Cassie had been up on the sixth floor alone. They didn't know who was living up there or why.

Their reasons could be innocent enough, but even if they were, that didn't mean whoever it was would take kindly to Cassie finding them. People didn't always react rationally when their secrets were exposed.

Knowing they weren't likely to have more answers before morning, Jesse got himself a drink of water, then headed back to bed and the warm body waiting for him. Cassie's declaration of love had been unexpected. He knew she cared for him. The fact she trusted him to restrain her proved that. Hearing her say the words, though, had done something to him.

Logically, he knew there was a process that should be followed.

Their relationship was new. They needed time to get to know each other more, test the waters.

His heart, however, had already made its decision. Cassie was the one. The woman he wanted to marry. She'd be his in every way and he'd be hers.

Cassie was snoring softly as he slipped into the large bed. He didn't want to disturb her, but he also needed her close.

She released a sigh as he gathered her against his chest, spooning her. Her ass was cradled against his hips, exactly where it was supposed to be.

He rested his head on his pillow, one arm above his head, and closed his eyes as his other hand cupped her naked breast. This was about as perfect as life could get.

The next morning, there weren't any new messages from Craig or his dad. He didn't know if that meant they didn't have anything, or if they just hadn't shared it with him.

Jesse walked Cassie to her desk. "No going up to the sixth floor alone."

"I won't."

He wanted to kiss her, but he knew that would create even more office drama. "I'll see you at lunch."

"Um. I have a lunch meeting today."

He raised an eyebrow in question.

"All the assistants go out for lunch once a month."

A memory from his teenage years popped into his head. He'd come to work with his dad not long before he'd left for Europe and his assistant at the time, Martha, had gone to lunch with the other administrative assistants. His dad had said it was great for building teamwork between the support staff.

Jesse nodded. "Text me when you get back to your desk."

She cocked her head to the side as if trying to figure out what he was thinking. "Okay."

Before he could do something he shouldn't, Jesse turned and made his way to the elevator.

He was sitting at his desk two hours later when there was a knock on the door. Considering Stephanie hadn't called to let him know someone was here to see him, he assumed it was her. "Come in."

It wasn't. His father's head of security strolled into Jesse's office and closed the door behind him.

Jesse stood. "Did you find something?"

Craig shook his head. "Not yet. I had to be discreet when placing the cameras last night. I didn't want to spook whoever it is before we get a face. They might move their things and then we're back to square one."

Although Craig hadn't been directly involved in the accounting mess Jesse had walked into or the missing contract, he was aware of them. Especially given he oversaw security for not only the building, but his father's personal security as well.

Craig crossed his arms in front of his chest. "I've been thinking about everything that has happened over the last year and what's happened since you've taken over the department."

Jesse sat back down. "I took over after the pervious manager failed to deliver a balanced set of numbers for multiple quarters."

"Yes, but who compiles those numbers?"

It only took Jesse a few moments to realize where he was going with his line of thought, and he didn't like it. His defenses went up. "Cassie's not responsible for the numbers not adding up."

"No. Not Cassie."

Jesse relaxed. "Then..." He let his mind drift. "You're thinking it was Travers's assistant?"

"I think it's possible. I never liked Travers, but he didn't strike me as a thief. Neither did Crystal, but I could see her fudging numbers if she had an incentive." He paused. "Or if someone was putting some pressure on her. Travers implied as much when he was let go."

"That's a lot of ifs."

"Which is why I haven't said anything to your father. I need more proof."

Another lightbulb went off in Jesse's head. "What do you need from me?"

"I'm thinking you and I aren't likely to get any information if we start asking questions, but maybe your assistant. Or Miss Ross would."

"I won't put Cassie or Stephanie in danger." The thought of intentionally putting any woman in harm's way made the hairs on the back of his neck stand up.

"Neither do I. But having someone running around unchecked with full access to this building and the people in it doesn't sit well with me either."

Craig didn't need to elaborate. Whoever was living on the sixth floor had been coming and going without detection for who knows how long. They had no idea what their intentions were, and that was dangerous for everyone.

"I'll ask, but I'm not pushing either of them."

"Understood." Craig opened the door and let himself out.

Jesse ran a hand over his face and picked up his phone. He dialed Cassie's desk.

"Blake Masters's office."

"Cass, it's Jesse."

"Hey. Why are you—"

"Sorry to interrupt you, but I need you to do me a favor," Jesse said.

She didn't hesitate. "Of course."

"When you're at your lunch today, can you ask about Zac Travers's assistant?"

"Crystal?"

"Yes." He knew she was confused about his request. "I'm trying to get a feel for how things worked before I took over." He paused, not wanting to give her any more information than he needed to. Not because he didn't trust her, but he didn't want her involved more than she needed to be. He didn't like her level of involvement as it was.

"Oh. Well, Stephanie should be able to help with that. I mean, I knew Crystal from our assistants' lunches, but it's not like I hung out with her or anything."

"I know, and I plan on asking her as well. But from my

understanding, Crystal was in this position for a while. I'd like to get a feel for who she trusted."

Cassie was silent on the other line. "You think she had something to do with the missing…information?" Her words were said in a whisper. While her desk was somewhat isolated, that didn't mean people didn't walk close enough to overhear her.

"You know more about what my father is working on than anyone else. You have access to everything he does. That means she had access to everything Travers did."

He didn't fill in the rest, and luckily, he didn't have to.

"I'll ask around. See what I can dig up. Find out who she was friends with at the office."

"Thank you."

"It's hard for me to say no to you."

Jesse smiled. "I know."

Cassie giggled. They both knew they were no longer talking about Crystal or work. "I need to go. Lots of work to do before lunch."

"One more thing."

"Yes?"

"We'll be spending the night at your apartment tonight, so you might want to give Brie a heads-up. She may need to swing by the store and buy some noise-canceling headphones."

"You can't say stuff like that to me at work," she said in a harsh whisper.

Jesse laughed. "Enjoy your lunch. I'll be at your desk to pick you up at five."

He disconnected the call and stood. Stephanie was next. He only hoped that between Cassie and Stephanie, they'd be able to find some trail of useful information for Craig to follow up on. That, or whoever their mystery guest was showed their face. Either way, he was hoping they'd have answers soon.

* * *

Cassie logged off her computer at eleven fifty-eight. She knocked on her boss's door and reminded him of her lunch with the other assistants and made her way to the lobby.

Within five minutes, the lobby was full of the company's administrative assistant. They walked the block and a half to the restaurant, chatting amongst themselves. Cassie had made their reservation over a week ago, so the hostess was waiting on them. They were promptly shown to an area in the back.

As everyone took their seats, Cassie took inventory of the room. Most of the assistants were women, but there was one man. He worked as an assistant to Grayson Hyde, the head of the IT department. She'd talked to him a few times, but she wouldn't say she knew him.

Her gaze landed on Stephanie, and they locked eyes for a moment. A silent communication passed between them. They were both here on a mission.

Two servers came to take the group's orders. It didn't take long. Given they came to the same restaurant every month, most of them ordered the same thing every time. It made things easier for everyone.

Conversations continued as the servers went around the table, so Cassie figured she'd get to work. She turned to the woman beside her, Janice. "How are things going in accounts payable?"

"Oh, you know. Same old, same old. IT updated some of our software, so I've been fighting with that." Janice rolled her eyes.

Cassie had to log into accounts payable from time to time, so she knew what the woman was talking about. "I can only imagine. Anytime I've logged into the system over the last week, I've had to call down to the help desk."

Janice grinned. "What about you? How are things on the executive floor?"

"Good. I've been helping Mr. Masters with some new projects."

There was a gleam in Janice's eye. "Are we talking about your boss or the other Mr. Masters?"

Cassie had walked into that one. "My boss. Jesse and I try to keep our relationship out of the office."

The woman on the other side of Janice snorted. "He brings you to work every day and comes to your desk to pick you up."

"I heard you got caught making out in the executive conference room," Betsy said.

Cassie was trying to figure out how to respond when Stephanie chimed in. "I doubt that. I've seen them together in the office and they've always kept things professional."

Betsy pursed her lips, not liking how Stephanie shut her down.

Janice patted Cassie's arm. "Try not to let Betsy over here bother you. She's just not getting any at home, so she has to live vicariously."

Betsy narrowed her eyes, but everyone around them laughed.

"Maybe we should change the subject," Stephanie said. "Did either of you know the woman who used to have my position? I think her name was Crystal."

Janice nods. "I knew her. Not well, but she used to come to these lunches." She paused. "You know, if you want to find out more about her, the best person to ask is Sandy."

Cassie had no idea who Sandy was. "Is she another assistant?"

Betsy shook her head. "No. She works in accounts receivable. They used to go to lunch all the time. I think they hung out outside of work, too. I saw them leaving together a few times."

As much as Cassie wasn't a fan of office gossip, for once it was working in her favor.

"I know Sandy. She hangs out with Shannon a lot. Long, blond hair, wears it up in a bun most of the time."

"That's the one," Betsy said.

Given the direction of the conversation, Cassie let Stephanie take the lead. "Do you know if they still hang out? I might want to pick her brain. I'm still trying to get a handle on some things."

"I'm not sure." Betsy looked at the other side of Cassie. "Maxine, do you know if Sandy's still in contact with Crystal?"

"That's a strange question."

The tone in Maxine's voice piqued Cassie's interest. "Why do you say that?"

"Because they're sisters."

"I didn't know that," Janice said.

Betsy spoke up next. "Neither did I."

"I didn't think relatives could work together in the same department?" Cassie said, knowing she was walking a bit of a line. Even though she and Jesse weren't related, she was working for his dad. That created a conflict of interest, or at least, a potential one.

Maxine waved a dismissive hand in the air. "I don't think they're blood related. I think they're stepsisters or something."

The food started coming out then and the conversation about Crystal and Sandy dissolved into comments on lunch.

Cassie caught Stephanie's gaze a couple of times, but there was no way they could have a private conversation. She'd been hoping to corner her on the walk back, but one of the other ladies, Kris, Cassie thought her name was, made a beeline for Stephanie as soon as they stood up from the table.

Deciding to take a chance, Cassie lingered in the lobby until everyone else had gone back to their respective floors, then took the elevator to the billing department. Stephanie almost never came to the executive floor, so if Cassie wanted to talk to her, she was going to have to go to her.

The doors opened to the third floor and Cassie was immediately hit by how different it looked to the executive level. There were cubicles everywhere. Rows and rows of them.

She was heading for Jesse's office when she overheard a woman talking. It was coming from the break room.

"Why did you say that?" The woman paused and Cassie realized she must be talking to someone on the phone. "Well, you should have kept your mouth shut."

Cassie paused by the door, glancing inside. A blond woman looked up, noticing her. Her hair was piled on top of her head in a loose bun. The woman matched Maxine's description of Sandy.

"Can I help you with something?" the woman asked, her smile overly sweet.

"I'm looking for Stephanie?" Cassie took a step forward. "I don't think we've met. I'm Cassie." She held out her hand for the woman, trying to both be polite and confirm her suspicions.

It took a moment for the woman to shake Cassie's extended hand. "Sandy. Stephanie's desk is down the hall to the left. Just after the stairwell."

Cassie forced a smile. Although the woman had answered her question, she was getting frosty vibes from her. "Thanks. It was nice meeting you."

Stephanie wasn't at her desk. The door to Jesse's office was open, however, and she could hear voices.

Jesse saw her first. "Hey."

"Hey."

Stephanie glanced at them both. "I'll give you two some privacy."

"No," Cassie said, stopping her. "I came to see you. I wanted to discuss lunch."

"Close the door," Jesse said.

With the door closed, Cassie and Stephanie brought Jesse up to date.

"How did we not know this?" he asked.

"Maybe we did. Or at least, someone did. Craig's only been handling security for the last three years. Both Crystal and Sandy were hired before that."

Jesse's eyebrows rose in question.

"Sandy started in the mailroom like me. We worked together for six months before she was transferred to accounts receivable. If I remember correctly, Mr. Travers approved the transfer himself."

"That still doesn't help us find the missing contract," Cassie said.

"No, but it adds another piece to the puzzle." Jesse reached for his phone. "I'll update Craig and see where he wants to go from here. For now, though, there's not much we can do. As far as we know, Sandy hasn't done anything."

Cassie thought about mentioning Sandy's phone call but decided to let it go. Like Jesse said, right now they didn't know Sandy, or Crystal, for that matter, had done anything wrong.

Saying goodbye to Jesse and Stephanie, Cassie headed for the elevator. The missing contract seemed to be the key to a lot of their unanswered questions, but it was like finding a needle in a haystack. They didn't even know if it was still in the building.

The elevator doors opened to her floor, and she made her way to her desk. Her gaze landed on a piece of paper that hadn't been there previously.

You're wrong.

Cassie had been away from her desk for over an hour, but she scanned the area anyway.

It was useless, of course. The office buzzed with its usual activity.

She picked up her phone and dialed Jesse's office, but he didn't answer. Next, she tried his cell, but again it went to voicemail.

Something told her ignoring the message was a bad idea, so she crossed to her boss's office and knocked. No one answered.

She was considering her options when she heard something that sounded like someone was bouncing a ball against the stairwell door. It wasn't loud exactly, but it was consistent. And it wasn't increasing or decreasing in volume like it would be if it came from someone going up or down the stairs.

At first, Cassie ignored it, remembering Jesse's instructions not to go to the sixth floor by herself. But the noise persisted. Never getting louder. Never getting softer.

He didn't say I couldn't go into the stairwell. It could be a leaking pipe or something. She didn't want it to cause a bigger issue.

Convincing herself it would be okay if she looked, Cassie walked to the heavy metal door that led to the stairwell and opened it.

CHAPTER 26

ALMOST AS SOON AS Cassie left his office, Jesse got a call from his dad saying he was needed in IT. There was a problem with the newest software update and his dad had been called away by one of their largest clients.

It took him over an hour to get things sorted. Someone had buried a bogus code into the old software. When they'd upgraded it, the new system didn't know what to do with the code and kept trying to merge it with the new software.

The kicker was the code was tied to his department. It was possible it was being used to skim money through a customer's account. Jesse was willing to bet, if that was in fact what was happening, it was somehow connected to the missing contract.

He wasn't sure how yet, but the best news of the day was now they had a trail to follow. Even if they couldn't find the missing contract, they might be able to find who entered the code and where the money was being funneled. Grayson Hyde, the head of IT, just needed time to flush it out.

When Jesse returned to his desk, Stephanie was typing away. She looked up from her keyboard as he approached. "Craig Allen came by to see you. He asked that you give him a call as soon as you returned."

Jesse nodded and went into his office, closing the door behind him. Taking a seat behind his desk, he dialed Craig as he began logging into his computer.

"We have a problem," Craig said in greeting.

Jesse stopped typing. "What kind of a problem?"

"I've been researching Crystal and Sandy's history. Crystal's dad married Sandy's mom when the girls were young. They lived together for two years, then the couple split. There was nothing in either of their files to suggest they'd stayed in touch, until I found they were both sent to a summer camp as pre-teens."

"They stayed in touch after that, I'm assuming."

"It appears so," Craig said. "I've found some social media posts where one commented on the other's photos. Nothing crazy, but one can assume they were communicating through private messages."

"Can you get access to those?" Jesse asked.

"Legally?"

Jesse shook his head. "Okay, I won't ask. Plausible deniability."

"Good call."

Jesse wasn't sure how this new information constituted a problem. "But we already knew they were communicating. They worked together."

"While scrolling through the pictures, I came across some of Crystal and a man."

The first person who came to mind was Travers. Was that why Sandy had been in on the gossip regarding him and Cassie? "Was it Travers?"

"No." Craig paused, and the suspense was killing him. "It was Grayson Hyde."

Jesse's eyes almost popped out of his head. He was on his feet faster than he thought possible. "We have to get to IT. Now."

"We don't have any proof—"

"Trust me, we do. And if we don't get down there right now, he's going to make it disappear."

Jesse didn't bother hanging up the phone as he raced out of his office. He headed for the stairwell. It was only one floor down and the stairs were closer.

As he entered the stairwell, there was a noise above him, but he barely registered it as he bounded down the stairs to the second floor.

The IT department was humming with a weird energy that only rooms full of computers seem to generate. Jesse scanned the floor, looking for Grayson, but he didn't seem him.

The elevator dinged and Craig appeared. He saw Jesse and nodded in the opposite direction. Jesse hadn't had time to explain why they had to get to Grayson quickly, but to his credit, Craig was willing to give Jesse the benefit of the doubt.

They each made their way across the large room, coming from opposite directions. Grayson's office was in the back along the wall. Jesse didn't want to spook him, but he also didn't want to give him time to destroy evidence.

Jesse reached his office door first with Craig hot on his heels. They shared another look before Jesse knocked twice on Grayson's partially closed door.

"Hey," Jesse said, a fake smile on his face as he peeked his head into the office.

Grayson looked up from his computer. "Hey. I didn't expect to see you again so soon."

Jesse stepped into the room, Craig following behind him. "I wanted you to show Craig what your team found."

Grayson hesitated. "Sure. I was just working on it now."

Luckily, Craig took over. He strode toward Grayson's desk, rounded it, and stood towering over the much leaner man. "I'm not a computer expert, but I'd like to see what you found." Although Craig had made it sound like a request, it was obvious by his posture it wasn't.

Sweat began to bead on Grayson's forehead. Any doubts Jesse had been harboring disappeared. Craig was being assertive, but he wasn't acting threatening. There was no need for Grayson to be nervous unless he was guilty of something.

Before Grayson could bring up the file, there was another knock at the door. The person didn't wait to be given permission to enter. He walked right in.

Jesse recognized the man but didn't know him by name. He was Craig's computer guy and Jesse got the impression he could find anything if it was on the web.

"Oh, good, Adian. You're here." Craig didn't relax his stance, still hovering over Grayson. "Hyde was about to show me the code his team found."

The new arrival stood on the other side of Grayson, waiting. When the man didn't move, it was Adian who took the lead. He twisted the keyboard toward him and began typing.

"What are you doing?" Grayson asked. Jesse could hear a slight tremble in his voice as he spoke.

Adian didn't respond until he'd found what he was looking for. "I think I found it."

Jesse moved to look, although he had no clue what he was looking at. Numbers he could do in his sleep. Computer code was something else entirely.

"I was about to begin tracing its origins," Grayson said, puffing out his chest with what little bravado he could muster.

Adian began typing again. "I'll take it from here."

"But—"

Standing tall, Adian looked at his boss. "I'll let you know as soon as I have something."

Craig nodded and Adian left, closing the door behind him.

"Tell me about your relationship with Crystal Carter," Craig said, going right to the heart of the issue.

"Who?"

"We found pictures of you on her social media, so drop the act."

Grayson looked at Jesse as if he'd somehow save him from being interrogated by Craig.

Instead, Jesse asked a question of his own. "Were you two seeing each other? Romantically?"

The man didn't say anything, but his body language spoke volumes.

"Right now, my man is backtracking that code. Is it going to lead him to Crystal or to you?" Craig paused. "Or is this all about Sandy?"

"Sandy?" Grayson asked in surprise.

Not missing a beat, Craig continued pressing. "Okay, not Sandy then. Where's Crystal?"

"I don't know."

Craig raised an eyebrow.

"I don't." Grayson glanced at his computer screen, then something in him changed. He pressed his lips together and narrowed his eyes. "I'm not saying anything else to either of you."

"Very well." Craig wrapped his hand around Grayson's forearm and lifted him from his chair. "You can make yourself comfortable in my office until my guy has time to do his thing."

"Stop manhandling me."

Craig ignored his protests. "Walk."

Jesse thought Grayson might be stupid enough to resist, but he must have thought better of it.

Figuring Craig could handle Grayson, Jesse parted ways with them at the elevator and headed back to his office. He had no idea how long it would take for Adian to trace the code.

A part of him wanted to call Cassie and give her an update on what was going on, but what did he know really? Grayson and Crystal knew each other. They were possibly in a relationship. And Sandy and Crystal were stepsiblings for two years when they were in elementary school.

It wasn't exactly news to write home about.

Stephanie was still at her desk when he returned. She studied him. "Everything all right? You took off like your office was on fire."

"Yeah. I just realized something needed my immediate attention." He could tell by the look on her face she didn't believe him, but he wasn't ready to share. Not yet. Not until they knew something for certain. "I'll be in my office if anyone needs me."

* * *

Cassie's head felt like it was going to explode and there was a ringing in her ears. She had no idea what happened. One minute, she was trying to find where the knocking noise was coming from. The next, she felt like she'd been hit by a wrecking ball.

She tried to open her eyes, but she couldn't see anything. Something was covering her eyes.

Her first instinct was to remove whatever it was, but as she tried to bring her hand to her face, she met resistance. Her hands were tied behind her back.

Tightness gripped her chest at the thought of being restrained. She tested her legs to see if her feet were bound, but they moved freely.

Not that it helped her much. She didn't know where she was or even if she was alone. Who had done this to her and why?

The pounding of her heart wasn't helping the weight on her chest. With every pump of blood through her veins, she felt a sharp pain at the back of her skull. Had someone hit her over the head?

It was the only explanation that made sense.

Panic was building inside her. Memories of being restrained against her will and what had happened to her. She couldn't go through it again. Couldn't let someone take from her like that.

Thoughts of Jesse replaced her fear. How long would it take before he noticed she was gone?

She knew he'd look for her, but that wouldn't be until five o'clock. What time was it? How long had she been unconscious?

Cassie had no answers.

If someone came, she had to buy time. Time for Jesse to find her… to realize she was missing.

Time passed and still no one came. Cassie was alone as far as she could tell, so she began trying to focus on details. She knew from all those movies she and Brie had watched over the years that sometimes it was the little things that solved the case. Or in this case, might save her life.

It was then she realized it wasn't quiet. In fact, there was a hum all around her. A mechanical hum.

Was she on the sixth floor?

Their mystery person. Had they been the one to hit her over the head and drag her up here?

But why?

The pounding in her head, while still there, wasn't as intense as it had been, and she was able to think a little more clearly. The notes that had been left on her desk. Had they been from the person staying on the sixth floor?

They'd made no sense. They still didn't. But it was the only thing she had to go on.

I know what you did.

You're wrong.

What did it mean?

Or maybe it didn't mean anything. Cassie was grasping at straws, and she knew it.

She was deep in thought when something caught her attention. Footsteps. At least, that's what she thought they were.

Then, a voice.

No. More than one voice.

They were far away, and she couldn't make out what they were saying, but she thought it was two people.

Cassie tugged at her restraints again, but they were still as tight as they'd been before and without being able to see, she didn't know if there was anything nearby she could use to set herself free.

Her best option, the only one she had at the moment, was to listen in on the conversation. Maybe if she could figure out who was holding her, she could convince them to let her go.

She knew it was a long shot, but it was her best plan given her current circumstances.

The voices got louder, then faded away again. Whoever it was, they were moving around.

Then the voices stopped completely. All she could hear was the dull hum of the mechanical room.

It felt like forever, but it was probably only a few minutes before she heard footsteps coming toward her. Cassie froze. Should she lie down? Had they already seen she was awake?

Her question was answered a moment later when her captor spoke. "You're awake."

It was a woman's voice. "Crystal?"

"So much for just letting her go." The second voice confirmed the other person she'd heard was still there. Given the situation and the conversation in Jesse's office, she was willing to bet the second person was Sandy.

Cassie was having trouble thinking past the throbbing in her head, but she knew she had to. While Jesse would come looking for her eventually, she had no idea how long she'd been unconscious. Nor did she know what Sandy's statement that they couldn't just let her go meant.

She decided to play dumb. "What's going on?"

"This is all your fault," Sandy said, although Cassie had no idea if she was talking to her or to Crystal.

"Shut up." Crystal's response did nothing to help clarify.

"Can someone please tell me what's going on?" Cassie asked.

"No," they both said in unison.

Cassie was determined not to give up. If they were talking, it would buy time for Jesse to find her. "I can't help if I don't understand what the issue is."

Sandy's response was sharp. "You've helped enough already. We wouldn't even be here if you'd kept your nose out of things that didn't concern you."

"What did I do?" She had a feeling she knew, but she wanted confirmation.

"Oh, let me count the ways." It was Sandy who'd answered, although her reply hadn't really answered anything.

"This isn't helping." This time Crystal's voice came from farther away. "It wasn't meant to be like this."

"How was it supposed to be, then?" Sandy asked.

"I just wanted what was mine. Grayson said it would be easy. No one was supposed to get hurt." Crystal sounded as if she were on the verge of tears.

The whole thing made no sense. The only Grayson she knew was the head of IT. "Grayson Hyde?"

A slap resonated from somewhere nearby. "There you go again. Why don't you just tell her everything."

Cassie ignored Sandy's comment and pressed on. She had to keep Crystal talking. "What did Grayson say would be easy?"

Neither woman spoke for several moments, but Cassie could feel the tension in the room.

"Crystal?" Cassie kept her voice calm even though she felt anything but.

"He said there was a way to skim money from the accounts. It wasn't supposed to be a big deal. He said no one would miss it. Blake wouldn't miss it."

Blake? What did Jesse's dad have to do with this?

"But you found it," Sandy said with a level of disdain Cassie didn't understand.

Ignoring Sandy, Cassie directed her question to Crystal, who seemed more willing to share information. "Why would you want to take money from Blake?" It felt strange calling her boss by his first name like that, but she decided to go with it.

Again, there was no response for the longest time. So long, in fact, Cassie didn't think she was going to get an answer. And when she did get an answer, it didn't come from Crystal. "It's the least he owes her. Jesse and Beks have had everything in life handed to them."

It took her muddled brain a moment to make the connection. Jesse and Beks? What…?

Somehow everything began to make sense in a strange sort of way. The missing money. The missing contract. And even Crystal's part in it all.

Cassie didn't want to believe it, but whether it was true or not, it was clear Crystal did. "Crystal, is Blake Master's your father?"

CHAPTER 27

JESSE HAD BEEN GOING over a client issue someone had brought to his attention when his father knocked on his office door. It was rare Blake Masters visited the other departments. Most of the time, they came to him.

"I didn't expect to see you down here in the trenches."

Blake smiled. "I thought I'd make an exception today."

He motioned for his dad to take a seat. "I'm guessing Craig brought you up to speed?"

"Yes." Blake frowned. "I'm still trying to figure out why. He's not only ruined his career, but he's looking at jail time."

"Maybe he thought he wouldn't get caught."

"Maybe. But he knew we were looking at the discrepancies in the accounting. Why take the chance?"

Jesse didn't have an answer. "Craig getting anything out of him?"

"Not so far. They've managed to get him to admit the code was his, but he seems to be digging in his heels. I'm hoping Adian can find the information we need to connect the dots."

A confession was, at least, something, but it still didn't explain why he'd done it in the first place, nor did it answer the question about the missing contract. "Did he clarify his relationship with Crystal and Sandy?"

Blake shook his head. "No. He almost seemed protective of them in some way." He paused. "I'm glad we're getting answers, but the answers are leading to more questions."

Jesse chuckled. "That's usually how it goes."

"I'm glad you were here and figured out the connection. Who knows what would have happened otherwise."

"You don't have to thank me," Jesse said. "It's my job as both your son and your head of accounting."

His father held his gaze for a long moment and Jesse would be lying if he said he didn't get a warm feeling from the pride radiating from his dad's eyes.

After a long moment, Blake stood. "I should get upstairs."

Jesse nodded and Blake left. He had a mountain of reports to get through, and he'd wasted half his afternoon dealing with Grayson Hyde.

Thirty minutes later, Jesse's cell phone rang. His first thought was that it was Craig, calling to give him an update, but the name that came across the screen was his dad's. He felt a note of unease bubble up in his gut. "Dad?"

"Have you heard from Cassie?"

"She's not at her desk?" Jesse asked, already knowing the answer.

"No. She wasn't at her desk when I returned. I didn't think anything of it. She often runs to other departments throughout the day. But it's been almost a half hour, and I haven't seen or heard from her. Given what's been going on, I'm getting concerned."

For the second time that day, Jesse bolted from his chair. He went to his door and peeked his head out of his office. "Hey."

Stephanie turned to look at him.

"Have you heard from Cassie since she left my office earlier?"

"No." She shook her head.

Jesse headed for the stairwell. "I'll be right up."

He hung up the phone as he entered the stairwell. A memory of hearing something earlier flashed through his mind, but he dismissed it. He'd told her not to go to the sixth floor alone. Surely, she wouldn't have…

Taking two steps at a time, Jesse reached the fifth floor where the executive suites were located. He glanced around, looking for any sign of Cassie.

Something red on the railing caught his eye. He wanted to touch it, see if it was what he thought it was, but he knew if it was Cassie's blood, it wouldn't be smart to disturb evidence.

The panic he'd been trying to clamp down on took over as the door behind him opened. He whipped around and came face-to-face with Craig.

Jesse didn't wait. He took off up the stairs toward the maintenance room—Craig following close behind.

* * *

Cassie didn't know what she'd expected, but it wasn't the sharp sting of a slap to her face. She gasped. "What was that for?"

Her blindfold was ripped from her eyes. The sixth floor wasn't full of bright lights, but she'd had her sight impaired for a while. She blinked, trying to get her eyes to adjust and process what she was seeing.

Sandy kneeled in front of her, her face contorted in an angry sneer. "Because I felt like it. This is all your fault anyway."

While she didn't want to be slapped again, she needed to know. "What's my fault?"

"You got me fired," Crystal said.

Sandy stood and began pacing. "You don't need to tell her anything." She turned to Crystal. "What are we going to do with her? We can't just let her go? She'll have us arrested for sure."

They'd be arrested anyway. Even if they made her disappear.

Cassie didn't want to think about that. How would they make her disappear? What would her family do? Jesse?

She figured her only hope was to appeal to Crystal and try to get to the bottom of this whole thing. Sandy seemed hell-bent on getting rid of her. Crystal, on the other hand, seemed genuinely distraught. "Crystal, there must be a way to work this out. Does Blake know you're his daughter?"

It was a risk bringing Blake up again, but it was one she was willing to take.

Sandy answered, "Of course he knows."

A moment later, Crystal responded, "I don't know."

Sandy put her hands on her hips as she looked at Crystal. "How could the man not know he fathered a child? Your mom talked about him all the time. It's why my dad and your mom broke up. She was still hung up on Blake Masters." She said his name with disdain.

"Have you talked to him?" Cassie asked Crystal, ignoring Sandy.

"No." She looked down at the floor. "I tried once, but I couldn't bring myself to do it. He's very intimidating."

While Cassie wasn't intimidated by her boss, she could understand why some people were. He could be an imposing figure, especially when he was upset about something.

Then, because she needed to know, she asked, "Are you the one who left the notes on my desk? The one that said you knew what I did and the one today saying I was wrong?"

"I left the one today," Crystal said. "I don't—"

"The other one was from me. It's because of you that Crystal was left homeless. All because you found that stupid accounting discrepancy."

"I was doing my job."

Sandy didn't seem to hear her. That, or she was ignoring her. "It was so small. Why couldn't you leave it alone?"

"That's not how it works."

"How does it work, then, huh?" Sandy stormed over to Cassie again. "Blake's other kids get everything their hearts desire, while Crystal here has to scrape by. Why shouldn't she have a piece of the Masters empire? It's the least she deserves."

Cassie continued to focus on Crystal. "Why didn't your mom get child support or a settlement or something?"

"I think—"

There was a noise that drew all their attention at once. They all looked in that direction.

"Someone's coming," Sandy whispered.

Cassie didn't stop to think. She screamed as loud as she could.

CHAPTER 28

A woman's voice pierced through the industrial overhead lighting, bouncing off the metal and obscuring the direction of the sound. Fear settled in his gut as he took off toward where they'd found the bedding and clothes.

Given the blood on the stair railing, Jesse figured Cassie was hurt. His heart was pounding in his ears as he rushed by pipes and machines, Craig keeping pace with him. The other man didn't question where he was going.

As they drew closer, he heard voices, but they were moving away. He was about to adjust his direction when he saw her. Cassie was on the floor. She was sitting, her back against a pipe.

She didn't notice him at first. Her head was turned in the opposite direction.

"Cassie?"

She turned, her eyes wild, her face red and a little swollen on the left side. At the sight of him, she let out a sound he couldn't quite describe. It was somewhere between a sigh and a whimper. "Jesse."

He rushed to her side. It was then he noticed her hands were behind her back. He cupped her face in his hands. "Are you okay?"

"Yes." She nodded. "They tied my hands. I can't get free."

Jesse dropped his hands from her face and reached behind her. He'd hoped they'd used rope to secure her hands—he was good with rope and knots—but no such luck. They'd used a large zip tie to secure her wrists. Her arms had been looped around a pipe sticking out from the floor. It went all the way to the ceiling.

He looked at Craig, who was on the phone, barking orders to whoever was on the other end.

"Knife?"

Craig didn't miss a beat. He kneeled on one knee, raised his pant leg, and unsheathed a six-inch blade. He handed it to Jesse as he continued to talk to his man on the phone.

Jesse's attention went back to Cassie. "Lean forward as much as you can. I don't want to cut you."

She bent forward, stretching the zip ties at her wrists.

There wasn't much room between her wrists, the zip tie, and the pipe, so it took longer than he'd like to set her free. Eventually, the plastic broke, and her arms fell to her side.

Cassie's head fell against his chest. He dropped the knife and gathered her into his arms. He could already feel her tears soaking his dress shirt.

"You're safe now. I'm here." It was then he noticed the gash on the back of her head. It was bleeding, but head wounds tended to do that. He couldn't tell how bad it was, but the fact she was conscious and talking was a good sign.

Craig took a step toward them and picked up the knife Jesse had dropped. He lifted his pant leg and returned the weapon to its sheath. "I need to ask you some questions."

Cassie clung to Jesse, the blood from her wrists staining his dress shirt.

Jesse didn't care about the blood. Shirts could be replaced. "Who did this to you?"

She met Jesse's gaze, then looked at Craig. "I don't know who knocked me out. I think it was Crystal, but it may have been Sandy. I didn't see."

"They were both here?" Craig pulled out his phone again.

Cassie tried to nod but stopped herself mid-movement. She gripped the sides of her head with both hands. "Yes."

"We need to get you checked out by a doctor." Jesse began helping her to stand.

"Paramedics are already on their way, as are the police." Craig turned his attention back to the phone. "We're looking for Sandy Green and Crystal Carter. Check all the security cameras. I don't want either of them leaving the building."

"Can you stand?" Jesse asked Cassie.

She met his gaze. "I think so."

Rocking back on his heels, Jesse stood and offered her his hands for support. She took them, pulling herself up. He didn't miss her wince, nor the way she swayed on her feet. Bending, he placed one arm under her knees and the other behind her back, lifting her into his arms.

Cassie didn't protest, telling him more than she could with words. She was hurting.

He pressed a kiss to her forehead and followed Craig to the stairwell.

Her warm breath against his neck reminded him she was safe in his arms. Why the hell had she gone into the stairwell in the first place?

He held on a little tighter as they made it to the fifth-floor landing and entered the executive floor. The paramedics were already there, waiting for them.

As soon as Jesse laid her on the stretcher, two paramedics began working. They asked about her injuries and did a quick assessment.

Jesse didn't like feeling helpless. Why had she put herself in danger like that?

The paramedics finished their examination. "We're going to want a doctor to check you out. You might have a concussion."

Instead of answering the paramedic, she turned to Jesse. "Where's your dad?"

"I'm sure he's around somewhere. We'll see him later." His father's whereabouts were the farthest thing from Jesse's mind. Cassie had been on the sixth floor. Somewhere he'd told her not to go. And she was hurt. "I'm more concerned with you at the moment."

Before she could argue, Jesse made eye contact with the paramedic. The man nodded and they started toward the elevator.

Being Blake Masters's son came with its share of benefits. One of them was that no one questioned him when he climbed into the ambulance next to Cassie.

He held her hand as they drove to the hospital. His head was swirling with questions, but they weren't alone. His questions would have to wait until later.

The hospital was bustling with activity when they arrived. They were set up in a room and left to wait.

Jesse sat next to her, not able to take his gaze off the marks on her wrists.

"I'm okay." Her whispered words did nothing to calm him.

"You were lucky. What possessed you to go into the stairwell alone after I'd told you not to go to the sixth floor?"

She paled at the reminder. "I heard a noise."

He stood and walked the length of the room before looking at her again.

There was a knock on the door a second before it opened and a woman wearing scrubs walked in. She spent the next ten minutes going over Cassie's chart and checking her vitals.

He stood in the corner, observing while she worked.

When the nurse finished, she let them know the doctor would be in soon and left, closing the door behind her.

Several moments passed in silence before Cassie spoke. "I'm sorry."

He met her gaze and held it. "Do you not understand how important you are to me? How much I love you? This isn't a game to me, Cass."

"It's not a game to me, either. I love you, too."

To his surprise, there was another knock at the door, but it wasn't the doctor. It was two police detectives. They asked a lot of questions, and Cassie relayed what had happened to her.

"Did either of the women give any indication of why they'd done this?" the male detective asked.

Instead of answering, Cassie closed her eyes and brought a hand up to her head like it was pounding. He wasn't sure why, but he got the impression she didn't want to answer the detective's question.

"We should let you get some rest. I know it's been a long day." The female detective removed a card from her pocket and handed it to Jesse. "We'll be in touch in a day or so, but if she thinks of anything before then, give us a call."

"Thanks." Jesse tucked the card into his pocket.

The two detectives left the room, leaving them alone again. He was going to ask Cassie why she'd avoided the question, but there was another knock at the door.

A man stressed in scrubs walked into the room and introduced himself as Dr. Jasper. He inspected Cassie's injuries, taking some extra time looking over her head wound. Cassie lay there stoically, allowing the doctor to poke and prod, only wincing a couple of times.

Jesse wanted to do something. He didn't like this feeling of helplessness he felt. When they'd left, Craig's men hadn't yet found Sandy or Crystal and Jesse hadn't wanted to step away from Cassie long enough to see if they'd been located.

Once the doctor was finished, he wrote some notes on his tablet, then addressed Cassie. "I don't think you have a concussion, but I'd like you to rest for the next three days. No television. No reading. And try to avoid bright lights. I'd rather be safe than sorry when it comes to head trauma." The doctor looked toward Jesse. "It would be best if she wasn't left alone."

"She won't be." He'd make sure of it.

"Does that mean I can go home?" Cassie asked.

The doctor smiled at her, the first one he'd seen from the man since he strolled into the room. "I'll send the nurse in to get your bandaged up, then we'll get your discharge paperwork going and get you out of here, all right?"

"Thanks." Cassie smiled, although it didn't quite reach her eyes. She looked exhausted.

It took another hour for the nurse to bandage all of Cassie's wounds and the doctor to complete her discharge paperwork. Not knowing what was going on with Crystal and Sandy was driving Jesse nuts, but there was no way he was leaving Cassie alone.

When they walked out of the ER and into the waiting room, Jesse was ready to call for a ride when he noticed his dad's driver, Micheal, sitting near the entrance. Jesse wheeled Cassie over to him.

Micheal stood. "Your dad thought you might need a ride."

Jesse and Cassie waited in front of the building while Micheal went to get the car. It had gotten dark, but the temperature was still mild. He was grateful for the gentle breeze, but he wondered if it was too much for Cassie. "Are you cold?"

"No. I'm good. The breeze feels good."

Micheal stopped the car in front of them and Jesse wasted no time opening the back door. He helped Cassie into the seat, returned the wheelchair inside, then climbed in next to her. "Take us to my condo, please."

Jesse placed his arm around Cassie, and she snuggled against him. Her hair smelled of the disinfectant they used to clean her head wound, and it brought his anger to the surface again.

Cassie must have felt the shift in his mood. "I'm sorry I put myself in danger."

"We'll talk about that later."

She was quiet for a long moment. "I need to talk to your dad."

"I'll call him once we get you settled and let him know what the doctor said."

"No. I need to talk to him. In person." She paused. "I know it's late, but do you think he could come over tonight?"

Jesse tilted his head so he could see her face. "What's going on?"

She pressed her lips together and played with his tie. "Crystal said something I think he should know."

"What did she say?"

Her gaze darted toward the driver. While Jesse knew Micheal could be trusted, Cassie obviously didn't want to discuss whatever it was in front of him.

Jesse wasn't sure what to think about that, but he didn't want to argue with her. The doctor said she needed rest, so he wouldn't push her. Not yet anyway.

His dad's driver brought them to the front entrance of Jesse's condo building. He waited while Jesse lifted Cassie from the vehicle, then held open the door to the building. "I've got it from here."

Micheal nodded.

Cassie rested her head on his shoulder as they made their way up in the elevator. Once they reached the door to his condo, it was a little more of a challenge. "Can you stand?"

"Yes."

Jesse set her down on her feet, making sure she wasn't going to lose her balance before digging his keys out of his pocket and opening the door. He flipped on the lights and lifted her into his arms again.

She giggled and his heart warmed at the sound.

It was quickly followed by the realization that he could have lost her had his dad not called him to let him know she was missing. Had he and Craig not gone looking for her.

Jesse got her settled on the couch with a blanket and pillow. "Are you hungry?" The doctor had warned him Cassie's appetite might be off for the next few days.

"I'm starving."

He pressed a kiss to her temple, then headed into the kitchen to see what he could whip up.

"Jesse?" Her voice was softer than usual, but he still heard her.

"Yes?"

"Can I borrow your phone? Mine's still at the office."

* * *

Cassie was nervous as she waited for Blake to arrive. She had no idea why. It wasn't her secret. And she wasn't even sure if it was real.

Jesse had tried to get her to explain why she needed to see his dad, but it didn't feel right for her to tell Jesse before she told Blake. This whole secret thing put her in a weird position she didn't like.

At ten o'clock, there was a knock at the door and Jesse went to let his father in.

"How is she?" Blake's asked.

"Tired and in need of rest."

Blake's gaze shifted to where she was reclining on the couch. "I won't stay long."

Cassie tried to sit up a little straighter. Even though this wasn't work related, Blake Masters was still her boss. "Thank you for coming. I know it's late."

Blake waved her comment away and sat down on the chair across from her. "I'm just happy to hear you weren't seriously hurt."

"Me too."

When she didn't say any more, Blake decided to take charge of the situation. "What is it you needed to talk to me about?"

Her gaze shifted to Jesse. She wasn't sure she wanted him to find out like this, even if it was true, but she couldn't exactly ask him to leave his own living room. And even if she did, she wasn't sure he'd go. "Have you talked to Crystal?"

"Personally? No." Blake's jaw tightened. "Craig got a few minutes with her before the police took her away, but she wasn't talking. Did she say something to you?"

Cassie played with the blanket draped over her lap. "She said Grayson Hyde created the code to skim money from the company."

Blake nodded. "That's consistent with what Grayson told Craig." He paused. "Did she say why he did it?"

This was where it got complicated. "She said he did it for her." Cassie glanced at Jesse before continuing. "That the money was supposed to be her inheritance."

Jesse took a step forward. "Her inheritance?"

Cassie licked her lips, suddenly feeling parched. "She said she's your daughter."

Blake froze.

"That's impossible. Crystal's around my age. That's…" The words died in Jesse's throat when he saw the look on his dad's face. "Dad? Tell me it isn't true. It's not possible."

Instead of answering Jesse's question, Blake stood and walked to the large bank of windows overlooking the city. "I can't tell you that. I wish I could."

"What about Mom? How could you—"

Blake turned to face his son. "After you were born, your mom and I had some difficulty adjusting. She went into a deep depression, and we separated for a few months."

"And you cheated on her?" Jesse's voice was hard.

His dad didn't deny it.

Jesse blew out an angry breath. "Does she know?"

"About my dalliance? Yes."

"Dalliance?" Jesse's eyes were wild. She'd never seen him this way. Not even when he found her tied up.

Blake's mind seemed to be elsewhere. "I need to go."

"You're leaving?" Jesse asked.

His father walked past them both and headed for the door. "Get some rest, Cassie." Then he looked at Jesse. "Take care of her. She's a keeper, you know."

Jesse didn't respond.

When the door closed behind his father, Jesse sat down next to her on the couch. He ran a frustrated hand through his hair before turning to look at her. "Now I understand why you didn't want to tell me."

"It's not so much I didn't want to tell you as I thought I needed to tell your dad first." She placed a hand on his thigh. "How are you holding up?"

"Not great." He stood. "Let's get you to bed?"

"Did you want to talk about this?" The news was a big blow.

He shook his head. "Not right now. Right now, I want to punch something. Or fuck you until you can't walk straight. As I can't do either at the moment, I'm going to take you to bed and hold you in my arms until the need to pummel something dissipates."

CHAPTER 29

THE NEXT FEW days were rough. Jesse worked from home, taking care of Cassie. Stephanie stopped by on Friday to bring him some papers he needed to sign, and on Sunday, Brie brought Cassie some more clothes.

He'd given Cassie and her friend some time alone, retreating to his study to check his email. Brie had stayed for about an hour and when she left, Cassie was pensive. He waited until after dinner to broach the subject. "How was your visit with Brie?"

"Good." Cassie paused. "She told me Kaden proposed. She wants me to be her maid of honor."

Jesse crossed his ankles and leaned against the headboard. "Kaden's a good guy."

"I know. He's almost as good as you are."

He smiled at the compliment. "Is that your way of trying to butter me up?"

"No. It's the truth." She paused. "Besides, why would I need to butter you up?"

Jesse had held off addressing her disobedience given her injuries, but it would have to be dealt with. She needed to understand her obligations in their relationship. "I figured you might be trying to convince me to go easy on you."

A deep crease formed in her brow. "Easy on me?"

It had been three days since he'd found her tied to a pipe on the sixth floor. He'd made sure she'd done nothing but rest and listen to relaxing music. Jesse had contented himself with holding her and knowing she was safe. But their family doctor had cleared her. He said she could go back to work on Monday. The thought of her being out of his sight for any length of time caused him anxiety.

It wasn't logical, he knew. She'd be fine. The threat had been removed. Or at least, the physical threat. Grayson was being charged with theft, along with several other cybercrimes. Sandy had been charged with kidnapping and assault for helping Crystal hold Cassie.

Then, there was Crystal. She'd also been charged with kidnapping and assault. During her interrogation, she'd admitted to living on the sixth floor for the last two months. She'd been having an affair with Travers, her boss. When they were both fired, he'd kicked her to the curb.

The whole thing felt like a soap opera to Jesse. He didn't like the chaos.

Meeting Cassie's gaze, he kept his voice firm and even. "You disobeyed me. I told you not to go to the sixth floor."

"I didn't."

He raised an eyebrow in disbelief.

"I didn't." This time, it was said with less conviction. She broke eye contact, her gaze on the sheets in front of her. "I went into the stairwell." When he didn't say anything, she continued. "Okay, maybe I shouldn't have gone into the stairwell. Maybe I should have called maintenance instead of going to check it out myself. I know that now."

"Cass, look at me."

She lifted her gaze.

Jesse held it for a long moment before speaking. "You are mine. When we're together, I take care of your needs. I make sure you're safe and protected. But when I can't be there, it's your job to take care of what's mine. You didn't do that. You disregarded your own safety. You disrespected me and our relationship."

Her eyes widened, then sadness came over her. "I didn't mean to." Cassie ran her teeth over her bottom lip, stretching it taut. "What happens now?"

He knew what she was asking. "I discipline you.

She swallowed. "How?"

"As this is your first offense, and you're still healing, I thought we'd keep it simple."

"Meaning?"

He was enjoying watching her sweat. "Tomorrow I'll be working from home. You'll spend the day serving me however I choose."

"But I have work of my own to do. I should go into the office—"

"My dad's already brought in a temp to cover for you this next week."

"He can't do that."

Jesse smirked. "He can, and he has." Jesse didn't go into the conversation he had with his father. They weren't on the best of terms right now, but certain things had to be taken care of. Cassie being one of them. Her health and well-being were one thing they could agree on.

Cassie was quiet for a long moment. "You two shouldn't be making decisions for me."

The look Jesse gave her spoke volumes and it only took her a few seconds for what she said to register.

"I meant when it comes to my career. Jesse, you can't make deals with my boss behind my back."

He took her chin in his hand, holding it firm in his grasp, making sure she was focused only on him. "You are my priority. My responsibility. And right now, you need to concentrate on healing, not being my father's gopher."

"That's not all I do."

"That's not what I meant, and you know it." He paused. "My father can function without you for a few days. Your job can be hectic sometimes. I don't want you running around wearing yourself out."

She opened her mouth to protest, but he cut her off. "This isn't up for debate. If you must, look at it as part of your punishment. Maybe you'll think twice before you go looking for trouble next time. And if you keep this up, I'll drape you over my lap and give you a reminder of who's in charge here."

"That's not what I did."

"We'll have to agree to disagree on that." Jesse pressed a quick kiss to her lips. "I need to clean up the kitchen. I'll be back to check on you."

Jesse knew she was fuming when he left her, but she was going to have to work through it.

* * *

Cassie stared at Jesse's back as he left the room. She couldn't believe what had happened. He'd talked to his dad about her without her knowledge. Granted, it was in relation to the injury she'd sustained and her healing, but still, she should have been consulted.

Grabbing her phone, she dialed Brie.

"Miss me already?" her best friend asked.

"Always."

"Hey, what's wrong?" Brie had always been able to tell when something was wrong with Cassie. She'd known something had happened with Trent before Cassie had told anyone about the breakup.

"How would you feel if Kaden talked to your boss and arranged for you to take a week off? And he didn't say anything to you about it until after."

Brie didn't answer right away. "I'm assuming we're talking about Jesse and not Kaden, and considering what happened to you…"

"You don't think it's crossing some sort of line?"

Brie was taking all the air out of Cassie's sails.

"No." Brie paused. "Do you?"

"I don't know. Maybe a little?"

"I saw the way he looked at you. I think you scared him. And if having you take a week off makes him feel better, then take a week off."

All the bluster Cassie had been feeling left her in a rush. "You're right."

"I'm always right."

Cassie laughed. "Thanks."

"Anytime."

Placing the phone on the nightstand, Cassie climbed out of bed. The shirt she was wearing, one of Jesse's, hit her mid-thigh as she stood. She hadn't gotten dressed in days and there was no use doing so now even though being almost naked made her feel more vulnerable.

Normally, she wouldn't care. She liked feeling that way when she was with Jesse, but not when she had to find him and apologize. For some reason, she wanted the protection of clothes.

She found him in the kitchen, exactly where he said he'd be. He closed the dishwasher, wiped his hands on a towel, and spotted her walking toward him.

Jesse didn't say anything as she came to a stop in front of him. They hadn't done anything beyond since she was injured. Not because she didn't want to, but because he said he didn't want to hurt her. She'd gone years without sex before she met him. Now, it seemed to be something she craved whenever he was around.

But what she was feeling now wasn't only about sex. She'd been wrong. She'd screwed up. When he'd mentioned how he was going to punish her, her defenses had gone up. Then, at his declaration that she was going to stay home from work and spend the day serving him, she'd lashed out.

Not stopping to think about it, Cassie lowered herself to the floor, kneeling in front of him. "I'm sorry, Sir. I shouldn't have said those things. I know you're trying to take care of me."

His fingers grazed over her hair, avoiding the still sensitive area on her head. He didn't say anything, so she rested her head against his leg, her face almost even with his crotch. It was strange. Before she'd met him, she would have found this position humiliating. Now, it somehow felt right, comforting.

He continued to stroke her hair. The dishwasher hummed in the background, adding to the feeling of contentment she felt.

For years she'd tried to find her footing, her place. Who knew her place would be kneeling at Jesse's feet?

As they continued to stand in the kitchen, the bulge in his pants began to grow. It was impossible to miss.

She pressed her lips against his growing erection and his fingers flexed. "Cass," he warned.

"Yes, Sir?" Her voice was full of an innocence she didn't feel.

"The doctor said you needed rest."

"He said to rest for three days. It's been three days." She pressed another kiss to his now fully erect cock. "I miss you." Her words were whispered, but he'd heard them.

Before she knew it, she was being lifted off her feet and carried to the couch. He set her down and turned her to face away from him. "Kneel on the couch and brace yourself against the back. I don't want you to hit your head while I fuck you."

Heat flooded through her at his words and she did as he asked.

The sound of his zipper being released sent a shiver of anticipation through her. She heard foil being ripped open and knew he was putting on a condom. He'd asked her to go see her doctor about birth control, but she hadn't gotten around to it. Yet another way she was failing as his submissive. She'd have to do better. He deserved better.

Without preamble, Jesse moved between her legs. He pushed her panties to the side and pressed the tip of his cock against her sex. Something inside her came alive, a primal feeling of connection. "Please, Sir. I need you."

He placed both hands on her hips and thrust his hips forward. His cock sank into the depths of her pussy, filling her in the most delicious way. Tears pricked her eyes as he plunged into her again and again. Not because she was in any physical pain, but because she finally realized what he'd been trying to say to her earlier. She was his. His to take. His to love. His.

But what she hadn't realized at the time was that he was hers as well. She had caused him pain by disobeying him. Pain that was purely her fault.

Jesse's arms wrapped around her, pulling her torso up to rest against his. He pressed a kiss to her shoulder. "Shh, baby. I've got you."

That only made the tears stream down her cheeks faster.

His thrusts slowed. "Sir, don't stop. Please."

Jesse nuzzled her neck as he continued his steady movements, holding her tight. "You're mine," he whispered in her ear. "Mine. Now and always."

"Yours."

He trailed one hand down her front until his fingers found her clit. "Come for me, Cass."

She felt the energy building, coiling as he played with her. When her orgasm hit, she felt it deep in every muscle…down to her bones.

Pain radiated from where she'd hit her head, but it was secondary to the pleasure she felt. She could handle the pain.

Jesse grunted twice before giving one final thrust and letting go, his own climax rocking him as he clung to her.

"You're moving in with me," he said as soon as he'd caught his breath again. It wasn't a question. He was making a declaration.

He cupped her cheek, turning her head so he could look at her. The evidence of her tears marred her face, and he brushed them away.

His lips captured hers in a way that had her wanting him all over again. "I need to go clean up," he said after breaking the kiss.

A whine escaped her throat before she could stop it.

He smiled and kissed the tip of her nose. "I'll be right back. I promise. Make yourself comfortable on the couch while I'm gone."

True to his word, Jesse returned within a few minutes. He'd removed his clothes, which was fine with her. She was kind of hoping he'd be willing to go again in the not-too-distant future.

Jesse snatched a blanket from the ottoman before joining her on the couch. He eased behind her, covering them both in the blanket before gathering her in his arms. "Are you hurting anywhere?"

"My head's pounding a little, but it was worth it." She ran her fingers over his lips. "You're going to have to meet my dad soon. Especially if we're going to be living together."

"As soon as things settle down here, we'll arrange it."

Cassie's gaze met his. "When you talked to your dad, did you also talk about Crystal?"

His lips pressed together in a hard line. "He wants a DNA test."

"That's a good idea." Cassie paused. "How's your mom taking it?"

"Better than I am. She knew about the affair."

"And she chose to stay with him."

Jesse sighed. "Yes."

Silence lingered in the condo with each one of them lost in thought. "What are you going to do?"

He shook his head. "There's not much I can do. If she's my sister, then I'll deal with it once the test results come back. If not…"

Jesse didn't say the words, but Cassie knew the implication. If this was a ploy, a way to try and drive a wedge between the family, then Jesse and his family would use their resources to make sure she received the harshest punishment possible.

CHAPTER 30

Cassie woke up wrapped in Jesse's arms. His warm body pressed against hers, sending prickles of awareness to her core.

He was still sleeping. His chest rising and falling with each breath. They'd been up late the night before.

She pressed a kiss to his neck and started to move away.

"Where do you think you're going?" His voice was deeper than usual.

"I need to use the bathroom."

He peeked one eye open. "Start the shower. I'll join you in a few minutes."

It was then Cassie remembered that today, she was at his mercy. She was to serve him, all day. Did that mean she was going to have to kneel to take a shower?

She scrambled off the bed and padded to the bathroom to take care of business. After washing her hands, she turned the water on in the shower, allowing it to heat up.

The bathroom door opened, and Jesse strolled in. He walked over to the toilet and relieved himself, not seeming to mind she was watching.

Jesse didn't comment as he finished up and headed into the

shower. He held out his hand toward her, and she took it, letting him lead her into the spray.

Turning her so her back was to the water, he wet her hair, then took a step back. He moved her out of the water and reached for the shampoo bottle.

She closed her eyes, enjoying the feel of his hands in her hair. He was careful around the tender spot on her head but made sure to remove any dried blood from the area.

He rinsed the suds from her hair before squeezing a large glob of conditioner into his hand. She could stand here all day if he continued to touch her like this, his fingers massaging her scalp.

Once the conditioner was on, he focused on washing her body, taking his time as he worked over her skin from head to toe. She was a ball of nerves by the time he was done. All she needed was a little pressure on her clit and she'd explode.

But he didn't touch her there. Not like she wanted him to.

He used the detachable shower head to rinse between her legs, opening her folds so he could clean her, but it was all very clinical. The only attention her clit got was when the water hit it as he moved it over her skin. It wasn't enough to do anything but tease her.

Jesse replaced the shower head and rinsed her hair before shifting her to the side and wetting his own hair. He lathered his head with shampoo, rinsed, then picked up the conditioner. She didn't know what to do. "Would you like me to wash you, Sir?"

He rinsed his hair before answering her. "You can wash me after."

"After?"

He reached behind her and tossed what looked like a garden mat onto the tile in front of him. "On your knees."

Cassie looked down at the mat, then lowered herself onto it. She'd been wondering when her punishment would start. Although she wasn't sure how sucking his cock would be viewed as punishment. She enjoyed the feel of him in her mouth. Loved hearing his breathy moans as she pleasured him.

His erection stood proud, pointing directly at her. She wasted no time circling her fingers around his base, opening her lips, and taking him inside.

Jesse put one hand at the base of her neck. He cupped her cheek with the other, careful to avoid her tender spots. His thumb grazed the side of her face as she bobbed her head, rubbing her tongue against his length.

Her clit was pulsing with need as she serviced him. She was so horny, she wanted to reach between her legs and relieve the pressure.

With her free hand, Cassie went to touch herself.

"No." His grip tightened on her neck.

She froze.

"You are not allowed to touch yourself without my permission."

Cassie balled her hand into a fist and pressed it against her leg. She began bobbing her head along his erection again, but it must not have been to his satisfaction because he started moving his hips, driving his cock into her mouth faster and harder. She was having trouble keeping up with the pace.

She concentrated on her breathing as he used her mouth. His cock hit the back of her throat and she tried her best not to gag. Then he was coming down her throat, the saltiness coating her tongue.

Jesse pulled out of her, his erection softening. He tilted her head up, making her look at him. His thumbs brushed the tears from her cheeks—tears she hadn't realized had fallen.

He helped her to stand, then handed her the soap. "You may wash me now."

Blindly, she ran the soap over his body. She could still taste him, her sex still aching with need. When she washed his cock, he stood stoically while she did it, as if it were no big deal for her to have her hands on him—as if he hadn't been in her mouth minutes before.

When she finished soaping up his feet, he helped her to stand once more and leaned into the water to rinse. He made sure her hands were free of soap, then turned off the water.

Jesse was waiting with a towel when she exited the shower. She felt self-conscious, exposed. More so than she'd ever felt with him.

He dried them both, then went to his closet to dress. She had a feeling she'd be left naked for the day, and she'd been right. Sort of.

After dressing himself, he disappeared into his closet for a few minutes. When he returned, he held a pair of red heels in one hand and something she couldn't make out in the other.

He set the heels in front of her and offered a hand to steady her as she slipped them on. They were taller than she was used to, which made her feel unsteady. Jesse was patient, allowing her time to adjust to them before releasing his hold on her.

It was then he opened his other hand, letting her see what else he'd brought with him from the closet. It looked to be two red hearts. She didn't get to look too closely, though, before he began securing the first one to her right nipple.

With that in place, he moved on to her left nipple. It was only then she got a good look at what he was putting on her. They looked like drop earrings, but instead of studs at the top to go through your ears, they had loops that went around her nipple.

He finished securing the second one, then backed away from her several paces to observe her from head to toe. She wasn't sure how she felt about this, but she was also positive he wasn't concerned with her feelings right now.

They moved into the kitchen, her heels clicking on the wood floor as she trailed behind him. He stopped in front of the table and patted the top. "Sit here and spread your legs. I want to see your pussy while I make us breakfast."

Cassie hopped onto the table. She opened her legs, but they weren't wide enough for his liking. "Lean back on your elbows."

She complied—the new position causing her back to arch and her chest to push forward.

"Hm. Almost there." Jesse lifted her legs, bending them and setting her feet on top of the table. Her legs were spread wide, her pussy on full display. "That's better," he muttered before turning his back on her and going to get something out of the refrigerator.

She stayed there until he'd finished cooking, then he helped her to stand. Again, he made sure she was steady before letting her go. He placed a pillow beside his chair and had her kneeling at his feet. The tiny hearts swung from her nipples, reminding her they were there.

He speared a piece of melon on his fork and held it in front of her mouth. She opened her lips, and he fed it to her. It was strangely sensual having him feed her like that. Not to mention, the cool air wafting over her naked body. She was both turned on and self-conscious at the same time.

After they'd finished eating, he cleaned up and moved them to his study. "Wait here."

He left her standing naked beside his desk. She had no idea what he had planned for her today and she was pretty sure she wasn't going to love it.

A few moments later, he returned with the coffee table. He placed it a few feet in front of his desk, turned the opposite way.

Cassie knew what was coming before he said it. "Lie down on the coffee table and spread your pussy for me. I want to enjoy the view while I work."

She lay down, her back flat this time, and propped her heels on the edge of the table. Her nipples were hard and her pussy was wet, but she was so embarrassed she wanted to hide.

Jesse stood over her, gazing down at her body. He ran a single finger down her torso but stopped at her bellybutton. "Why are you here?"

Cassie swallowed. "Because I disobeyed you and put myself in danger."

He looked her over once more, then walked to his desk and took a seat. She stayed in that position while he checked his email and made a couple of calls. He'd ignored her for the most part, but every now and then she'd feel his gaze on her.

She had no idea how long she'd lain there before he addressed her. "Go get me some water and make me some popcorn. I need a snack."

He was talking to her. There was no one else in the room.

Cassie closed her legs and turned to put her feet on the ground before sitting up. Her legs were a little stiff from being in the same position for so long, but it wasn't too bad. The worst part was her nipples. They'd been hard this entire time and even the slightest movement was sending little zings to her clit.

When she returned with his snack, he began eating it without any instruction on what she was supposed to do. She felt lost. Was she supposed to stay standing there or go back to the coffee table?

She wanted to ask but decided against it. He was proving a point. She was starting to get it, and it was making her feel even worse than she had before.

At ten thirty, Jesse closed his laptop, moved it to the side and pushed back from his chair. He lifted her up and set her on top of his desk.

He stood, towering over her, a hungry look in his eyes. Her breath hitched in her throat and that primal need clenched deep in her belly. She knew that look. Knew what it meant.

His lips crashed over hers, his tongue plunging inside her mouth. He cupped her breast, kneading it and brushing his thumb over the already sensitive tip. It reminded her of the time he took her against the wall. It was raw and full of need.

With his other hand, he inserted two fingers into her pussy. She spread her legs open for him, needing his touch more than she could explain. But all too soon, it was gone. He was gone.

She opened her eyes, and he was already rolling on a condom. He lined himself up and pushed his hips forward. "You're calling your doctor tomorrow. I'm tired of these fucking condoms."

Her pussy throbbed, needing more of him. "Yes, Sir."

He pushed her back onto his desk, digging his fingers into her hips as he took what he wanted. He fucked her hard, bouncing her against the desk until he found his release. Not once going near her clit.

Again, her body was humming, even more than it had been before, and she was being denied.

She knew why. He'd told her this would be punishment, but she hadn't truly understood what he'd meant until now. This was torture. Not in the traditional way. Not because of physical pain, but because she wanted to be his in every way. To feel the connection with him as they both found release. Both found pleasure in each other.

By putting herself in danger, she'd disregarded that connection. She'd disregarded him.

Cassie spent the rest of the morning at his feet, resting her head in his lap. He hadn't required it, but she'd needed to feel close to him and his only reaction was to run a hand over her head in much the same way one would pet a cat.

Jesse made them lunch, then moved to the couch. He brought the coffee table back to the living room and had her lying on it while he worked on his laptop. Later in the day, he had a conversation with Craig and his dad. She'd only heard one side of the conversation, but she didn't get the impression any of them were happy.

It was almost four when he finished his last call. She stayed where she was, unsure what came next. The workday wasn't technically over, but he'd made no move to call anyone else or reach for his laptop.

"Come here."

She rose from her perch on the coffee table and went to him. He had her lying down on the couch, her head in his lap. She snuggled against him, needing to feel his touch.

His fingers trailed down her arm, tickling her skin before traveling back up again. Over and over, he did this until goose bumps started to form.

"Crystal agreed to a DNA test."

"How do you feel about that?" She'd been quiet for most of the day, not speaking unless he asked her a direct question.

"I don't know. Glad, I guess. I want answers and this is how we get them."

She nodded.

His hand strayed from her arm to her breast, absentmindedly massaging her. "How are you doing?"

Cassie tried to ignore the way her body came to life. She'd been wet all day, and he hadn't allowed her any release. "Fine."

He chuckled. "Even I know that when a woman says she's fine, she's anything but."

That made her laugh, but it was short-lived. He tugged at the nipple jewelry she was wearing, and a surge of energy went directly to her clit. "Please don't tease me, Sir. I'm not sure I can take any more."

Instead of stopping, he did it again, this time on the other nipple. "Are you wet for me, Cass?"

"Yes, Sir."

"Does your pussy want to be fucked?"

She pressed her legs together, looking for some kind of relief even though she knew she wouldn't get it. Not from that anyway. "Yes, Sir."

He helped her to sit up and straddle him. "I need you to tell me if this is what you want. Not just the sex, but this kind of relationship. With me."

Cassie had a lot of time to think over the course of the day. Even though it had been humiliating being on display as she had been, the worst of it was when he ignored her. When he used her and seemed to discard her. It had driven the point home. "Yes. I want to be yours."

He nodded. "Unzip my slacks and take out my cock."

She did as he instructed. He lifted his hips, allowing her to free his erection.

Out of nowhere, he handed her a condom and she rolled it down his length. She could feel the heat from her pussy radiating against his thighs.

Jesse lifted her up and set her down on his cock. He felt bigger like this but still so very right. She'd never get over how wonderful it felt having him inside her.

"Ride me," he said, leaning back against the couch, his arms at his sides.

Cassie lifted herself up, then sank back down, reveling in the feel of him stretching her. She braced her hands on his shoulders and her eyes drifted shut.

"Look at me, Cass. I want to see you when you take me into you. I want you to know who you belong to."

"I know who I belong to."

"Say it." His voice was possessive.

"I belong to you."

He took hold of her hips again, digging his fingers into her skin. "And you won't put yourself in danger again."

It wasn't a question, but she answered anyway. "No, Sir. I won't put myself in danger again."

Jesse kissed her hard, using one hand to hold her head in place while the other guided their movements. He was lifting his hips at the same time he was driving hers downward, their bodies crashing into one another.

Cassie felt her climax building. She hoped he wouldn't leave her hanging again, but she had no way of knowing. His mouth dominated hers, taking it to the point she could barely breathe.

A deep rumble vibrated from his chest right before he stiffened. She whimpered, knowing he'd climaxed and fearing he was going to leave her wanting again. Then she felt his thumb on her clit. "Come."

His sharp command was all it took. Her body had been coiled tight from all the teasing he'd done throughout the day, and it burst with so much force it was almost painful. She cried out, digging her fingernails into his shoulders as her orgasm rocked through her.

Jesse covered her mouth with his, capturing her scream. Pleasure rippled through her, seeming to go on and on.

He held her tight until her orgasm had subsided. She buried her face in his neck, trying to regulate her breathing again. Her body was coated with sweat, and now that she wasn't frantic with need, she was getting cold.

As if reading her mind, Jesse stood. She wrapped her legs around him, not caring where they were going, just knowing she didn't want to let go of him.

They ended up in his bathroom. He turned on the shower, not releasing her, and waited for the water to heat before carrying her inside. "Baby, I need to get rid of the condom. Put your feet down on the tile."

She let her legs fall, but she didn't release him.

Jesse chuckled as he untangled her arms from around his neck. He gave her a kiss. "Two seconds."

He left her in the shower so he could dispose of the condom and his clothes. A few seconds later, he was back. He pulled her into his arms, crushing her against him.

His hands were gentle against her skin as he washed her. He kissed her neck, her shoulder, her lips. She felt cared for and loved.

She looked up at him, knowing this was the man she wanted to spend the rest of her life with. "I love you."

Jesse brought their mouths together for another lingering kiss. "I love you, too, baby. Always."

EPILOGUE

TWO WEEKS LATER, Jesse sat at his parents' dining room table, Cassie next to him, waiting for his father to read the results of the DNA test.

So much had happened over the last two weeks. Grayson, Crystal, and Sandy were arrested. They'd thought maybe Shannon was involved as well, but Craig determined her only crime was that she liked office gossip.

The missing contract was never located. They did find the extra inventory, however. Or the credit generated from the extra inventory. It had landed in Crystal's bank account not long before the code first appeared in their software.

There were still a lot of unanswered questions, and he wasn't sure they were ever going to get the whole story. Not unless Crystal, Grayson, or Sandy decided to share.

His dad was at the head of the table. His mom sat next to him, looking every bit the wife of a wealthy businessman.

She hadn't said much since this whole thing with Crystal began to unfold. It was almost as if she'd resigned herself to whatever happened.

Jesse didn't like it, but there wasn't much he could do.

He and his father weren't on the best of terms. They spoke but kept their conversations brief and focused on work-related items.

Beks sat across from Jesse, her arms crossed. She wasn't taking the news of their father's infidelity any better than he was.

His dad's best friend, Cole, was also in attendance. The man was like a brother to their dad, so it wasn't strange having him there. Beks, however, seemed to be bothered by his presence. She kept shooting him glances. Or maybe they'd be better described as death glares.

Granted, Beks didn't know Cole as well as Jesse did. He'd moved out of state when she was a baby, only returning for brief visits. She never really viewed him as an uncle figure like Jesse did. Still, her reaction to him struck Jesse as odd. To his knowledge, she'd never had an issue with Cole before.

Craig slipped in through the side door, closing it behind him.

"Okay," Blake said, releasing a sigh. "Let's get this over with." He picked up the yellow envelope and tore it open.

Everyone waited for him to read the contents of the letter out loud, but he didn't. Instead, he ran a hand over his face, set the papers on the table, and walked to the liquor cabinet in the corner of the room.

Their mom picked up the discarded papers. Color drained from her face as she read them.

She returned the papers to the table, stood, and walked out of the room.

"I guess we know what the results were." No one disputed Cole's assessment.

The room grew quiet for several long moments. Beks was the one to break the silence. "What happens now?"

His dad downed a shot of whiskey. Blake Masters was in a difficult position. Grayson and Crystal, with Sandy's help, had stolen from his company. He couldn't let that go. Yet, Crystal was his flesh and blood. He knew his father well enough to know Blake would feel a debt to Crystal. Maybe even more so than he did to Jesse and Beks.

"Craig."

His dad's head of security came to attention. "Yes, sir?"

Blake set his glass down with too much force. "Does she still need to be bonded out?"

"Yes."

Jesse knew what was coming before his dad said the words. "Pay her bail. Today. And see if the prosecutor will drop the charges."

"You can't just have her roaming around free. We don't know anything about her." Jesse had been doing research on Crystal, but he hadn't found much outside of her work history and an associate's degree she'd gotten at a community college.

Craig took a step forward. "I must agree."

Jesse was glad he and Craig were on the same page.

"The information we have on her is limited," Craig said.

"So what do you suggest?" Cole seemed to be the voice of reason in this.

"Let me assign one of my men as her bodyguard."

"You think she's going to agree to a man following her around twenty-four seven?" Beks's voice dripped with sarcasm.

Craig nodded in agreement. "We can make it a condition of bonding her out."

"We're blackmailing her?"

Jesse had to agree with Beks on this one. It did sound a lot like blackmail.

"Call it what you want, but it's my job to protect this family. If she's now part of it, then she's going to have to get used to everything that comes with it." Craig's tone was matter-of-fact. The man was still beating himself up over what happened.

After a lot of detective work, Craig had found an access tunnel that allowed Crystal to move through the building without using the main hallways. He'd gone over hundreds of hours of footage and had only had her show up a handful of times after she'd been let go from the company. Even then, the sightings were brief.

"Who are you thinking?" Cassie asked, speaking up for the first time.

"Adian. He's been involved in the investigation from the beginning."

"Your computer guy?" He would have been the last person on Craig's team Jesse would have chosen.

"He's a computer whiz, yes, but he also spent a fair amount of time on the front lines. There isn't anything she can dish out he can't handle."

"It's settled then." His dad walked out of the room, effectively dismissing everyone.

Craig left out through the same door he entered, and Cole followed Blake.

Jesse was glad his dad had someone because he wasn't in the mood to provide any comfort to his father.

Cassie laced her fingers through Jesse's. He gave them a squeeze, grateful she was there with him.

Beks stood. "I'm going to find Mom."

His sister closed the door behind her, leaving Jesse and Cassie alone in the large dining room. The size of his parents' house had never bothered him before, but for some reason, it felt almost claustrophobic now.

Cassie rested her head on his shoulder. "Are you okay?"

"I have a sister."

"You have two."

Jesse snorted. "Yeah."

"Do you want to stay with your mom? I can get Brie to pick me up if you want to stay."

He kissed the top of her head. Her wound had completely healed, and hair was already starting to grow back in the damaged area. "No. Beks will take care of her. I'll call her later."

* * *

They made their way back to the condo in silence. Jesse had helped Cassie move all her stuff to his place last weekend. Brie was happy for her but sad at the same time. They'd lived together since college. But they were both starting new phases in their lives. Brie with Kaden and her with Jesse.

The closer they got to home, the more Jesse touched her. She spread her legs, grateful she wore a dress today. His fingers skimmed the outside of her panties, but he didn't go any farther than that while he drove.

After her punishment, things had been different between them. Better. She understood her role in the relationship more and she was learning to embrace it.

He parked and helped her from the vehicle. They rode the elevator to their floor, and he opened the door for them.

Cassie stood waiting while he locked up, her body already anticipating what was going to happen next.

He cupped the side of her cheek, brushing his thumb along her jaw. "Wait for me in the bedroom."

"Yes, Sir."

She entered the bedroom, removed her clothes, and kneeled beside the bed to wait. A month ago, she would have been full of nerves. Now, she was calm as she waited for her Dom.

Jesse didn't make her wait long. He strolled into the room, unbuttoning his shirt. He walked over to her, ran a hand over her head, and smiled.

Warmth spread through her chest. This was still new. He'd begun adding certain routines now that they were living together full-time. She was finding she loved serving him in a variety of ways, not just sexually.

This, for example. Yes, she was kneeling naked before him, but it felt intimate rather than sexual.

He didn't say anything right away, just stood there, petting her hair.

She leaned into his hand, enjoying his touch.

"Undress me." His words were no more than a whisper, but they sounded loud in the quiet room.

Cassie reached for his belt, her fingers grazing the skin beneath. He held still while she removed his pants, only lifting his leg to help her when needed.

After taking off his socks, she stood to remove his shirt. He'd already taken care of most of the buttons. All she had to do was release the cuffs and push it off his shoulder. The fabric fell to the floor at his feet.

He stood there gloriously naked, his cock standing proud and hard. She wanted to touch him. Before her punishment, she would have. Now, she waited for his instructions.

Jesse cupped her face with both hands and brought her mouth to his. She closed her eyes and relished the feel of his lips, loving the way his tongue dipped and licked, stoking the fire within her to the surface.

He walked them toward the bed until the backs of her legs hit the mattress. With one arm braced behind her, he lowered them to the bed and went to work making her body sing for him.

* * *

Crystal sat alone in her cell, contemplating how her life had gone wrong. Was it the day she decided to apply at Blake Masters's company? Or was it the day she was born? Or maybe it was the day she met Grayson Hyde.

It didn't really matter, did it? Wherever her life went off the rails, it didn't change the fact that she was now sitting in a cell, waiting to go on trial for stealing money from Blake Masters's—her biological father's—company.

She rested her head in her hands, listening to the sounds around her. Some of the other people in the jail were hardened criminals. She didn't belong here.

Yet, she did. She knew that. But the anger she felt didn't comfort her.

The sound of footsteps in the hallway brought her head up. A guard stopped outside her cell, keys in hand.

She stood. "What's going on?"

"You're getting released."

Crystal's heart skipped a beat. "Why?"

"Someone paid your bail."

Not wanting to question it, Crystal exited the cell and followed the guard down the hall. She looked around for Sandy or Grayson, but all she saw were other officers and a man in a suit that looked like it had been tailor-made for him. He was staring right at her, making her want to squirm.

"Here are your things. You need to sign here." The officer's voice dragged her gaze away from the man.

She took her purse, made sure everything was in there, and signed the papers. "Um, can I call someone to give me a ride?" She had no idea where she was going to go. Sandy's maybe? But she didn't know what had happened to her friend. Was she still in jail or had she been bonded out too?

"Your ride's right over there." The officer pointed to the man in the suit.

"Who is he?"

The officer shrugged. "I believe he's the one who paid your bond."

Crystal walked over to him. "Hi. I'm told you're the one who paid my bail."

He gave a curt nod.

"Well, thank you. I appreciate it. I—"

"There's no need to thank me. I'm just doing my job."

His job? "I don't understand."

"I work for Mr. Masters. I'm your bodyguard for the foreseeable future."

***

Are you READY FOR MORE from Sherri Hayes? Start reading her BDSM Club series by reading the prequel, Welcome to Serpent's Kiss, for FREE. Click HERE to download it and start reading today!

CAN'T WAIT FOR SHERRI'S NEXT BOOK?

Let her know by leaving a review and telling her what you liked about
FALLING FOR THE BOSS'S SON(HEAD OVER HEELS #1)

Strictly Professional

A Christmas Proposal

<u>Head Over Heels</u>

Falling for the Boss's Son

<u>Novellas</u>

Tangled In His Embrace

<u>Box Sets</u>

Finding Anna Boxed Set (Books 1-4)

Daniels Brothers Box Set (Books 1-4)

Boys In Blue: Everyday Heroes

ACKNOWLEDGMENTS

Thank you to Mack and Rae who make sure all the BDSM elements are accurate. They are the first ones to see the story, including all my typos.

Beta readers are key to catching inconsistencies and plot holes in a novel. Authors are focused on moving the story forward and sometimes we forget what we wrote ten chapters ago. A big thank you to Marci who went through Falling for the Boss's Son with a fine tooth comb.

Editors and proofreaders are the unsung heroes of the book world. Without them, our books wouldn't be nearly as good. They painstakingly go through each and every word to help us clean up and polish our work. Thank you to Emily Lawrence for all the work she did to help get this story ready to be published.

Covers are often the first thing a reader notices about a book, so a great cover design is important. A huge thank you to GetCovers for a beautiful cover.

ABOUT THE AUTHOR

Sherri picked up her first romance novel when she was twelve and immediately she was hooked. She would stay up reading long after everyone else in her house had gone to bed, needing to see the hero and heroine get their happily ever after. But Sherri never imagined becoming an author.

At the age of thirty, all that changed. After getting frustrated with the direction a television show was taking two of its characters, Sherri decided to try her hand at writing an alternative ending to give the characters the happy ending they deserved.

Since then, writing has become a creative outlet that allows her to explore a wide range of emotions, while having fun taking her characters through all the twists and turns she can create.